The Princess of Chaos

Candice Wright

The Princess of Chaos Copyright © 2020
Candice Wright

This is a work of fiction. Names, characters, places, and incidents either are the products of the author's imagination or are used fictitiously.
Any resemblance to actual persons, living or dead, businesses, companies, events, or locales is entirely coincidental.
All Rights Reserved.
No part of this book may be reproduced or used in any manner without the express written permission of the publisher except for the use of brief quotations in a book review.
This eBook is licenced for your personal enjoyment only. This eBook may not be re-sold or given away to other people. If you would like to share this book with another person, please purchase an additional copy for each recipient.

For T
I'd take a bullet for you. Well, a Nerf bullet, but that still counts right?

CONTENTS

Chapter 1	1
Chapter 2	13
Chapter 3	18
Chapter 4	40
Chapter 5	46
Chapter 6	57
Chapter 7	72
Chapter 8	87
Chapter 9	101
Chapter 10	112
Chapter 11	127
Chapter 12	137
Chapter 13	152
Chapter 14	166
Chapter 15	180
Chapter 16	201
Chapter 17	215
Chapter 18	231
Chapter 19	243
Chapter 20	264
Chapter 21	274
Chapter 22	288
Chapter 23	295
Chapter 24	309
Chapter 25	319
Chapter 26	334
Sneak Peek: The Queen of Carnage	354

Also by Candice Wright	363
Acknowledgments	365
About the Author	367

When they tell you that you can't do it,
Do it twice.

CHAPTER ONE

Megan

Don't throw up. Don't throw up. Don't throw up. I chant silently to myself, feeling nausea swirl inside me as my legs threaten to buckle in protest of every step I take.

I might not be able to hear the sound of my heart rapidly trying to beat its way out of my chest, but I sure can feel it. With each of my hands firmly held by the imposing bikers either side of me, I find myself being led out of the Carnage clubhouse towards the two shiny black Harleys parked near the huge iron gates that protect the Kings of Carnage property from the outside world.

The Carnage MC members look dark and formidable as they part to let us through. None of them are happy with this shitty situation, but we all know my going with two Chaos

Demons is the only way this truce between the two clubs will work.

The Kings of Carnage won't attack the Chaos Demons and risk me getting hurt. In return, the Chaos Demons won't damage their shiny new pawn and run the risk of Carnage burning their compound to the ground in retaliation.

The Carnage members watch me avidly, looking for any signal that I might need them to step in. The risk is too high to let that happen, so I keep my eyes focused forward, pull my shoulders back, and hold my head up high. Fake it until you make it, right?

I watch as the man they call Viper, the new president of the Chaos Demons, the club that is home to most of my nightmares, climbs onto one of the chrome beasts and waits. Zero, the guy still holding my hand, lets go before placing both of his hands gently on my waist and lifting me behind Viper.

I loosely grip Viper's waist and turn to look back towards the Carnage clubhouse where both my brothers stand with their arms crossed over their chests and angry scowls adorn their faces. Standing between them is my best friend Luna, the soon-to-be mother of my niece or nephew. That little baby is the reason I'm on the back of this bike, heading back to the Chaos Demons' clubhouse, the very place I spent so long trying to escape.

Oh, Luna would have come instead of me. She tried fighting me over it, knowing just how much going back there was going to kill me, but I would be fucking damned if I let anyone I love anywhere near that godforsaken place. It had already taken so much from me. I refuse to let it take anymore.

Don't throw up. Just think of the truce, I remind myself. My reluctant stay at Chaos is the only way to ensure peace between our clubs. At least until they can learn to trust each other.

My eyes lock onto Luna. If I have to play at being a pawn for a little while so the queen doesn't sacrifice herself, then so be it.

I try to blank my emotions but I know she sees right through me when she starts signing.

You've got this. You are so fucking strong that I'm humbled by you. I have a feeling you're going to bring that club and those men to their knees.

I frown in confusion. What is she trying to say?

Time to take back that crown, sweetheart.

I snort and roll my eyes at that. I might have been raised as a Chaos Demon but I was far from their princess.

Oh, and Megan, I have eyes on you. Take care.

My eyes widen at her words. Things to know about my friend? She could be batshit crazy when she wanted to be, and she was ridiculously protective.

What did you do? I sign to her.

Say hi to my brothers for me. She smiles and I can't help it, I smile back. Luna's brothers Oz and Zig are as crazy as she is.

I can tell when Viper starts the bike, feeling the engine

3

vibrate as it comes to life beneath me. He pulls away, making me hold his waist tightly. Unable to sign anymore, I offer Luna a reassuring wink as we leave behind my family and head back to the hellhole I was raised in.

I tighten my grip and swallow the bile in my throat. One hour. That's how long I have until everything I thought I had survived gets a second chance to start taking shots at my soul.

The hour passes in the blink of an eye, my nerves growing as I recognize where we are. I turn my head in the direction of the compound, but instead of turning right towards it, we veer left and continue down a gravel road for a few miles until we pull up outside a small wood-stained cabin with a wraparound porch. I remember this building from when I was a kid, but I've never been inside it.

The bikes stop and the vibrations cut out as the engine shuts down. I look around and see nothing but trees filled with pretty blooms of baby pink and crisp white cherry blossoms that sway in the early spring breeze.

As pretty as it is, I can't help the shiver that travels down my spine at how isolated it is here.

I eye Zero warily as he climbs off his bike and offers me his hand. I stare at it for a beat, like it's covered in flesh-eating ants, before slipping mine into his. He helps me slide off as Viper holds the bike steady. When I try to pull away from Zero, he tightens his grip, making me swallow hard. I stop tugging and let him hold my hand, for now, quickly reminding myself to pick my battles wisely.

Zero says something to Viper, but he's not looking directly at me so I can't read what he's saying. Whatever it is, Viper nods in agreement as he climbs off his bike. He jogs up the steps and opens the door, holding it for us to pass through.

Zero finally lets go of my hand, so I quickly wrap my arms around myself before he can snag it again.

It's dark in here, now that the evening is drawing in, so Viper flicks a lamp on, bathing the place in artificial light.

I take in the large space, all open, one-room seamlessly leading into the next so you can see everyone no matter where you are.

The living room seems cozy enough—'lived in' is the phrase that pops to mind—with a couple of brown leather sofas facing a large flat-screen television that's mounted on the wall above a huge brick fireplace.

Just in front of that is a dark wood coffee table situated in the perfect position to put your feet up while you kick back and watch TV. Judging by the empty beer bottles and pizza boxes that litter the top of it, I would say this space is *very* well used.

A hand on my shoulder has me reacting before my brain can kick in. Lucky for me, Zero's reflexes kick in just as quickly and he catches my fist swinging towards him before it connects with his jaw.

"Shit!" His lips form the words as he glares at me. I look down, embarrassed, and wait for him to let go of my hand. A finger under my chin tips it up until I'm eye to eye with his pretty green ones. My eyes drop to his lips when he starts speaking.

"You react like that a lot, or just for handsome bikers like myself?" he asks, making me roll my eyes.

I don't answer him, obviously, but he refuses to let go of my chin, searching my eyes, for what, I have no idea.

"We can't sign at all, so this is fucking hard."

A movement out of the corner of my eye has me pulling free from Zero's hold to face Viper, who is walking towards me with a pen and notebook in his hands.

"You write, though, yeah?"

I snatch the paper and scribble fast, letting my anger take over. I shove it against his chest and stomp over to one of the sofas, sitting down on the edge of it so I can keep my eyes on them both.

Viper reads my words, "No, I'm a dumb illiterate bitch."

"Being deaf doesn't make you stupid, asshole," he continues to read before he lifts his head and glares at me, then stomps over. I swallow hard when he grips my chin, which he doesn't miss. Sighing, he loosens his hold and makes sure I'm watching him before he speaks.

"You can make your time here as easy or as difficult as you like, Megan, but making an enemy out of Zero and me won't do you any favors."

I hold my hand out for the stupid notepad and when he gives it to me, I start to write.

I don't need any favors from you. I'm afraid to even ask what the price of a favor would cost me. No, I think I will take my chances, just keeping myself to myself.

I hold the paper up for him to read. He shakes his head but doesn't say anything else.

What are the rules? I write and wait for him to read it.

"What are the rules for you while you are here?" he clarifies, making me nod.

"Tonight, you will stay here. Zero and I will head over to the compound and make everyone aware of what is going on. You will have a prospect on you, so don't even think about running."

I flip him off. I won't run without provocation. I'll never willingly put my family in any unnecessary danger.

He reaches out, grips my hair, and pulls me up until his face is as close to mine as it can get while remaining just far enough away for me to be able to read his lips.

"Be very careful with that attitude of yours, Megan. It doesn't matter what you think of Zero and me, or this club. It doesn't change the fact that I am the goddamn president and you will treat me and my brothers with some fucking respect." The vibrations of his voice rumble over my skin. He lets go of my hair and pushes me back down onto the arm of the sofa before taking a step back.

"Tomorrow we will be moving into the compound."

My face must pale because his aggression disappears.

"You'll be safe there, Megan. The Chaos Demons have enemies and while we are sorting through this shit, I will feel better knowing that you are protected."

I don't respond. He has no clue what being back behind those gates will do to me and I doubt very much that I will be any safer in there than I will out here.

What about work? I write.

"You can still go to work, you just need someone with you. Give us a week to get you settled in and I'll make sure someone is available to take you every day, okay?"

I nod my agreement, knowing that if they wanted to they could stop me from going completely. My shop is my baby. I can't stand the thought of not being able to be there. Thankfully, I haven't reopened it yet since all the shit that went down with Stokey, that traitor my brothers knew as Weasel. I've just been doing the cleanup. It's ready now but another week won't hurt in the grand scheme of things, being as Wyatt is still filling and shipping orders from the warehouse.

"That will do for now. You grew up in an MC, Megan, you know the rest of the rules. They all still apply to you."

I turn when Zero steps up to me and snags a piece of hair and starts twirling it around his fingers.

"—Food in the fridge." I catch the words on his lips, missing the start as I was too busy trying unsuccessfully to pull my hair back.

"There are three rooms. Find a bed and crash. There is no point waiting up for us; it's going to be a long-ass night," he tells me, letting go of my hair and stepping back. They both turn to the door and stare at it for a moment. Viper heads towards it and pulls it open, revealing a red-haired guy an inch or two shorter than Viper's six-foot-three frame. He looks to be the same height as Zero, maybe six-one, at a guess. I take in how differently they all look. Viper, with his inky black hair and ice-blue eyes that are intense and laser-focused. And then you have Zero with his deep mischievous green eyes and I-just-rolled-out-of-bed-this-way sexy blond hair. A redhead, a brunette, and a blonde. Sounds like the beginning of a joke. Lord, please don't let me be the punch line.

The leather jacket, or cut as the MC calls them, the redhead is wearing has a badge declaring him a prospect, which surprises me. He has an air of confidence about him that you don't usually get when you are the lowest ranking person on the premises, and that's basically what a prospect is. They're little more than glorified servants until they prove their worth and their loyalty.

Viper says something to him. I can't make out what it is from here, but the prospect nods and heads back outside.

"Be good, Megan," Zero tells me before making his way over to Viper and out the door. Viper throws a look my way that I can't decipher before following Zero out and closing the door behind him.

I take a deep breath and crumple to the sofa.

Shit, shit, shit. I can't do this. Lifting a shaky hand, I wipe a stray tear from my face, born more from frustration than fear. Taking a deep breath, I try to calm myself down. I need to mentally prep for what's going to happen tomorrow.

I close my eyes and count to ten, breathing in slow and

deep, fighting down the memories that try to make themselves known. I have fought too damn hard and long to make my way out of the darkness to give in so easily now.

Growing up in the heart of the Chaos Demons' territories taught me many lessons. How to be seen and not heard. How to keep my mouth shut and my head down. How to blend in. It worked for the most part—except when it came to Crogan. Being the president's daughter should have offered me some kind of protection, but for that, my father would have had to acknowledge my existence, wouldn't he? Most of my life, I thought my mother was one of the club girls who had gotten pregnant, much to the disgust of his old lady Wanda. It wasn't until years later that I learned the truth. My father wasn't my father at all. That title belonged to the recently disgraced and deceased Joker—the former president of the Kings of Carnage. It also came to light that my mother wasn't so much a club whore as she was a hostage, as I, her only daughter, was held as ransom.

I don't know who is privy to the truth, or if they will even care. Despite everything, nothing can change that my mother killed the president of the Chaos Demons and his stepson, Crogan, before turning the gun on herself. The whys don't matter anymore, if they ever really did to begin with.

I stand and shake off my bleak mood. Strolling down memory lane changes nothing. I walk over to the clean, if slightly dated, kitchen and open the fridge before slamming it shut again. Eating with my churning stomach is not a good idea. I look over to the huge TV before turning to the hallway, which leads to the bedrooms and decide to just sleep the rest of this fucked-up day away before the worries eat me from the inside out.

The hall has two doors on each side. One reveals a bathroom, the other three lead to masculine bedrooms. I pick the one on the other side of the bathroom as it looks into the woods at the back and is the farthest away from the prospect stationed at the door.

The room is tidy and the bed is made, which is good enough for me. Lord knows I've slept in worse.

I tug open one of the drawers of a tall pine dresser and find some T-shirts. Snagging the first one my hand touches, I take it with me to the white nondescript bathroom and take a quick shower after making sure the door is locked behind me. I'm as quick as I can be, drying myself off with a huge navy blue towel before donning the soft gray T-shirt I've claimed to sleep in. It falls to my knees and covers everything it needs to in order to preserve my modesty. Not that I think they will try anything after how hard they pushed for this truce between the two clubs. Me being here is meant to keep the peace between them until they learn to trust each other.

Besides, fondling the Carnage president and VP's sister the first night she is under their roof wouldn't do them any favors. I take a quick look in the mirror and take in my pale face and wide, large blue eyes that are so much like my brothers', noticing just how tired and stressed out I appear.

My long black curly hair reaches all the way down my back and at the moment, is beginning to soak the back of my

T-shirt. I quickly braid it before moving to switch off the light and heading back to the room with my clothes bundled under my arm. Tossing them on top of the dresser, I climb between the cool black and gray checkered cotton sheets. I doubt I will be able to sleep. With so much swirling around in my brain, it will be a miracle if it calms enough for me to actually rest. But as the slight pine scent washes over me from the pillow I'm lying upon, I find myself drifting off almost immediately. I guess today's events have taken their toll and I have reached my emotional limit. Fuck it, I'm not complaining. I can deal with reality tomorrow. For right now I just want to sleep and pretend my life hasn't just been one series of clusterfucks after another.

CHAPTER TWO

Zero

"Did you manage to get ahold of Grim?" Viper asks, sipping his beer from beside me.

"Nope, nothing. I was surprised he wasn't still passed out when we got back. Something's got to give with him because if he carries on, he'll kill himself long before he ever finds his sister."

Viper sighs before finishing off his beer in three swigs.

"It's the not knowing that's killing him. If she was dead, at least he could grieve and move on like with his mother. But I think he's convinced himself she's living in hell, waiting for her big brother to come save her."

"What do you think happened to her?" I ask, curiously. Kids go missing every day, but it's not as easy as you might think to disappear without a trace in this day and age, what with computers and facial recognition software. Especially fourteen-year-old girls who looked like she did. I'd never met her in person, but I'd seen the photos Grim had kept above his bunk when we were deployed. She looked like she had gone straight from a young girl to a pin-up model, bypassing the awkwardness of puberty most teenagers go through.

The problem with that is there are many people out there that find the combination of beauty and innocence irresistible. Especially in young girls. And I can't help but think that, with the kind of world we live in, that poor girl got chewed up and spat out like many others before her.

"Honestly, it's more than likely she's dead in a ditch somewhere. With the resources that have been plowed into locating her, I find it too hard to believe she could have evaded us for so long unless it's not us she's hiding from."

"Yeah, that's what I figure too. So what are we going to do about Grim?"

"We keep looking. We'll search until we find the answers he needs regardless of what we think." Viper slaps me on the back before standing and putting his fingers between his lips to whistle loudly. "Right, listen up. Normally I'd bring this up at church, but it was a spur of the moment decision that Zero and I made and you all need to be aware of it," he tells them, looking at the club bunnies and old ladies to push his point home. Church is a meeting just for patched in officers. No prospects or women, and he's right, this affects everyone.

"We have brokered a tentative peace deal with the Kings of Carnage."

A few groans ring out from the room but nobody voices their grievances too loudly.

"And we trust Joker to keep his word? I know he plays for both sides, but that doesn't make the slick asshole worthy of trust." The massive bald-headed rotund man we aptly named Shrek pipes in with a skeptical tone.

"Joker's dead and so is King. They have a new generation of leaders, Orion and Diesel, just like we do. It's time to work on an alliance instead of a war, especially with the cartels trying to take over more territory," I tell them firmly.

"The question still stands though, Vipe. How can we guarantee they will keep their word?" Shrek replies, unconvinced.

"They'll keep it because I have their sister," Viper tells them in a flat voice like he's talking about the weather and not the feisty beauty tucked away in our cabin.

"Fuck, yeah. Is she hot?" someone calls out from the back of the room, making me glare in that direction. If anyone touches her, I'll snap their fucking fingers off.

"She is off-limits. I mean it. If anyone fucks with her, they will have me to answer to. While Megan's here, she is under my protection."

"Megan?" Rock asks, a flare of recognition in his eyes.

"Megan Cooper. I'm sure some of you remember her," Viper tells the room, which is now a lot louder than before.

Interesting how the thought of calling a truce with a rival club causes less of a stir than one small slip of a girl.

The faces in front of me frown with displeasure at the news of the returning princess. They are not pleased, yelling and complaining that this is a mistake.

"I'm not sure that's a good idea," Viper's uncle warns him.

"Well, Rock, I wasn't asking for your permission, now, was I?"

"You know..." I step up next to Viper, letting the room know exactly where my loyalties lie and where they always will. "It dumbfounds me how much hostility you all feel for a girl none of you have seen since she was sixteen," I tell them pointedly, watching as a couple of the old ladies' expressions take on a downright frosty look.

"You were gone a long time, boys," Rock adds quietly.

"She has a traitor's blood running through her veins. Can't say it's a surprise to find out she has Carnage in her too. We'll never be able to trust her," Fender adds with a disgruntled huff.

"You act like you didn't know Melly had sons with King before coming here. You would have known they were her brothers before she did, so don't give me that. Regardless of how you all feel, Megan is here and she will remain so until I say differently. This isn't open for debate. Understood?" It's tense while I wait for people to nod their agreement. Not everyone's happy, fuck, a blind man could see that but they'll get over it.

The club girls are the only ones who seem unfazed. At

least they know their place. I admit, I'm surprised by their lack of response but I'm grateful for it. Megan is going to find it hard enough fitting back in here without club girls making it worse with their catty comments and unfounded claims on us because we'd fucked once or twice.

Viper and I sit back at the bar but this time I get the prospect to pour us glasses of whiskey neat.

"To truces," I offer, holding up my glass to his.

"To raven-haired beauties who have no idea what they've gotten themselves into," he adds before clinking his glass against mine and taking a sip of the amber liquid. I snort at that. It's not like we gave her a choice.

"I wouldn't be too sure about that if I were you, Viper. Something tells me that she shouldn't be underestimated."

He shrugs off my words as I take a sip of my own drink.

"It makes no difference to me. She'll bend, and then she'll beg. The thought of all that silky hair spread out across the pillow as those big blue eyes of hers stare up at me in submission..." He groans and takes another sip.

I laugh but shake my head. "I'm man enough to admit that I think that little vixen will have us on our knees long before we get her on hers.

"We shall see, my friend. We shall see."

CHAPTER THREE

Megan

It was the warm breath on the side of my neck that pulled me from my troubled sleep, finally clearing the fog enough for me to realize that I wasn't still trapped in a nightmare. No, my nightmare has manifested and now the creeping claws of fear that tear into me nightly are groping my breast as a bearded face rubs the side of my face and neck.

My body locks down, paralyzed by fear as my memories blur with my reality.

When I was sixteen, Crogan – a patched member of Chaos – tried to rape me in my bed in the middle of the night. I've replayed the attack over and over in my head for years, wishing I had done things differently and planning out what I would do if I ever found myself in that kind of situation again.

I swore I would fight and kick and bite and scream but instead, my body is frozen solid, my scream trapped in my throat, refusing to leave my lips.

I can't breathe, why can't I breathe? I stare into the darkness as the large rough hand slides under my T-shirt and cups my bare breast before lips press firmly against mine. I can't move. My terror so absolute, it's like I'm floating above myself looking down. I'm trapped in a body that won't respond as my mind begins to shut down, preparing itself for the inevitable.

I can taste whiskey and smoke before the lips pull back and the man buries his head against my shoulder again. The hand cupping my breast goes still as the body covering most of mine goes heavy. My already shallow breathing grows slower as the weight of my attacker presses down upon me. When a fuzzy dark hue clouds everything and my eyes slip closed, I don't fight it. I welcome the oblivion, part of me hoping that maybe this time I won't wake up.

There are hands-on my body, pulling, shaking. A slap on my face has my eyes snapping open. Viper is looking down at me with a look of concern on his face, but it barely registers as I fly off the bed and scramble into the corner, clipping my hip painfully on the bedside table. I make myself as small as I can and wrap my arms tightly around myself in a pathetic sense of self-preservation.

Zero crouches down in front of me, making me whimper

and pull back. He frowns and looks up at Viper, who looks livid. They speak to each other, but I'm too freaked out to concentrate on what they are saying. I tuck my head against my knees and wrap my shaking hands around my legs, rocking myself a little. My breath wheezes in and out as I desperately try to find some way, any way, to soothe myself. When a hand touches my arm, I don't think, I react, lashing out and scoring lines down the side of Zero's face with my nails. He falls back in shock but doesn't get any closer. I lean my head on my knees again but keep my eyes on the room this time. I struggle to stay focused but at least nobody can sneak up and surprise me now.

I don't know how long I sit here. Physically, I'm here but mentally I'm a million miles away. Eventually, I become aware of another person in the room. I focus on the faded blue denim of their jeans and follow that up to a white T-shirt with an oil smear across the front, up over a broad chest to a neat silver beard and into familiar silvery blue eyes.

Rock. The man who was the vice president when I was growing up and the only one who ever tried to show me any kindness. He was also the guy who got me out of this hellhole the first time around, even tracking me down years later to give me my inheritance, which enabled me to start up my shop.

He bends down on his knees, looking remorseful before opening his arms wide.

"Little Bird." I see his lips forming the nickname the club gave me many years ago on account of me being quiet and flighty. I hated it then, and I hate it now, but it doesn't stop me from throwing myself into his arms so forcefully, I almost make him lose his balance. I haven't seen him in years but I still draw comfort from the familiarity of him.

The tears I had valiantly tried to keep at bay slide down my cheeks, blazing a trail of shame and humiliation. Humiliation that again I was an easy target, and shame because I didn't fight back. It's like the woman I grew up to be reverted back to the sixteen-year-old girl who just had her world shattered into a million pieces.

He picks me up, carries me out to the living room, and sits on one of the sofas with me cradled in his lap. He smooths my hair back and places a kiss at my hairline. I know we aren't alone. I can't see anyone else but I can sense them close by. I don't look up or acknowledge them, not knowing which one of them decided that my body was theirs to play with.

Eventually, when I'm all cried out and too weak to fight anymore, Rock turns us both so we are facing the others. Zero and Viper are next to each other on the sofa opposite us but there is another guy sitting on the very edge of the coffee table. His face is swollen and littered with bruises, and he has dried blood around his nose. He looks at me with anguish-filled eyes that I can't place, but know I've seen somewhere before.

"My name's Grim." I don't answer him. He means nothing to me. "I'm sorry," he tells me as I watch his lips move.

I frown and burrow a little deeper into Rock's shoulder, not really knowing what he is sorry for, unless—my body goes rigid even as Rock tries to soothe me by running his large hand up and down my back.

"I didn't expect to find you in my bed. I was drunk as fuck and thought you were a club whore; they've been known to sneak in occasionally," he tells me solemnly.

I lift my trembling hands and sign to him but he looks pained when I do. Shit, right, they don't understand me. I look over at Viper and he seems to know what I want, disappearing and coming back with the notepad and paper I left in the kitchen yesterday.

I write what I just signed, ignoring Rock's body going solid beneath mine, needing to know the answer before I figure out my next move. I turn the notebook and hold it up for him to see.

"What did you do to me when I passed out?" I watch his lips move as he reads my words. The horror in his eyes and the color bleeding from his face has me bracing for the worst, but I need to know what happened.

"Nothing, I swear it." He shakes his head frantically, making it hard for me to pick up the words, but he repeats them enough that I manage to catch them all.

"I passed out too and woke up to these two pulling me off you," he tells me. I look over to Zero who is watching me intently.

He nods his head. "We came back and found him asleep on top of you. Both of you were wearing what you have on now. We pulled him off and I beat the shit out of him while Viper tried to wake you up. For a second there, we thought you were dead. What the fuck was that, Megan?"

Is he mad at me? Seriously? I look away from his face, effectively blocking him out. I don't want to be here. I want to run far, far away so that I never have to deal with Chaos again.

Viper's hand on my jaw has me cringing away from him, but he lets go and resumes his position next to Zero when he knows he has my attention.

"Tell me what happened. Why did you react like that?" he asks again but I'm shaking my head before he finishes.

He doesn't need my story, it's not his to have.

"Tell me," he orders.

I try to write but my hands are still shaking so it's making everything ten times harder.

Finally, I manage to write just one line but it's enough to encompass how I feel.

"You are not my president," he reads the words when I flip the paper around for him to see.

"Well, that's your choice to make but your options are either you're a guest or a prisoner so choose wisely."

Rock's large hand covers mine before I can write anymore, catching my attention. I tip my head up to look at him.

"Just tell him what happened," he implores with a sad look on his face.

I shake my head no but his face is set with steely determination.

"Either you tell him or I will. If you are staying here, he needs to know the truth." I don't bother writing anything down. Nothing I say matters. They are just going to do and say what they want, they always do.

"I'll explain what I know and you can just fill in the blanks while you get yourself together?" I nod sharply, twisting a little so I can watch Rock speak more clearly as he spills my story. As much as I don't want him to tell them, I'm going to make sure if he tells it, he tells it right.

"You guys remember Crogan?" He asks. I flinch just watching his name fall from Rock's lips.

I spare a glance at the guys to see if they noticed and Zero's frown tells me he didn't miss a thing.

"Yeah, slimy fucker and the oldest son of John's old lady, Wanda. He was the one that Melinda shot, right?" Viper asks, staring at me as he tries to figure out what he is missing. I turn to Rock to see what he says next.

"Do you know why she shot him?" Rock asks.

I focus on Viper who looks at Zero before answering.

"The only version we know is the Chaos Demons' version. After hearing a little about what Melinda—your mother—went through from you and Luna, I'm inclined to believe it's bullshit," he tells me. I shrug my shoulders, faking indifference, having no idea what the bastardized version of the story is.

"Let me start from the beginning. As you all know, John

was my stepbrother. He came on the scene when Gettie and I were ten and he was eight." Rock starts when I turn back to face him, enunciating his words clearly so I can understand him.

I quickly scrawl on the notepad and wait for him to read it.

"Who's Gettie? You never met her?" he asks. I shake my head, thinking Gettie isn't a common name so it's unlikely.

"Gettie is my twin sister and Viper's mother," he clarifies. "This used to be her place but she married someone new and now lives in Australia, of all places.

I frown then, realizing something. They wait patiently as I write. I twist the paper and show it to Viper, who reads it out.

"So John wasn't really your uncle by blood, but by marriage. Like a step-uncle or something?"

"Yeah, I mean, we never really made the distinction as kids, though. Both Rock and John were always just uncles to me."

I nod and wave for Rock to continue, for some reason feeling relieved that John's blood isn't coursing through Viper's veins. I have to hold back a snort at that. I have Joker's running through mine. The former Kings of Carnage President was a traitor and an asshole to boot. I snap out of my thoughts and focus back on Rock's mouth as he speaks.

"Truth be told, I didn't really like him then anymore as a kid than I did when he was an adult, but that is a story for a different day. John, Joker, and King were biker royalty. They were given the keys to open a club away from the mother chapter of Carnage way back in the day.

"I was off fucking my way around the world and it suited me for a while before the urge to settle down snuck in. I came back, thinking of prospecting for Carnage as my father and John had before me, only to find that John had left Carnage and begun rounding up folks to make up a new club. He offered me a spot as the VP and I snatched it up, not once thinking about why I didn't have to do any of the grunt work like the others. I sure as fuck wasn't looking a gift horse in the mouth. I should have fucking realized there would be strings attached. I ignored the shady shit. We're an MC, it's expected, right? But there was always something not quite right about John.

"He had been sleeping with this chick, Wanda, for years. She was a stripper over at our club, Elusive, but she was also someone else's old lady. Had two boys—Stokey and Crogan—with him and everything, but when John left Carnage and started Chaos, Wanda's old man miraculously had a bike accident and died. Wanda became John's old lady a day later."

Zero waves his hand to get my attention.

"We were told that Wanda was partly the reason that Melinda went into a fit of rage. When John wouldn't leave Wanda and make Melly his old lady in her place, she lost it, shooting Crogan and John in retaliation. When she realized what she had done, she turned the gun on herself," he tells me.

I look up at Rock in shock. I fight back the unbridled sadness that even in death, my mother is still cast as the villain. Rock squeezes my knee and picks up where he left off.

"As I'm sure you've heard by now, Melly— sorry, Melinda —wasn't here by choice. John took her as a fuck you to his former club and friends. He kept Melly locked up and only pulled her out when he wanted to play. When she fell pregnant with Megan, she was given some more freedom under the threat of harm coming to Megan if she tried to leave.

"So, she stayed. To keep her little girl safe, she played her role of club whore, but when Crogan attacked Megan and all John gave him was a slap on the wrist, something inside her snapped. She took out Crogan and John, and I got Megan the hell away from here."

"He attacked you?" Viper asks. Even though I can't hear him, I know he's livid by the red flush on his face and his angry frown.

I hold my tears at bay and swallow around the lump in my throat before nodding. I resist the urge to turn away from them, feeling uncomfortable with all eyes on me. Zero's glare shows he is pissed as Viper and Grim looks sick.

"You thought I was Crogan," Grim states when my eyes fall on him. I nod. I know he's dead but it doesn't mean that I'm not afraid of ghosts.

"He raped you?" he asks me with a gulp. I scribble down

what I need to say, conscious of Viper now pacing in agitation.

Twisting around, I hand the note to Grim.

"He never managed to get that far, but it came pretty close. I screamed my head off while he punched me over and over to shut me up. When I woke up, everything was different. I had no family, no club, and no hearing. I finally had my freedom, but it came at a price." Grim tosses the notepad beside me and stands up, making me sink into myself again. He pulls his gun from behind him so I close my eyes and try to make peace with myself that this is it. I jump when I feel a hand on my leg and snap my eyes open, only to find Grim's green ones staring into mine. He tugs my hand and places his gun into it, closing my fingers tightly around the cool metal.

"Keep this until the next time I see you. Someone tries to hurt you, shoot them." I swallow hard, strangely comforted by his gesture. He inclines his head at me and again I feel this odd sense of familiarity.

I keep hold of the gun but reach over and grab the notebook and pen before writing my question.

"Where do I know you from?" Rock reads my words out loud.

"I'm going to make some coffee," Grim tells me before turning, but I grip his arm as his words tug at a memory. He bends back down to face me and I see the look of uncertainty wash over his face.

I mouth one word – "Kibble."

He grimaces, but nods. I write fast, feeling angry and confused before tossing it to him.

"You were at my store that day with Luna. You brought me coffee. Do the Kings of Carnage know you're a traitor?"

He looks at me warily before answering. "I know you have no reason to believe me but I have my reasons for what I did. I'm not a bad guy, Megan, despite all the evidence that's suggesting otherwise. As for Carnage knowing," he shrugs, "Luna knows, so I imagine every Carnage chapter has a most wanted poster of me hanging up behind their bar."

My lips twitch a little in response to that, even if it's inappropriate. Luna is a force to be reckoned with and I'm sure he's not far off the mark. I point for him to hand me back my notepad and write quickly.

"Do I call you Grim or Kibble?" He frowns at the pad when I flip it around for him to see.

"Grim. I fucking hated Kibble." He stares at me for a moment before continuing.

"I really am sorry, Megan," he says, looking right at me without flinching and despite what I know about him and everything he stands for, I find myself believing him.

"I swear to you, what happened last night will never happen again." He turns a little, listening as someone else speaks, drawing my attention over his shoulder to Viper just in time to see his lips move.

"Oh, you don't need to worry about that. Megan will be spending the rest of her nights here lying between Zero and me. At least that way we can keep the little hell-raiser out of trouble."

I glare at him and mouth, "Not a fucking chance."

"Oh, it's happening, Megan, even if I have to handcuff you to the bedframe myself," Viper tells me, wearing a no bullshit expression on his face.

Well. Fuck.

* * *

MY PROTESTS FALL on deaf ears. Yes, I've got jokes. Even after a shower and redressing in the same clothes—minus panties—I'm still feeling like a regular little ball of homicidal sunshine right now as we pull up to the Chaos clubhouse.

Bathed in the early morning sunshine, the differences between the Carnage and Chaos clubhouses are obvious. Instead of one huge building housing everything and everyone, Chaos took over what used to be a motel. Sure, it had been built on and adapted over the years to suit the wants and needs of the MC, but its bones are still the same. The most noticeable difference would be the eight-foot barbed wire-topped gate and fence that encompasses the club, keeping nosy civilians out and in some cases, captives within. Two prospects are manning the gate, swinging it wide when we approach in a cloud of dust and debris that coats the dirt road leading up to it. We pull through slowly. I grip Zero's cut with clammy hands as a sense of foreboding washes over me. I'm returning to the hell I once crawled out of with no way of knowing for sure if this time I'll make it back out alive.

It looks the same as before, maybe a little more dated, but then time stands still for no man.

We pull up and park in front of the diner that sits in the center of everything and is fully functioning as it was in its former life. It's a place where most of the MC comes to eat throughout various times of the day and night.

The colossal building behind it was where the offices and bar were and the other two sides that face each other are all the rooms that used to be paid for by the hour. Now they house the many bikers that call Chaos home.

I climb down from behind Zero and pull the borrowed helmet from my head, shaking my hair free and allowing it to tumble down over my shoulders, offering a curtain that separates me from the world.

Viper snags my hand after climbing off his own bike and tugs me behind him. He pulls the door to the diner open and ushers us through. Like a car crash on the highway, everyone turns to stare. I pull my shoulders back and lift my chin defiantly, refusing to let these assholes intimidate me. Viper walks to the back of the room, never loosening his grip, ushering us into the last booth in the far corner. He slides himself across the cracked red faux leather seat and tugs me in beside him. Zero follows suit, sandwiching me between the two of them. Any normal person would have sat opposite us but then, I forgot, I'm not dealing with normal people anymore. MC members don't believe in fucking boundaries unless it suits them. I guess I should be grateful that Grim and Rock had other business to deal with or this would have been one hell of a squeeze.

Viper slings his arm across the back of the seat as Zero signals for one of the waitresses to head our way. He reaches up to play with my hair, making me scowl at him again, but he just grins and tugs harder.

"Hey, boys, what can I get you?" the easily pushing forty redheaded waitress asks—and I use the term waitress loosely. In the outfit she's wearing, I'm guessing she is on the menu as an extra. I mean, sure, it technically could be called a uniform, but her chest looks like it's one sneeze away from making its escape and the hem of her pink shift dress is so short that if she bends over I'll be able to see if she waxes or shaves.

"Coffee for me, Betty," Viper answers.

She waits for Zero's reply but I don't turn to see what he says, choosing instead to watch Betty.

Her pouty smile morphs into a sneer when she looks at me, waiting for me to give her my order. I hold my hand out for her pad and pen and wait.

"I realize you might not be the brightest bulb but I'm the one who takes the orders," she tells me. I know she knows who I am from the way she slows her words and exaggerates them like a dumbass. I wasn't deaf when I was here, no, that was my parting gift, but everyone heard my story, or at least some kind of version of it, afterward.

I don't drop my hand and just raise my eyebrow, waiting.

When she still doesn't speak, I turn to face Viper who is looking at me with his jaw clenched tight. What the heck is his problem now?

"Just get her a coffee, Betty," Viper orders. Before I can tell her I need some freaking food, she walks off, putting so much sway in her hips I'm surprised she doesn't dislocate them. If I wasn't so pissed I might have found it comical.

I turn my head and glare at the side of Viper's face. A face that is taking in the other diners and completely ignoring me. The asshat. Fuck this shit. I slip down between the seats and crawl under the table and pop up the other side, enjoying the incredulous looks on their faces. I turn and stomp over to Betty, who is leaning over the counter talking to another MC member and yep, I was right in my guess, she definitely shaves. Gross. I spot her pad and pen sitting on the counter beside her so I snatch them up while she is distracted and write.

I'm deaf, not stupid. Do you know sign language? No? Then how the fuck do you expect to understand me when I speak? I asked for the pad so I could write it down for you, I didn't realize I broke some waitress' rule. My Bad. I'll take a stack of pancakes and bacon as well as the coffee, thank you.

I rip off the page before tapping her on the shoulder and when she turns to face me, I slap the piece of paper against her perky boobs before she can even protest.

Turning on my heel, I stomp back to the booth, this time sliding into the empty seat across from them and with Betty's pad and pen in my hand.

"You might want to rein the attitude in a little, princess. You won't make any friends here like that," Viper oh so sagely advises.

I scribble the pen across the paper, writing fast, pushing the pen so hard, I'm surprised the nib doesn't snap off. Once I'm finished, I rip the paper from the pad before scrawling five words on a clean sheet and ripping that off too. I toss the short note to Viper and slide the other one over to Zero, who is watching me with an infuriating smirk on his lips.

Viper reads his first, scowling down at the words *You, sir, are a dick.* Zero reads the words over his shoulder and snorts.

"Well, can't say she's lying, can we, Pres?" he teases and picks up his own note from the top of the table before reading it aloud.

Refusing to let me go back for my pen and notebook was a dick move. This place took my hearing, I refuse to let you take my voice too.

Viper interrupts him before he carries on.

"Getting a little dramatic there, aren't we, Megan? I realize I never thought through not going back for it but it was an honest mistake and we managed to order coffee just fine without you having to write it down for me. I'm a big boy, I've been ordering coffee for a long time."

I'm writing as soon as he stops speaking. I don't need to hear his voice to know he's being a condescending prick, I can pick up on all that from the smug look he threw me. I throw the pad at him when I'm done, wishing it was a fucking brick.

I haven't eaten in over twenty-four hours. Food would be good or am I getting punished like I used to?

I see his jaw clench so I know I struck a nerve. He doesn't apologize, which isn't really a surprise, but he backs down and lets Zero finish reading.

"You brought me here. Trust me when I say I would rather peel my skin off and roll myself in salt than be stuck here. But that doesn't change the fact that I am. Even still, there is no need to be assholes about it. Don't treat me like I'm stupid because it will be you who looks like an idiot in the end."

He doesn't say anything else as Betty places a coffee in front of both the guys before disappearing for a second and returning with a stack of pancakes and coffee for me. She places them down in front of me with far less finesse then she used for Viper and Zero, letting her petty agitation show for a few minutes before smirking down at me.

"Enjoy your food, little bird." I see the words her lips make and even though I can't hear the inflection behind them, it doesn't take a rocket scientist to figure out the disdain she so obviously used to coat her words.

I watch as she looks at the food, trying to hide a small vindictive smile for me. Bitch.

I slide the food over to Viper and indicate for him to take a bite. He shakes his head and sips his coffee but I nudge his hand with the edge of the plate.

"Not hungry, Megan," he tells me, but I nod pointedly at the food, then up at a nervous-looking Betty. Following my

35

train of thought, he finally looks at the food, then at Betty before picking up the fork and cutting a wedge of the pancakes with it.

"Betty wouldn't do anything to your food, Megan. She's not that petty. She sure as hell wouldn't let her president eat them if she had. She wouldn't like the consequences." He lifts the fork to his mouth.

I watch as Betty drops her head before calling out, "Wait."

"Yes?" he questions with the food hovering precariously at the end of the fork.

"Let me get you something fresh." She tries to snag the plate but Viper pulls it away from her. Zero stands and without the smirk on his face, he looks as pissed as Viper. I'd feel sorry for her if she hadn't brought it on herself. He pushes her into his seat beside Viper before moving over to sit beside me. I slide across, putting some space between us, but of course, that means nothing to Zero. He follows me, effectively pinning me in the corner, his thick thigh pressed firmly against mine. I frown up at him but he ignores me, snagging a strand of my hair and twisting it between his fingers

"Take a load off, Betty, help yourself." Zero indicates the plate of pancakes in front of her.

"N-no. That's okay, I should really get back." She tries to stand but Viper wraps his hand around her bicep, stopping her.

"I insist. Eat," he barks out. She shakes her head, her eyes wide.

"Got something to tell me?" Viper asks her.

"It's got—" She drops her head so I don't catch the rest of her words but whatever she says turns Zero to stone beside me.

Viper looks ready to explode, which seems a little extreme over a little spit in my food, but I'd be lying if I said I didn't like the fact that these guys are pissed off on my behalf. Pushing Betty out of the booth none too gently, he follows her out and then drags her over to where I assume the kitchen is.

I turn my head to look up at Zero and find him watching me with a fierce look on his face. I don't know what he's thinking but all that intensity focused solely on me does strange things to my libido, stirring up a need within me.

You have got to be fucking shitting me! These guys are basically using me to suit their needs and yet I've got the strangest urge to rub myself against his leg like a cat in heat. I must have lost my ever-loving mind. I mean, I like sex as much as the next person, but getting involved with these goons, no matter how ridiculously hot they are, is just asking for trouble. Even knowing that, it doesn't stop my eyes from watching his mouth as he bites his lower lip.

Whatever look he sees on my face has his eyes going molten. He slides his hand into my hair, gripping it tightly before speaking.

"Trust me?" he questions. I'm horny, not dumb, so I tell him the truth, shaking my head to let him know not a chance.

"Good girl." He smiles before his lips are on mine. I'm so surprised that for a minute, I'm completely frozen but his persistence has me melting into his touch. I open for him unconsciously, giving myself over to the sensations he evokes in me and savoring the feel of his tongue dueling against mine.

I don't know how long we kiss. As cliché as it sounds, the room disappears and in this moment nothing else matters beyond him and me.

When he pulls away, I sit with my eyes closed for a moment in a daze. When I open them and see Viper standing at the end of the booth looking down at me with lust across his face, reality comes rushing back in. I feel my face flush with embarrassment and tears prick my eyes as I try to fight off my humiliation. Was this some kind of set up? It sure as fuck wouldn't be the first time I'd fallen for something like this.

A hand on my chin tips my head up. Viper is leaning over the table with his eyes roving over my face. I don't know what he's looking for but whatever it is, he must find it. He indicates for Zero to slide out of the booth, which he does.

Expecting Viper to slide in beside me, I'm caught off guard when he pulls me gently, making me follow Zero out. As soon as I get to my feet, Viper is right there, crowding me until I look up at him with a scowl. I see his lips move, forming the words "fuck it" seconds before his hands are on my ass, hoisting me up into the air. My legs wrap around his waist, seemingly with a mind of their own, as my heart threatens to beat out of my chest for perhaps the hundredth time in the last twenty-four hours.

Then he's kissing me, hard, rough, and unyielding. Kissing lips that have, minutes before, been ravaged by Zero. Somehow I manage to find the strength of mind to pull away, my blissed-out brain filling with confusion. What the fuckity fuck are they playing at?

I try to drop my legs but Viper just tightens his grip on me even as I feel Zero press up against my back and place a soft kiss against the side of my neck, making me shiver.

Okay, where are the damn cameras? This has to be a joke, right? But even as I think it, I can feel the evidence of how much Viper liked our kiss pressed between us.

Viper turns his head and addresses the room, his mouth at the wrong angle for me to read his lips, even though I can tell he's speaking. I turn to watch the other patrons and find them all staring with various looks of disbelief and anger at whatever Viper is saying. I turn back to see him look down at me just as he finishes his speech. I might have missed all but the last few words, but what I did catch was enough to know I'm one hundred percent utterly fucked and not in the fun kind of way.

Viper just declared me their old lady, which in this biker world is a bond stronger even than marriage. I know now that this was all one big set up. They never had any intention of letting me go. The air rushes out of me along with one word, giving away the fact that I can speak.

"Fuck."

CHAPTER FOUR

Viper

"Fuck." It's barely above a whisper, but it's enough to have Zero and me snapping our heads down to look at her. So, she can talk. I did wonder why she didn't. I'm about to yell at her for playing games when I notice how white she's gone. Her eyes glaze over moments before they roll into the back of her head.

"Shit." I tuck her head against my shoulder, my skin tingling with how right it feels to have her here, pressed against me. It makes me think of what it will feel like to have her pressed against me with a lot less clothing between us. I shake it off even as my dick stands up and starts saluting within the confines of my jeans.

I focus on Zero. "She's out cold. I don't want these guys sensing any kind of weakness or, like a bunch of rabid sharks that smell blood, they will strike when our backs are turned. Gonna make it look like we are off to fuck her into a coma. I feel like a dick doing this while she is out cold, but maybe it's better this way. At least my balls will stay attached to my body and not get fashioned into a set of earrings." He smirks at me, but I don't miss the look of apprehension that crosses his face when he looks down at her.

"What?" I ask him.

"I really don't want her to hate us," he tells me, picking up a strand of her hair and running his fingers over it.

"She won't hate us forever, I'll make sure of that. She'll be too busy falling for us to remember what assholes we really are." I glance out of the corner of my eye and see people still watching us with rabid fascination. Thankfully, with the way we are angled, Zero is blocking most of Megan from view. Time to get the fuck out of here.

I grip a handful of her hair and tip her head back far enough to slide my lips over hers. Keeping my eyes open, I follow Zero as he clears a path towards the door. She starts to come around, stirring in my arms and unintentionally rubbing herself on my dick, making me pick up my pace. We just make it outside when her eyes flutter open. She freezes, every muscle coiled tight for a second before she struggles to break free.

I start to whisper for her to calm down but remember she

can't hear me. Frustrated that she won't stop fighting, I lift her higher and toss her over my shoulder. When she starts pounding me on my back, I rain down two hard slaps upon her ass. Finally, the fight goes out of her. Instead of risking her starting again when I place her on the back of my bike, I decide to just walk it back to the cabin and hope the twenty minutes gives her enough time to calm her ass down.

Zero walks beside me, neither of us speaking as Megan lays docile over my shoulder. I wish I could say I felt bad about taking advantage of the situation, but I'd be lying. Megan's sweet lips have had me wondering if she is as sweet everywhere else.

"Well, this is going to be fun. Not quite the way we planned it though," Zero points out quietly despite the fact that Megan can't hear us.

We knew we wanted her. We were planning on seducing her into being our old lady, solidifying a permanent truce between Carnage and Chaos and getting to keep the girl who had me captivated the first time I laid eyes on her.

"They put cum in her pancake batter. Betty asked Fobbs and he had no qualms about 'teaching the little traitor' a lesson," I tell him, still fuming over what transpired.

"What the fuck? I'll kill the prick," Zero growls from beside me.

"Be my guest. You'll find him out cold next to the trash behind the diner." I sigh as we approach the ranch.

"I couldn't wait any longer to make her our old lady, Zero. It's the only guaranteed way to keep her safe."

"I get it but I can't help but feel like this is all going to blow up in our faces," he tells me when the cabin comes into view.

He climbs the steps and swings the door open before stepping aside to let me in. I lean down to lower Megan onto the sofa when she rears back with her fist and punches me in the eye.

"Fuck!" That's quite the swing she's got there. I'm sure I'd be impressed if it wasn't aimed at me. Zero grabs her from behind when she jumps up, pinning her arms behind her back but it doesn't stop her from struggling.

"I'll let you have that one shot, Megan, but if you are going to hit like a man, you better be prepared for me to hit you back." She doesn't need to know that's a load of bullshit.

She scowls, glaring daggers at me as Zero maneuvers her to the sofa and pulls her down onto his lap. She tries to pull herself free but he holds her tight, pulling her back against his chest. I lean down over her and make sure she can read my lips.

"So you can speak, huh?" If I thought she was going to answer me I would have been severely disappointed.

"If you answer me, we might be able to work something else out without you becoming my old lady." I'm lying and I'm guessing with the look of disgust she throws my way, she knows it too.

"Well, see now, here's the thing, Megan. If you want something, you are going to have to ask for it. No more pen and paper. I've got better things to do than cater to your petty bullshit," I tell her, trying to get a rise out of her.

"Are you trying to get her to castrate you in your sleep, asshole?" Zero questions. I don't know what I want but I can see her shutting down on me, and that won't do. There is more to this girl than anyone bothered to notice and I'll take her anger rather than a void of all emotions any day.

She ignores me completely. Looks like I'm going to have to call her bluff, then.

"Cuff her to the bed," I tell Zero, making sure she can see me.

"Christ, you have to do things the hard way," Zero mutters, standing and taking Megan with him. "I'm hoping she just cuts off your dick and leaves mine intact," he tosses over his shoulder as he ushers her down the hall to the bedrooms.

I sit on the sofa with a sigh. Nothing ever runs smoothly around here. I'm doing what I have to, though. If that means pissing people off, then so be it. I can't pussyfoot around Megan when there is a rot spreading its way through my club.

Zero walks back out, frowning.

"What? Let me guess, she clocked you one too?" She's feisty which, if I'm honest, just makes my dick hard. Mind you, I'm beginning to realize that when it comes to Megan, everything makes my dick hard.

"Nope. She's as docile as a mouse. She let me cuff her, calm as can be, then rolled over and dismissed me."

"She'll get over herself. Call Tanner over here to patrol. I want to call another meeting and get some shit sorted about our old lady. It seems some people didn't get the message." Calling her our old lady shouldn't feel so good given the circumstances, but fuck me, it does.

CHAPTER FIVE

Megan

I wait for maybe half an hour before I decide that needing to pee outweighs anything else. Using my free hand, I slip my fingers down the v at the front of my T-shirt and pick at the stitching on the seam of my bra until it gives way. After some wiggling, I manage to slip the wire free before using it to pick the lock on the cuffs. It pops open within seconds. Clearly, these are just for playing in the bedroom and not designed to hold someone hostage. The other kind are a bitch to get out of. I mean, I could do it, but it would take longer.

I stand from the bed as gracefully as I can and head to the open bathroom door opposite me. I take care of business before heading out the door and down the hallway. I'm kind of looking forward to seeing the looks on their faces when they realize I got out. But when I make it to the living room, I notice they're not there. Puzzled, I wonder if they're in one of the other rooms. I'm about to turn and look when I see a shadow pass by the window. I creep closer and see the red-headed prospect from before pacing backward and forward outside, smoking a cigarette, oblivious to me.

I head back down the hall, check the other rooms, and smile when it registers I'm alone. I should be offended that they so easily underestimated me but being as it works in my favor this time, I shrug it off. I go back to the kitchen area and make myself a cheese sandwich while I watch the prospect for a little while, figuring out his movements. I chew the last of it and stare hard, realizing he's only watching the front of the building. I head back to the room I was cuffed in and gaze out the back of the house facing the woods, waiting to see if anyone else is out there. After ten minutes, I figure I'm alone. I can't wait any longer as I have no idea when Viper and Zero might return.

I lift the window and slide it up, grateful that the house is all on one level, and climb out the window and down to the grass below.

I don't need to stop to get my bearings. I know this area like the back of my hand. I make my way over to the woods as quick as I can, needing the coverage the trees can provide before someone spots me.

I have no master plan beyond getting the fuck out of there. I take a deep breath as I step into the shaded woods and find myself wrapped in thick arms with a hand over my mouth. Before I rip off testicles, a body with a familiar face steps in front of me, making all the tension seep out. And because one of them is never far without the other, I know exactly who's holding me. As soon as the arms free me, I throw myself into the embrace of the guy in front and breathe him in as he holds me tight. Fuck, it feels so good to be held by someone who doesn't want anything other than to comfort me. Reluctantly, I pull away and smile through my tears at Zig, my friend and Luna's brother. I turn to face his twin, Oz, and offer him a peck on the cheek before he goes to stand next to his brother. They both stand there with their arms folded across their chests, their stance as clear to read as if they had asked the question, "Who do we need to kill?"

I sign, a feeling of completeness running through me. You never know how isolating it can be until you're stuck in a room with people who can't speak your language.

I've missed you guys so freaking much, I tell them.

We missed you too. Now tell me what's going on and why you're crying. Did they hurt you? Zig signs back rapidly, taking me a moment to catch it all. Their deceased gramps was deaf, so these guys have been signing longer than me. Sometimes they forget that not all of us sign at the speed of light.

I lift my hands to reply, then falter for a second. Does what's happened change anything? I'm pissed as hell that they made this play, but if I go with Zig and Oz now, they will take me back to the Carnage clubhouse. In doing so, the house of cards this truce is built on will come tumbling down. Leaving now won't just break the truce, it will start a war, thanks to the "old lady" label that's been placed on me.

I settle on *I'm okay, a little overwhelmed. I just miss you all.* All of it true, just minus the important stuff.

I know, Meg, but you've got this. You are not the same little girl that ran out of here. Show them the kickass chick we know you are, Oz replies with a grin.

We have cameras set up around the perimeter— Zig starts but I wave my hand to cut him off.

No, Zig. He frowns at me, ready to argue, but I don't let him. *You need to take them away. I know you are just trying to keep me safe, but if they find them, they'll go nuts. How would my brothers feel if Chaos set up cameras around Carnage? They would lose their shit and you know it. We can't go into a truce with one foot out the door. We either give them a shot or we call the whole thing off.*

We just want you safe, Meg, Zig signs.

I know, and I love you all for it, but I need you guys to pull back. Looking behind them, I walk toward the huge oak tree with the low branches that I used to climb when I was a little girl. I rub at a patch towards the base where I had carved my initials as a kid and damn near took off my pinky.

Place a fully charged cell—switched off, naturally—a gun, a knife, and some cash in a plastic bag—two would be even better—and bury them here at the base of the tree. I can get them if I need them and call you guys to get me if things turn bad. They look at me without saying anything, contemplating my words. Luna would flat out shut me down. That girl is protective to the

49

power of ten but these two understand that sometimes bulldozing your way in the front door is messier than sneaking quietly in the back undetected.

Okay, fine, but you need to be checking in regular or all bets are off. Deal? Zig pushes.

Deal, I agree, knowing that Viper and Zero already agreed for me to contact home regularly.

I've got to go back, I tell them. Figures my botched escape attempt will only remind me of all the reasons I have to stay.

Tell everyone I love them and I hope I'll see you all soon. I hug them both before they notice my tears. I won't be going home, at least not to Carnage. I know that now. Being an old lady makes me something I never wanted to be ever again.

A Chaos Demon.

I turn and walk away without looking back but I know they watch me until I disappear from view.

I climb back through the window, still undetected, and make my way back to the bedroom. My stomach growls as I climb onto the bed, letting me know a sandwich does not make a meal, but that will have to wait for now.

Without knowing when they'll be back, I don't want to risk getting caught so I slip my wrist back into the cuff and lay my head on the pillow. As much as I would like to see their faces when they realize I could get free, I think I'll keep my ability to pick a lock to myself for a little longer. You never know when that's going to come in handy around here.

I must drift off to sleep because the next thing I'm aware of is my hand being released and my wrist being rubbed. I try to pull it to my chest, but whoever is holding it refuses to let go. I open my eyes and glare at Zero lying in front of me with a smile on his face.

"We were longer than we thought we would be," he tells me, which I'm assuming he thinks means "sorry." I don't respond and wait for what comes next. He pulls himself closer, placing my wrist against his chest before sliding his hand to my hip. I feel the vibration of his voice against my forehead so tip my head up to see his mouth.

"Do you need the bathroom?"

Well, I didn't until he mentioned it, and now I can't think of anything else. I nod in confirmation and let him pull me up off the bed to my feet. I half expect him to follow me in. He doesn't, so I take care of business and wash my hands. I glance at my reflection in the mirror and wince. My hair is a tangled mess and my face has an imprint embedded on it where I must have fallen asleep on the seam of my jacket sleeve. Yikes, I mean, I'm not trying to impress anyone but I could give Medusa a run for her money.

I step out into the hallway and run into Zero who must have been waiting outside the door for me. Yeah, that's not disturbing at all. I might not be able to hear myself pee but it doesn't mean I want everyone else to.

I quirk an eyebrow and wait for him to speak but he doesn't, he just tugs a strand of my hair and twists it between his fingers. I stand there awkwardly, not knowing what else to do until Viper appears at the end of the hall with a beer bottle in his hand. He watches Zero play with my hair as I observe him, making this already odd situation even more bizarre.

"Why don't you speak?" Viper asks me, letting me know he is very much aware of me watching him. I don't answer, naturally, but he doesn't seem fazed by that.

"Guess we can add stubborn to your list of attributes." He trails his eyes down to my chest and holds them there for a second, letting me know exactly which attributes he's referring to. I frown and pull my jacket tighter around my shoulders.

"I meant what I said earlier. You will speak or you will go without. Now it's time for bed. Perhaps you just need some more time to think about it."

I could speak, lord knows I want to yell at him to go suck a dick, but I won't give him the satisfaction. I pull away from Zero and ignoring Viper, head back into the bedroom. I slip off my boots but leave everything else on, including my jacket. I'm not leaving myself exposed to these guys, especially after last night's fiasco.

I raise my leg to climb on the bed but I'm stopped by a hand on my arm. I turn to face Zero looking down at me.

"Don't you want to get undressed first?" he asks with a genuine frown that almost makes me want to laugh. Is he for real? I shake my head no and try to step back when I feel a presence behind me. I take a step forward, bringing me closer to Zero's chest. That's as far as I get before I find myself pulled back against a hard body. I know from the smell it's Viper but it does nothing to ease my nerves. If he is anything like his name implies, he could strike at any time, usually when least expected.

I feel his head dip. His breath skating across my neck causes an involuntary shiver to run over my body. I know he felt it when he gives me a little squeeze. I don't know how I know but I sense he likes the effect his body has on mine. Well, that makes one of us, at least. Viper must say something to Zero as something passes across Zero's face before he nods.

"Viper says to strip or he'll do it for you."

I stare at him, debating the merits of nut punching him, when the hands on my arms slide my jacket from my shoulders. Every possible scenario flits through my mind and none of the possible outcomes are appealing. My jacket gets tossed to Zero. He catches it in one hand before stepping back and making room for Viper who is now in front of me.

"If you want me to stop, just tell me."

I hold my arm up in a classic stop signal but he shakes his head as he reaches for the hem of my T-shirt.

"No, Megan. If you want me to stop, you need to tell me. Use your words."

So that's the game he wants to play. Okay, fine let's play.

I raise my hands, flip my middle fingers at him, and smile caustically before raising my arms above my head. He pauses for a second, surprise on his face and dare I say, a hint of respect. He wipes it all clear as his rough hands pull my T-shirt over my head, tossing it onto the bed, exposing my black lace bra.

Hands at my waist let me know Zero has moved behind me. My focus on Viper was so absolute, I didn't even see him move. Viper's hands move to the button of my jeans and pop it open before slowly sliding the zipper down. I don't break eye contact with him. I need to let him know that he might be calling the shots but I'm no one's bitch. When I still don't say anything, he shakes his head and hooks his fingers into the waist of my jeans, sliding them over my ass and down my legs. He stands back up and Zero takes over, freeing my feet as he keeps me balanced. Viper's eyes blaze up my legs to the apex of my thighs and to my mound that is scarcely hidden behind a scrap of black lace.

Zero's fingers trail up my outer thighs deliciously slowly, leaving a trail of goosebumps in their wake until they settle back on my hips. Their heat is so much more apparent now that my clothing isn't between us. I can tell he's waiting for Viper to decide what to do next, but he needn't have bothered. I know that Viper won't back down any more than I will.

I keep my eyes on Viper as I reach around and unhook my bra, letting my generous C-cup bust free. I toss the bra at him and smirk when it hits him in the face. I lick my lips, drawing his attention away from my eyes in case he can see how nervous I am. I move my hands to the pretty little ribbons that tie at the side of my panties and pull them. The material parts in my hands, allowing me to easily pull it away. I offer it to Viper with the sweetest smile I can muster, the little strip of fabric swinging from my finger, making his chest rise and fall rapidly as his breathing speeds up.

I feel Zero's ragged breath on the back of my neck and find a sick sense of satisfaction that I affect them as much as they affect me. A finger trails down my ribs to the curve of my hip, tracing over my tattoo. The black rose sits just under the curve of my breast. Its stem is made up of one of my favorite Atticus quotes—*She wasn't looking for a knight, she was looking for a sword*. I draw strength from those words now as I have many times over the years. They might be knights on chrome horses but I'm a motherfucking princess.

I open my mouth and my words flow out, my anger guiding me. "If you touch me, I will kill you." I glare at Viper as his eyes widen in shock but he doesn't wince or flinch so I'm guessing my volume is even enough.

"Fuck me!" Viper exclaims. I roll my eyes then climb onto the bed, aware I'm giving them even more of a show than before. I can't stand between them any longer, at least not without climbing one of them like a damn spider monkey.

"Think I just made my view on that clear," I tell them over my shoulder before lying down and pulling the blanket over me. I close my eyes and shut them out, all the while faking an outward appearance of calm.

A calm which goes out the window a few minutes later when I feel the bed dip on either side of me. My eyes snap open to find an amused-looking Zero staring back at me.

"I'm guessing you forgot the part about you sleeping in between us."

I try to shrug nonchalantly. "It's your funeral." I'm about to close my eyes again when I feel his hand on my jaw at the same time I feel an arm wrap around my waist and a hot chest press against my back.

"We won't take anything from you that you're not willing to give." I'm sure his words were meant to bring me comfort but all they do is remind me of why I'm here.

"You already did," I tell them and close my eyes before he can reply.

CHAPTER SIX

Zero

Viper and I don't say anything until Megan's breathing evens out, letting us know she's fallen asleep.

"So how's this plan of yours working out, Viper, because I'm not seeing the benefits of your wisdom right now," I tell him as I turn on my back and look up at the ceiling.

"She's a stubborn little shit, that's what the problem is," he grunts out.

I snort at the irony. "You have no fucking room to talk, asshole. You are the most stubborn person I know. I get what you're trying to do, kind of, but you can't force her to trust us. If anything, you'll make her pull further away."

"And yet she felt safe enough to sleep between us naked,"

he points out, which is true. That means she trusts us at least on some kind of subconscious level.

"Just remember you can only push so far before you do some serious damage," I caution.

"I'm not going to hurt her, fuck!" he yells.

"Physically, no, but mentally we're skating on thin ice. We took her from her best friend and her brothers. We brought her back to a place she loathes where she hasn't exactly been made to feel welcome, then made her our old lady without even asking her, effectively tying her to us forever. The only reason she's asleep between us naked is because, yet again, we forced her hand. Tell me, Viper, how many times do you think we can bend her to our will before she breaks?"

He's quiet for a moment, thinking over my words.

"Fine. I'll try to rein it in. I just don't want any of the assholes around here starting shit with her," he tells me, frustrated.

"I know, but maybe playing it differently would mean I'd be lying here with my dick inside her as opposed to hoping it'll still be attached to my body if I accidentally touch something I shouldn't during the night."

He's quiet for a beat before he starts laughing. "Fuck. Okay, I'll work on it."

I nod. It's all I can ask for. At the end of the day, Viper is who he is. Asking him to change is like asking a zebra to wear spots.

We don't speak after that, each lost in our own thoughts. I think back to church earlier and all the disgruntled faces

THE PRINCESS OF CHAOS

when we told them that Megan was now our old lady and, as such, she fell under club protection, not just mine and Viper's. Anyone who fucks with her will not like the fucking consequences. Most agreed, even if it was somewhat reluctantly, but there are a few that I'm going to need to keep my eye on who remained silent and stoic. Nobody was stupid enough to say anything outright but then, Viper and I are considered wildcards.

Rock let a lot of shit slide when he found himself the president of a club he never wanted to rule. Viper and I, however, are a different breed altogether. We were born for this shit. We might be soldiers, but we were bikers first. We have oil in our veins.

Whimpering draws my attention back to Megan who seems to be huddling in on herself. I look over at Viper and see his attention is on her too.

"If he wasn't already dead, I would gut that motherfucker myself," he mumbles about Crogan, mostly to himself, but I agree wholeheartedly.

When she pulls her legs up into the fetal position, tucking them tight to her chest in some kind of protective move, I decide to risk a kick to the dick and turn on my side to face her. I slide my hand across her jaw and press my lips against her forehead. I mumble to her, inconsequential words, especially knowing she won't hear them, but hoping that the feel of my lips against her skin will bring her a measure of comfort.

She moves in her sleep and tucks herself under my chin,

almost like she's trying to reassure herself that I'm still here. I hold her tight and feel Viper move in closer behind her.

"It seems that at least in her sleep she needs us," he speaks softly before burying his face in her hair. While that's true, I'd rather she slept peacefully than have her dreams plagued with nightmares.

THE NEXT WEEK proves to be a test of willpower.

We moved what shit we would need over to the apartment we shared on the compound. Usually, it's little more than a fuck pad, but it's where Viper feels she'll be safer, so who am I to disagree?

The only one who hasn't seemed to notice our change of residence is Grim, who's been AWOL. I'd be lying if I said I wasn't worried, even more so with him refusing to answer my messages. I get that he's struggling being back at Chaos and that he feels like his last chance to find his sister has slipped away. But Viper is getting antsy waiting him out and I doubt Viper will give him more than another day or two before he sends me to hunt Grim's ass down.

I catch Megan out of the corner of my eye, stripping off her jeans before she pads into the bathroom on bare feet and closes the door behind her with a click.

All thoughts of Grim flee my mind. I sit on the queen-sized bed and rub a hand over my face and will my cock to calm the fuck down, but it ignores me as usual. Anytime I see those long-ass legs with their smooth, silky skin taunting me, all I can think about is what it would be like to have them wrapped around me.

My attention turns to the door as Viper strolls through it with a six-pack in his hand.

"Where is she?" he asks in greeting.

"Bathroom," I tell him and watch him walk to the fridge and place the bottles inside.

Our apartment is different than the others. Originally, it would have belonged to someone like the super or manager when it was an up and running motel. Instead of being a standard room with a bathroom and a minibar, we had an actual apartment made up of three bedrooms, two bathrooms, and a kitchen area. It actually started out as a two-bedroom apartment but we converted the living room into the third bedroom so that Grim, Viper, and I could stay together.

Of course, that meant the main door opened into the third bedroom, but you'd find yourself facing down the barrel of Viper's gun if you tried to enter without being invited.

None of the rooms were designated; we didn't care about shit like that. Like I said, for all intents and purposes, this was a fuck pad. But now that Megan is here, it seems somewhat lacking. What this place has that the cabin doesn't, is an eight-foot fence topped with razor wire and manned by armed prospects.

Megan walks out of the bathroom wearing one of my

baggy T-shirts but I know she's bare underneath. Viper finally relented and agreed to her wearing a T-shirt to make her feel more comfortable but she just laughed in his face at his reasoning. We all knew damn well it was because it was getting far too hard for us to have her naked between us and not lose control.

He wouldn't admit that, of course. To prove her point, she slept without any panties on.

I'm pretty sure these two are going to be the death of me.

She doesn't say anything as she walks over to the bedside table, snagging the bottle of lotion from the top of it. I'm glad I had the foresight to ask one of the club girls to pick it up along with some other essentials. Viper switches on the TV that's mounted on the wall facing the bed before stripping down to his boxers and lying down on the bed. I follow suit and leave a gap in the middle for the woman that is slowly fucking turning my balls blue.

Every night this week without fail, Viper and I have made sure we were back here to sleep with Megan, partly to ward off the nightmares, but also to work on building trust between us. It was slow going but each day I could see another chink appear in her amor.

I watch as she cocks her leg up onto the chair in the corner of the room and smears the lotion into her smooth, creamy legs.

"She's doing this shit on purpose," Viper grunts out, watching her just as avidly as I am.

"Oh, for sure. She knows exactly the effect she has on us."

I look down at my cock straining against the gray cotton of my boxers. "It's not like I can hide it."

Megan looks up then and smiles innocently at Viper and me before climbing between us.

Innocent my ass. This woman is the devil sent to try me. We've agreed not to make a move until she instigates it, we've pushed everything else, but not this. The ball is firmly in Megan's court. And my balls are firmly in her pocket.

I grunt as I adjust my dick and resign myself to another long fucking night.

Like usual, she falls asleep in moments, her ass pressed against my hip, her hair fanned out over Viper's shoulder.

We talk shop for a while, then watch some comedy show, but it isn't long before we lose interest in the TV and switch it off in favor of calling it a night.

Megan is heading back to her shop tomorrow so she's bound to wake us up at the ass crack of dawn.

The sound of her whimpers pulls my attention her way. It's always the same, every fucking night. None of her dreams seem to be very pleasant. She thrashes around before crying out and rolling over, burying her head against my chest, which she soaks in seconds with her tears.

I place my lips against her forehead, just like I do every time, and pull her close until she calms.

I know the second she wakes. Thankfully, it's not because she knees me in the dick for holding her but because she slides her hand behind my neck and yanks me down, planting her lips against mine. I react on instinct and the salty taste of her tears on my lips isn't enough to stop me from giving her exactly what she's asking for. What I've wanted since I kissed her in the diner. Fucking finally. A sharp pinch on my arm has me pulling back abruptly, giving my sanity time to kick back in.

"Control yourself, asshole," Viper barks at me. His sharp tone lets me know he's the one responsible for the pinching. My eyes squint when light spills into the room, making me realize that Viper has switched on the lamp beside him. I look down at Megan and see her watching me, chewing her swollen lips with a look of trepidation on her face.

"Erm…" Wow, look at me being all eloquent and shit. She smiles at me, something about me being at a loss for words seems to comfort her. Slowly, as if worried about startling me, she lifts herself onto one elbow before leaning over and placing her lips back on mine for a second. Pulling away, she looks into my eyes as I fist the sheets. She keeps her eyes on me as she licks over the seam of my lips, darting her tongue inside when I part them on a gasp, before retreating. She sits up and climbs from the bed without looking back, padding softly to the bathroom, closing the door behind her. I turn to look at Viper who looks just as confused as I am.

"Erm…" Yep, that's still the best I've got.

"Yeah, I have no idea either. What the fuck was that? It's been a week and she hasn't wanted anything to do with us and now, all of a sudden, she willingly makes out with you? I —" He shuts up when the door opens and Megan strolls back out, naked as the day she was born and completely at ease in her own skin as she makes her way back over toward us.

And fuck me, she should be comfortable. She has the kind of body reminiscent of a 1950s pinup girl. Full, perky breasts with rosy nipples just begging to be sucked, a tiny waist that I'm sure my hands would easily fit around that give way to wide, flaring hips. Toned, well-shaped thighs that make my already half-mast dick harden completely as I yet again imagine them wrapped around my waist. And that waxed smooth pussy that has my mouth-watering.

The icing on the cake—ink. Fuck me, is there anything sexier than a girl with ink on her skin? I swallow hard, hearing Viper groan beside me, not helping at all. She stands there for a second, taking us both in before she surprises the shit out of me by whipping the covers away from us, leaving Viper and me lying there with our dicks pointing north as they pitch tents in our boxers.

"Megan," Viper warns as she crawls up my body and plants her naked pussy directly over my boxer-clad cock. She doesn't answer him, having been focused completely on me she didn't see his lips move. When she starts rubbing herself backward and forward over me, I grip the sheets so I don't reach out and grab her hips so I can pull my dick free and thrust up inside her.

"Vipe," I say his name hoping like fuck he tells me what move he wants me to make here because as the material of my shorts becomes wet from my pre-cum and her arousal, I realize I'm two seconds away from losing my shit. When he doesn't answer, I turn to look at him and see his hand wrapped around his cock, his eyes fixed firmly on her breasts as they sway with every movement.

"Fuck it." I lift my hands and grab her hips, pulling her harder against me, my grip tight enough to leave bruises and I'll be damned if the thought of my fingerprints on her skin doesn't turn me on even more. She doesn't pull back or shy away from my touch, oh, no, not this little minx. She lifts her hands and cups her breasts, tossing her head back with a moan, the tendrils of hair tickling the skin of my thighs.

"Jesus Christ," Viper grunts out, his movements speeding up. I take control, sliding her up and down my cock faster and harder.

"Yes!" She lets out a breathy moan of her own. I watch as Viper lifts the hand he's not fucking himself with and places it on her ribs, below her breast, tracing the tattoo we both like so much.

She lifts her head and opens her eyes at his touch. She looks from me to Viper before sliding her hand over his and linking their fingers, dragging his hand up and over her breast. The sight of my best friend's hands, which I've seen stained with blood, being gentle against her silky white skin pushes me over the edge.

"Fuck, fuck, fuck!" I yell, pulling her against me so hard, I'm worried I'll hurt her. Instead, it sets her off. Seems our little princess likes a little pain with her pleasure. Viper must realize this too because when she lets go of his hand, he pinches her nipple hard, making her scream out loud as she throws her head back and creams all over my cock.

Viper grunts beside me, letting me know that he just followed her over the edge. None of us move for a while, our ragged breathing the only noise in the room, nobody wanting to break the haze of the moment. I think part of me is waiting for her to freak out, to come to her senses and realize what she instigated in her sleep-fueled brain and blame us for taking advantage. I watch as she looks down at me before looking over at Viper who is watching her with as much trepidation as I am. When she reaches over and runs her finger through the puddle of cum he shot over his stomach, he moans in surprise. When she lifts her hand and sucks her wet finger into her mouth, I feel my softening dick start to shout for an encore. She winks at him before climbing off my lap and walking back over to the bathroom, closing the door and locking it behind her.

"Tell me I'm awake and didn't just have the best dream of my fucking life," I beg Viper, still in shock over the turn of tonight's events.

"Oh, you're awake alright." He's quiet for a minute as we lie there listening to the shower turning on.

"Think she's going to come out of there and pretend nothing happened or do you think she's going to freak?" His question gives voice to my fears.

"I don't know, Vipe, I'm still a little shocked about how all that played out. I don't want her to look at it as a mistake and pull back. I don't know about you, but I want in there so fucking bad it took everything I had not to throw her down on the floor and fuck the shit out of her. It doesn't help that since we talked about us all being clean and tested the other night, all I've been able to think about is sliding inside her bare."

When I asked her if she needed contraceptive pills picked up, she told me she had the implant and had been tested. Then with a smirk, she said it wasn't necessary anyway as I wasn't getting my dirty dick near her. After pinning her to the bed and tickling her until she cried mercy, I kindly informed her that Grim, Viper, and I had just been tested too, and were all clear. She changed the subject after that but I'd had a one-track mind ever since.

Viper and I don't speak while we wait for the water to shut off and the fallout to occur. We look at each other and climb out of bed, making our way to the bathroom. The door opens, revealing Megan wrapped in a giant towel. She indicates with her hand for us to use it so we do, having no qualms about seeing each other naked as we have a hundred times over. We clean ourselves up and head out to the bedroom, expecting to find Megan back in bed, but the room is empty.

"Fuck," I grumble. "I guess freaking out won."

Turning, I blow out a relieved breath when I find her ass —at least that's the part I zero in on—bent over with her head in the fridge, wearing nothing but one of Viper's T-shirts this time. The shirt has lifted enough to show the bottom of her bare ass. She stands up abruptly with a yogurt in her hand, freezing when she sees us standing there, watching her.

"What?" she asks quietly, almost too quietly for me to hear. "I'm freaking starving." She pouts before pulling open a drawer, looking for a spoon.

Viper drags his hand through his hair before walking towards her. When she doesn't flinch, he places his hands on her hips and steals the spoonful of yogurt she was about to pop in her mouth. She watches his mouth as he sucks the spoon clean, her eyes widening as his tongue licks over his lips. Fuck yeah. I love how responsive she seems to be to us.

"I'll throw some frozen pizzas in the oven, then you, Zero, and I are going to have a little chat, okay?" He says it softly, with just a hint of a threat threaded into it, a habit formed way before he became the president of Chaos. It doesn't matter that she can't hear the cadence of his voice, it's part of who he is. She shrugs her shoulders, not negatively, more of a "whatever" kind of gesture, making me smile. Viper might ooze authority, but Megan is a natural-born rebel. These two are going to either come together like fireworks or C-4. Either way, there'll be an epic explosion.

She tosses her spoon and yogurt cup in the sink before walking towards me with a smile, plonking herself down on the edge of the bed again.

"It's so weird having a kitchen in the bedroom but I can't deny how handy it is," she comments, eyeing Viper as he rummages around in the freezer for the pizza.

I walk over to her and sit beside her as she tucks her long

legs up under her T-shirt. My fingers twitch as her hair falls over my arm. I snag a piece of it and twist it around my fingers, loving how soft and silky the strands feel.

"Why do you always play with my hair?" Her voice is loud, surprising me a little in the quiet room. It must show on my face as I look at her because she flushes and tries to turn away. I tug the hair in my hand, refusing to let go and preventing her from looking away. How can she stroll around the room like naked goodness then get embarrassed over something as silly as how loud she is? As Viper pulls up a chair and sits directly in front of her, I realize it might seem small and insignificant to me but it's a big fucking deal to her.

I answer her question to deflect the attention from her and give her a chance to regroup for a minute. "My mother was a junkie who only ever really cared about her next fix. Sure, sometimes she'd get clean and be the best mother a kid could ask for, but it wouldn't be long before she lost herself in a needle again. I think it was worse that way, you know? If she never got clean, then I'd never know what I was missing. Instead, I would get these glimpses of normality, of what life could be like in a parallel world where mothers loved their sons more than their next high. It was never long before the dream was snatched away and the nightmare that was real life returned." I pause for a second when I feel Megan's hand on my thigh, staring at it as if it were a lifeline, anchoring me in the here and now so I don't lose myself in the turbulent memories of my past. I slip my free hand over hers and weave our fingers together before continuing.

"When it was good, it was really good, but when it was bad—" I shake my head as visions of my mother's face float before me. "When it was bad, I would find her wherever she had passed out and lie as close as I could get and stare at her hair. It was how I measured how bad it was. She always liked it when I played with her hair when she was clean, but when she was jacked up her hair was often covered in vomit and jizz. She had to earn the drugs somehow, after all." I look at Megan, waiting for the pity, but it never comes. I guess her story isn't too dissimilar to mine. "That was all I knew when I was young, a cycle of dirty, clean, and repeat until she took too much. When I crawled over to her that last time, I knew she was gone by the glassy-eyed stare, so I played with her hair one last time, just the way she liked it, until they came and took me away." I cough to clear my throat. I keep my eyes on hers, which are wet with unshed tears.

"When I run my fingers through your hair, it's shiny and smooth and reminds me that I'm not that little boy anymore. That's not my life anymore, I'm now a man living in the parallel universe I once only dreamed about."

CHAPTER SEVEN

Megan

It's so easy to forget when your life is knocked off course, everyone else's isn't necessarily running smoothly. I run my finger over the back of his hand in comfort, thinking about how much everything has changed in the last week.

"Tell me why you don't speak," Zero asks me. If it had been Viper, I might have been able to play it off, but not with Zero. Not after that.

"I can't hear how loud I am. Sometimes I'm too quiet and people strain to hear me. Sometimes I'm too loud, making people startle uncomfortably." A hand on my knee has me turning to face Viper.

"Fuck them. They don't matter." He tells me something that, on a logical level, I already know.

"People fall into two categories: the ones who are trying to be nice and won't say anything, not realizing I can read their facial expressions or that their unease makes me uncomfortable. Then there are the assholes who think it's funny to mock the deaf girl, like I don't have enough shit to deal with. I should have thicker skin. I get that now, at twenty-two, but at sixteen, it was just one more blow to my already battered self-esteem.

"So I stopped talking, stopped giving people another means to make me feel less than them. Eventually, it became my norm," I shrug, remembering the moment I stopped talking and withdrew a little from the world. It's not that I haven't spoken at all since then. It's just not something I do if I can avoid it. Meeting new people makes it even easier because they don't know I can speak, so it feels less like a lie.

"Well, that shit stops now!" Viper answers, the scowl on his face showing just how angry he is on my behalf. I would find it endearing if he wasn't trying to dictate to me again.

"No, it won't. I'll speak to you guys but you can't make me speak to anyone else. If and when I'm ready, it will be my choice who I speak to. I don't trust anyone here enough to put myself out there," I state emphatically, knowing I won't back down on this either.

"If you don't give people a chance, you'll never earn their trust," he warns, making me shake my head. He just doesn't get it.

"I don't need to earn their trust. I owe these people nothing. They failed me as a child and abandoned me as an adult. They're the ones that need to earn my trust, not the other way around." He looks like he wants to disagree but wisely holds his tongue.

Zero squeezes my hand so I look at him. "You trust us, though, obviously." He nods his head towards the bed, so I'm gathering he's referring to the dry humping from before.

I snort at that. I can't help it.

"I trust you guys less than anyone."

When they both cross their arms across their chests and scowl at me, I can't stop my smile from forming.

"Seriously? You think because I rubbed myself against you I suddenly trust you?" I laugh.

"You bartered me away from my brothers like I was a possession, not a person, took me back to the place that haunts my dreams, handcuffed me to the bed, forgot to feed me, and forced me to comply with your wishes when I disagreed with you. Oh, and let's not forget the part about me being groped in my sleep by a stranger. Did I miss anything?" I ask them as Viper stills for a minute, as if listening to something before stomping off to the kitchen area, leaving Zero to stare at me.

"You missed the incident with the pancakes," he points out helpfully.

"Ah, yes, of course, thanks for the reminder. I won't be eating there anytime soon, that's for sure."

"They won't do anything now, I can promise you that," Zero assures as Viper walks over and hands Zero and me each a plate of pizza slices.

"You can't know that for sure." I raise my hand to Viper who sits with his own plate. "I know you can threaten them and kick their asses, but so do they. They'll just hide it better." I take a bite of the cheesy goodness and moan in contentment when the tangy tomato sauce hits my tongue. I swallow it down and lick my lips before opening my mouth to take another bite, when I find two pairs of eyes focused on me. I roll my eyes and ignore them. Hot sexy bikers they might be, but pizza is pizza.

Viper seems to be considering his words before he speaks, so I brace myself.

"You freaked out when Grim, you know, but with us..." He trails off again. I always feel like I'm filling in the blanks with these guys. Luckily, I speak idiot fluently.

"I'm not afraid of sex and I'm not afraid of being touched. I like my body and I'm happy in my skin. It took a long time for me to stop seeing all my flaws and focus on the good stuff. I mean, I have pretty eyes, right?" I ask Viper. He nods in agreement.

"And my boobs are spectacular, huh?" I ask Zero, making him choke on his pizza.

I shrug and take another bite, swallowing it down before continuing. "I have had enough people turn on me because they deemed me defective in some way. One day I woke up and decided I wasn't going to be one of those people too. It took time and I worked really hard on how I saw myself. I took chances, learned my body and the things I like. I experimented and let my curiosity flow. I know now what I like, what I might try again with the right partner, and what is a hard no. And spoiler alert, guys, I like sex. I like it sweet and slow and hot and dirty. I like it deep and tender while pushed up against the wall and fast and hard bent over the kitchen table as I'm pounded from behind." I smile as Viper adjusts himself.

"Waking up with a stranger pinning me down and groping me is a trigger. In all fairness, it would trigger most women. Given my history, my reactions are extreme. Unless I'm going to find myself pinned down by random strangers regularly, it shouldn't be an issue."

"That, I can guarantee, won't happen again," Viper promises.

Grim hasn't slept here at all since we relocated even though I've been safely sandwiched between these two each night.

"He's not a bad guy, Megan—" Zero defends him.

"But he's not exactly a good guy either, is he?" I place the plate on the bed and sigh.

"I need you to be honest with me. Did you know, when you made that deal with my brothers, that you were going to make me your old lady? Or was it a spur of the moment decision?" I already know the answer but I need to know if they are going to lie to me.

"Yes, we knew," Viper admits unapologetically. Yeah, that's what I thought.

"Why would you do that to me?" I ask him, my eyes boring into his.

"For protection. As our old lady, you'll be safe from anyone inside Chaos that still harbors ill will." It's cute that they think that but I suspect they just made me a bigger target.

"And when the truce between Chaos and Carnage is strong, you'll just let me walk away?"

Viper's face switches from remorse to anger at the drop of a hat. "Never."

"Yeah, that's what I thought." I start to stand but his hand stops me.

"I won't apologize, but I won't give you up either, Megan. You might hate me now but you won't always," he remarks, confident in his choice.

"I don't hate you, Viper. I'm just disappointed. I expected more, which is ridiculous, I know. You could have spoken to me—"

"Would you have agreed to be our old lady if I'd asked?"

"We'll never know now, will we, and that's the crux of it all. You'll never know. Not today, not in five weeks, nor in five years if I stayed because I wanted to or because you took my choice away from me."

This time he does let me stand. I take the plate to the sink and then make my way to the bathroom. I brush my teeth using the new toothbrush they got me and look at myself in the mirror. What to do, what to do? My staying is crucial for both clubs, now more than ever, but what about me? My whole sordid past is wrapped up in this club and now I'm supposed to just hand over my future too? Fuck! I toss the toothbrush back into the tumbler and pull the door open, ready to lay down some ground rules. I collide with Viper, who's standing in the doorway.

"Jesus—" Whatever else I was going to say is cut off by his mouth on mine and his hands on my ass lifting me off the ground. I wrap my legs around him and let out a grunt when my back slams against the wall as his lips move from my mouth, over my chin, and down my neck. I see Zero standing in the space Viper had occupied.

"Is this Viper speak for sorry?" I ask Zero, my last word coming out on a gasp as Viper sucks on a spot where my neck meets my shoulder.

"I told you," Viper lifts his head to speak, "I don't say sorry." He dips down again and presses a kiss against my skin, his warm breath making me shiver.

"Damn, and here I was ready to actively encourage you to be an asshole from now on. I'm all for this kind of apology."

His breath comes out harsher and it takes me a second to realize he's laughing.

"Okay, I get it. I accept your non-apology. But there are going to be some conditions."

His head snaps up at that.

"Oh dear, Mr. President doesn't like taking orders," I tease, making him frown.

"I'm the one that gives the orders and you'd do well to remember that."

I laugh in his face. "If you wanted obedience, you should have gotten a dog."

He tosses me over his shoulder before I can say anything else, giving Zero a nice view of my naked ass, which he promptly slaps as he lets us past.

"Ouch, Zero. I thought you were the nice one," I grumble.

Viper flings me unceremoniously onto the bed, making me bounce once before he straddles one of my thighs, leaving space for Zero to straddle the other. Holy fuck, watching them stare down at me half-naked, their eyes blazing with lust as the T-shirt I'm wearing exposes more than it covers. I think I just had a mini-orgasm.

"Zero isn't nice," Viper tells me, his hand trailing slowly up my leg.

"He's nicer than you." I squeal when he lightly pinches the inside of my thigh.

Zero smiles down at me.

"They call me Zero because I give Zero fucks about most things. If I'm coming after you, you'd better run. There's not a lot I care about so if someone tries to mess with what I do, they'll die. Does that freak you out, knowing the man that comes home to you will have broken skin on his knuckles and blood on his clothes?"

"Zero, I'm a woman. I've been washing blood-stained clothes since I was fourteen years old." His grin turns feral at that. Then I feel it, his hand on my leg, sliding its way up just like Viper's on the other one. My breathing picks up as they come closer to my core.

"Ground rules, guys," I manage to pant out even as I feel myself slicken thanks to their ministrations.

They both pause with their fingers just at the crease of my thigh.

"So, tell me these rules, Megan. What's number one?" Viper asks before he starts to gently tap his finger. Oh god, I feel myself getting wetter.

"I'm selfish. Given the fact that there are two sets of hands on me, I'm a goddamn hypocrite to boot, but I don't care. I won't share you with anyone else, so if we do this, there are no club whores for you while you're with me." Viper frowns, making me swallow. This is a deal breaker for me. They might have tied me to them but I won't sleep with them if they are getting it elsewhere.

"But you don't have any qualms about sleeping with all of us, right?" he asks.

"I know it sounds bad, but I'm flat out telling you I can't handle you being with anyone else."

He waves me off. "That's not an issue, Megan. I'm not interested in anyone else and I know how to keep my dick in my pants."

I nod in relief, then think over his words and frown. "Wait, what do you mean sleep with all of you?"

I jump when Zero's fingers run over the lips of my sex in a barely-there touch.

"Me, Viper..." His fingers trail up and down, over and over until I find myself grinding down on him, looking for more friction. "And Grim," he tells me before sliding two fingers inside me.

"I don't think..." I trail off as he withdraws his fingers, only for them to be replaced with Viper's.

"Nobody is going to force you. Just don't rule it out, okay?" Viper asks. I don't know if I'm ready for that conversation and as his fingers slide in and out of me, I realize it doesn't matter at the moment. So I agree and add it to the shit I need to deal with later in the back of my mind.

"Next rule?" Zero asks. I gasp before I feel him slide a finger in next to Viper's.

"Fuck me!" I groan.

Viper smirks at me. "Oh, we will, but I'm glad you want to make it a rule."

"Rule two." I ignore the smart-ass and carry on even as I suspect my voice takes on a husky tone. "Respect."

They both pause with their fingers inside me and wait for me to continue.

"I know how it works here. I'm supposed to show you nothing but respect in front of the club and I will *if* you return it. Don't put me in a position where I have no choice but to react because I won't change who I am for a club that will never accept me. Oh, I'll be good. I won't cause any trouble but I won't take shit lying down. You'd better believe if someone starts something, I won't back down."

"You'll come to us—" I shake my head before Viper can finish.

"No, I won't. I have to fight my own battles or I'll never know a moment's peace."

"I agree with the respect thing, of course. But, Megan, if

someone messes with you, you need to tell me." Viper punctuates his words by thrusting his fingers harder into me.

"Fuck!" I grunt.

"How about a compromise? If it's something I can't handle, I'll come to you. Anything trivial, you leave up to me." They don't seem happy but they're smart enough to know this is as good as it's going to get for them.

"Rule three?" Zero asks as he slips another finger in besides Viper's. I shake my head as I stretch to accommodate him.

"Less talking, more fucking. I can't think straight with your fingers inside me. Talking can wait," I pant, a sigh of disappointment escaping as they both pull their fingers free and slide off me. That is, until they slip out of their boxers and stand before me in all their naked glory.

"Mother of God," I whisper reverently. "You look like you've been photoshopped!"

Viper grins at my words but Zero reaches out with a look of determination on his face, snagging my ankle and yanking me down the bed.

"Now, what was it you said you liked? Oh, that's right, sweet and tender and up against the wall."

Not those exact words but when he scoops me up and I wrap my legs around his waist, I decide not to correct him. I gasp when he pushes my back against the cool wall but he doesn't pull back.

He slips a hand between us and uses some of my wetness to coat his dick before nudging it at my entrance. Moving his hands so they are both on my ass, he tips me back a touch farther and then, without further ado, he glides all the way home.

"Ohmygod," comes out all in one garbled breath as I go from empty to deliciously full in seconds. He pulls back agonizingly slowly before sliding back in to the hilt again.

"Fucking pussy like velvet," Zero forces out the words as I zone in on his lips.

"So hot and slick." He keeps his pace smooth and even, never speeding up, never slowing down until I'm a babbling mess.

"Harder, Zero. Faster," I plead, needing more.

"Not this time, Megan. Slow and sweet," he tells me before taking my lips in a scorching kiss. I forget about everything else: the club, my nightmares, even Viper. All I can think about is the sensation Zero evokes in me as he slowly pushes and pulls his cock in and out of me.

I close my eyes as I spasm around him, slipping my hand down to play with myself. It doesn't take much before I feel myself ready to topple over the edge.

"Zero," I say his name in warning but he cuts me off again with another kiss, biting down on my lip before soothing the sting with his tongue. He pushes himself inside me hard and holds still as I rub my clit, applying more and more pressure until I feel him pulse inside me, which pushes me over with him. I tighten around him, wrap my arms around his shoulders and sink my teeth into his shoulder to keep from screaming out his name.

"Fuck, you are even better than I imagined, and I have a pretty fucking good imagination." I watch his lips move before looking into his slightly glazed eyes. I open my mouth to speak but I find myself being snatched out of his arms and carried over to the vanity table in the corner of the bedroom.

Viper stands me on wobbly legs before using his arm to clear the table. I watch with awe as the little bottles of lotions and creams crash to the floor around us.

"What the fuck?" My question goes unanswered as I find myself being spun and bent over the vanity table a few seconds later.

My chest is pressed flat, a hand on the back of my neck holds me down and a rush of fresh arousal mixed with Zero's cum drips from me. A still naked Zero appears next to me as I feel Viper sliding his cock up and down my pussy lips.

Zero bends down and puts his face close enough that I can read his lips.

"Slow and sweet was pretty spectacular if I do say so myself. But Viper... well, Viper is all about hard and fast with you bent over the table. You want that?" Zero asks, giving me an out as Viper continues to tease me. I try to tell him yes but end up moaning when Viper reaches down and strokes my already swollen clit.

"What was that, Megan? I didn't hear you," Zero mocks, making me growl this time.

"Fuck me, Viper." I barely get the words out before he surges inside me. I gasp as I stretch to accommodate him.

Although Zero is long, Viper is thick, pushing me to my body's limits and leaving me cursing like a sailor.

Zero laughs, but I ignore him, relishing the feel of Viper fucking me with forceful strokes, making my hips jar against the table.

Letting Viper take me from behind is my way of giving him a little bit of trust. I realize it's not a big deal to most. It's just one page out of the *Kama Sutra* for many but without being able to hear him, it's a whole different ball game.

He could be calling me names, hell, he could be calling me by another girl's name for all I know. He could be filming me or taking photos and I would be none the wiser.

Not being able to see when you can't hear is honestly terrifying but for some reason, I feel safe in the knowledge that they won't hurt me or use this thing between us to humiliate me.

I feel my hair being gathered into a ponytail before it's pulled tightly backward, lifting my body up. My chest thrusts out and my head tips way back so I can see an upside-down view of Viper. The look on his face, a mix of raw lust and pure need, has my pussy rippling around him. He leans over me, kissing my lips with surprising softness, before pulling back and hammering into me, making me detonate around him. Eventually, he collapses on top of me, careful not to give me too much of his weight. The scruff of his day-old stubble scratches my skin as he grazes his lips between my shoulder blades, eliciting a shiver.

He lifts himself off me, leaving me already missing his

warmth. I try to catch my breath for a moment. I see Zero looking at me with such a smug expression on his face that I kind of want to punch him in his magic peen. Instead, I stand, making myself look as unaffected from the fuckathon as possible and hop up onto the edge of the table.

"So, rule number three..." I smile inside at the shock written on their faces but don't show it. I'm not going to let them see how rattled they make me, not yet anyway. Give a biker an inch and he'll fucking take a mile.

CHAPTER EIGHT

Viper

I sling my arm around her shoulder, a casual move to most, but nobody can mistake the possessiveness behind the gesture. I feel a tremor run through her but she has her game face on as I pull her into the dimly lit bar area of the compound.

It's not changed much since she was last here. As I feel her shake a little beside me, my rage bubbles thinking of all the shitty memories she has tied to this place. She was right when she said it had failed her before. Well, I'm the fucking president now, these fuckers can either bow down or fuck off. I won't accept anything less. I look over Megan's head at Zero, who has his hand tucked into the back pocket of her jeans, and watch him checking out who's in the room.

It's still pretty early so it's relatively quiet. Boner is passed out on the pool table in the corner with one of the club whores. The fucker's limp dick is still hanging out of his zipper like a wet noodle.

Surprisingly, Grim is sitting against the back wall. Unsurprisingly, he's nursing a beer. As it's only eight in the morning, I'm betting that fucker has been up all night.

I sigh and lead us over to him. He looks up as we approach and turns his attention toward Megan, focusing on her. He takes a long pull of his drink before slamming it down louder than necessary.

"Vipe, heard I got a new old lady. Forget to tell me something?" His voice is laced with anger and even though it's justified, it still pisses me off.

"We talked about this. You knew it was coming," I point out.

"Maybe down the line, but now? Fuck you, Viper. You tied me to a woman that hates me, and rightly so." He lifts his beer as Megan steps forward with her shoulders back and head held high, despite the nerves that I know are riding her.

She takes his bottle out of his hands and puts it on the table beside him before slipping her little notepad and pen from her pocket. After hearing her voice all night, it feels weird knowing she's going back to silence. There's a sick part of me that likes the fact that she only trusts Zero and me with that part of her, even if I did force her hand with it.

She scribbles on the paper and flips it around for him to see.

"I don't hate you," Grim reads aloud. "Well, you should, Megan. I'm a fuck up. Stick with Viper and Zero here and you'll be okay, but stay away from me. You don't need my brand of crazy fucking up your life," he tells her, reaching around her for the beer on the table. She stomps her foot, looking a little like an adorable fairy before spinning, snagging the bottle and tossing it through the air towards the pool table. It hits the leg of the table and explodes, making Boner wake with a start and leaving a puddle of glass and beer on the floor.

Grim frowns down at her in shock, wearing a similar expression to the one Zero and I've adopted. She taps her foot, waiting for something. When he does nothing other than stare at her like she has four tits, she picks up the pad and starts writing again.

"I'm waiting for you to hit me. Come on, I'm ready." His look morphs from shock to horror back to shock again.

"I'm not going to hit you. What the fuck?"

She carries on writing, scrawling across the page in her girly looping script before turning it around.

"That's what my punishment would usually be here for a spilled drink or a broken glass. The fact that that seems to horrify you tells me all I need to know. I think I can handle your brand of crazy just fine. So you fucked up, you fucked up a lot. We all do. Get the hell over it already and fix it. If I have to be stuck in this hellhole, I need a friend who has my back and I've decided that's going to be you," he reads.

I have to dip my head to hide my smile at the shocked

look of disbelief on his face. He's been drowning a little more every day and I get it. I do. Coming home after deployment to find your mother dead and your little sister missing is enough to send anyone off the deep end. Sending him undercover at Carnage seemed like a good idea since they had contact with Gemini, the gunrunner whose name had once popped up in connection with his sister's. Now that everything's fucked up, I'm questioning the call I made.

"Your friend? Have you lost your fucking mind?" he roars at her.

"Apparently, crazy loves company." She shrugs, holding up the words for him to see.

"That's misery," he bites out.

"Perfect," she writes. I read the words out for her as she continues. "I have plenty of time on my hands to make you miserable." His lips twitch at that, surprising the shit out of me, bringing home that I can't even remember the last time I saw my friend smile.

"You keep me safe and I'll make you miserable. Sounds like the perfect arrangement," she finishes, putting the pad on the table after I'm done reading it out. She holds her hand out for him to shake, leaving him standing there staring at it for a moment before his large one engulfs hers. I don't know what her play is here and I know she's still a little wary of him, but it's been a while since I've seen him anything other than angry or hostile. Something about Megan has him engaged again so I'm going to let her take the lead on this.

"Okay, Raven, you win," he concedes.

"Raven?" I ask, knowing she's reading our lips. We all have club names around here. Megan's was always "little bird" from what I've heard. It might have fit the scared little girl I remember but it doesn't fit the beguiling woman before me. Raven... hmm with all that inky black hair, it fits nicely.

"She's no little bird. A raven, however, is majestic, graceful, and intelligent," Grim tells her. She flushes and stares down at her feet to hide it as Grim looks straight at me. "A raven is also a death omen. Mark my words, she will be the downfall of Chaos," he warns me.

"The rot in this club is spreading, Grim, some of it is already dead. Maybe Raven will signal its rebirth instead," Zero tells him.

Whatever Grim was going to say next he holds back when Megan lifts her head again to face him.

"So, friends?" she asks him quietly, almost too quietly for us to hear, but Grim's shocked face shows it was loud enough for him. She gave him her words. I hope he gets how big of a deal that is for her.

He swallows, thinks about saying something, then changes his mind and squeezes the hand he's still holding gently.

"Friends," he agrees just as softly.

I lean down, brush my hand over her jaw and wait for her to tip her head back and look up at me.

"I have some stuff I need to do in the office and Zero has work in an hour. You wanna come with me or sit out here with Grim?" I ask her, giving her the option even as Grim scowls at me. He clearly would rather be off drowning in a bottle or a whore. Well, tough fucking shit.

"I need to go to work myself," she reminds me, even though I'm reluctant to let her out of my sight. "I also need my stuff. As much as I appreciate the bits you guys bought for me, I need more than three outfits to rotate. Plus there are only so many times I can wash my panties out in the bathroom sink," she mutters.

I notice the more she talks, the more even her voice is. Almost like when she stops thinking about it, the pitch naturally sets itself.

"You can't go alone," I tell her.

"I know that already but you said I could go if I had a prospect with me. Plus, Grim can come too."

Grim scowls down at her but then sighs when she bats her eyes in an exaggerated fashion. He mumbles something under his breath about doe eyes, making me smile before he throws his hands up in the air.

"Fine!" he agrees.

She smiles at him and looks back at me. "Will you ask the prospect to drive us all over? My car is at home."

"Fuck that. We can take my bike. I'm not letting some prospect drive me around like Miss fucking Daisy," Grim grumbles, grabbing his keys from his jacket.

Quick as can be, the keys are out of Grim's hands and down the front of Megan's T-shirt. All of us gape at her for a minute before Grim takes a menacing step closer to her, his front pressing against hers. I place a hand on her shoulder, warning him that I will go to bat for her, but he ignores me. He opens his mouth, I'm sure to rip her a new asshole as nobody messes with a man's bike or his ability to ride, when she beats him to it.

"You've been drinking. All night, by the smell of it," she says softly. There is no judgment in her voice, it's just a statement.

"I'm fine," he argues.

"You willing to bet my life on that?" I pause at her words. She's one hundred percent correct. What's worse, if she hadn't said it, I would have gone to my office and not given Grim's intoxication a second thought. Fuck. I'm a shitty president.

"For fuck sake. Fine. But, Raven, you owe me," he tells her, making me breathe a sigh of relief that he isn't going to push the issue.

"Be a good boy and I'll let you frisk me for your keys later," she sasses, surprising him again before turning to me and kissing my jaw. It's a surprisingly sweet move on her part and unexpected. When she realizes what she's done, she steps back and blushes again. She is such a contradiction. Sexy yet shy, sweet yet feisty. A good girl with a dirty mouth. A wild streak runs through her and I can't wait to see how deep it runs.

I pull her back to me and slam my mouth over hers, demanding entrance, which she gives willingly. I grip her head and feast on her, trying to get enough to last me through the day, before pulling away. Any more and I'll have her spread out naked across the bar.

"Damn. Now I'm hard as a rock," Zero mutters, adjusting himself.

"Zero, call Kaz and get him to bring a cage. Tell him he's on guard duty today," I order, never taking my eyes off Megan.

"You good?" I ask her, waiting for her to nod. I hold out my hand. "Phone?" She shakes her head, making me scowl.

"It's back at Carnage. It's not like you guys let me pack before you dragged me out here." Ah, good point. I consider my options. It would take a prospect ten minutes to get her a brand-new phone with all the bells and whistles on it, but something tells me she wouldn't appreciate it as much as having her own back. Ah, fuck. I pull out my phone and send a text to Orion, the Kings of Carnage newly appointed president and Megan's brother. I tell him Megan is fine and to send her things over sometime later today, including her phone so she can message them. She had been Skyping them nightly using my laptop so she could sign to them. I never even thought about her needing a phone until now.

"Is there anything else at Carnage you specifically need?" I ask her before hitting send.

She shakes her head no. "Everything else is at home."

"This is your home now, Megan."

She shrugs her shoulders and turns back to Grim, effectively shutting me out. I let it go for now but she better get used to it.

"Kaz is on his way. Said for you to meet him at the gate when you're ready," Zero informs Grim, sliding his phone back into his pocket. "I've gotta head to the garage." He tugs Megan's hair, making her look at him. He places a quick kiss against her lips before pulling back and smacking her on the ass, making her squeal.

"Be good." He turns and heads out before she can say anything else. It doesn't stop her from flipping him off though.

"Come on, Raven, let's get this shit over with," Grim grumbles, snagging her hand and guiding her towards the door. Just as he pulls her outside, a couple of other members stumble into the room bleary-eyed.

"Pres," Wizz greets me with a nod of his head. He's one of seven prospects we have at the moment and is a genius with a computer.

"Get me a coffee, Wizz, and bring it to my office."

"On it." He heads off to the kitchen, leaving me with Fender, one of the old-timers.

"You're up early this morning, Pres. I thought you'd be balls deep in that Carnage pussy still." My hand is around his neck as I smack his head down hard against the bar, holding him in place.

"That is my old lady you're talking about, Fender. I hear you speaking shit about her again and I will cut out your tongue, understood?"

"Understood," he gasps out when I squeeze his neck hard.

"Come on, Pres, he didn't mean anything by it." I look up and see Boner stumbling over, zipping his jeans up after tucking himself away.

"He needs to learn to keep his fucking mouth shut." I toss him on the floor and look down at him with my don't-piss-me-off face.

"Just a joke, Pres. Boner's right, I didn't mean nothing by it."

I let it go even though I know he's full of shit. But Megan's right, it's going to take time.

"Megan is Chaos, always has been, always will be, despite the shit this club put her through. Perhaps, for a change, we could show her some loyalty instead of treating her like a fucking pariah." He doesn't say anything but offers me a nod instead.

I walk off as Boner reaches out his hand to help him up. I head upstairs to my office and slam the door. There is always some asshole around willing to fuck up a perfectly good morning.

I sit in my chair just as there is a knock on the door.

"What?" I yell, not ready to deal with any more bullshit. Wizz opens the door with my coffee in his hand.

"Got your coffee, boss man," he snarls. If he was truly just a prospect, I would have backhanded the fucker for that shit. He deposits it on the table then plonks himself down in a chair on the other side of the desk.

"Get over yourself, Wizz. Everyone here was a prospect at one time or another. It's a rite of passage and you guys get more leeway than anyone else would because of who you are. If you blow your cover because you don't like being someone's errand boy, I will kick your ass myself."

"Relax, Viper, I'm not going to blow my cover, and fuck you for saying so. You know me better than that," he grumbles.

"Tell me what's got you acting like a damn drama queen then."

"You have no room to talk. Ever since Megan showed up, you've had your panties in a twist." He holds his hand up to silence the retort I was about to fire at him. "I'm not saying it's a bad thing. For what it's worth, I think she might be good for you guys. I haven't seen Grim this animated since we got home."

I nod in agreement, his words echoing my own thoughts. "I guess time will tell. So, what have you found?" I ask him, wanting to get down to business. The sooner I finish up here, the sooner I can track down my girl.

"The books are a fucking mess. I don't know if that was intentional or incompetence, yet. Either way, it's making things harder to track. What I can say is that there is a huge discrepancy in what's coming into this club and what's being fed back out."

"So someone's skimming," I summarize

"Skimming is too tame a word. Whoever it is got cocky. They've been taking huge chunks of change, which should make it easier to find. I just have to wade through all the other shit first. It wouldn't go well for us if I ended up pointing the finger at the wrong person."

I sigh, frustrated but knowing he's right. I'm not the most patient guy in the world and it doesn't sit well with me that I'm standing idly by while someone tries to mess with my club.

"Fuck." I run my hands through my hair, pissed off with the world. Some days I almost wish I was back in the sandbox. At least there I knew that my brothers were protecting my back not trying to stick a knife in it.

"Just keep working your magic. The sooner you find out who's messing with us, the sooner you can swap out that prospect patch for your real one. How are the others getting on?" I don't interact much with them because it would look suspicious if the Pres spent too much time with the prospects.

"Same as me, really. Frustrated for sure but they can see the big picture. What you're offering us here is a family, but like any family, there's always a bad seed. Don't worry, Viper, we'll find them. Me and the guys can manage just fine. We've had it worse." He smirks at me, making me smile. He's not lying, some of the shit we had seen while overseas will haunt us forever.

"Okay, get out of here and keep me posted. Kaz is on Megan duty today. Let the others know." We made it a rule to know where each other is. Can't be too careful when you have people so willing to take you out.

"No problem." He stands and heads to the door, turning just before opening it.

"Have you spoken to Wanda yet?" I tip my head up and groan at the ceiling, feeling a headache coming on.

"She's on my list."

"Well, don't leave it too long, Vipe, she isn't going to be happy that Megan's here."

That's an understatement if I've ever heard one.

"I know and in a way, I get it. She lost her old man and her son in one night but none of that was Megan's fault, so she is just going to have to deal with it."

"Just like that, huh?" The fucker looks far too amused.

"Yeah just like that. I'm the president, she won't go against a direct order," I tell him, sounding far more convinced than I actually feel.

"Whatever you say." He laughs as he heads out. I pick up a pen and lob it at him, but it hits the door as he closes it behind him. I might just leave the fucker on prospecting duty for the next six months. Let's see how fucking funny he finds this shit then.

I turn on the computer and log in. This thing has more security than the fucking Pentagon but if someone thinks they can sneak in here and mess with my shit they are sadly mistaken.

I read over the crap I have to do today and wonder if Grim has the right idea getting wasted in the morning.

All thoughts of Wanda slip from my mind as I work,

trying to straighten out the books as much as I can to make it easier for Wizz to do his digging. I see what he's talking about straight away, it's like whoever is doing it isn't even trying to hide the fact that they are pocketing the club's money.

What has me confused, though, is where most of the money seems to be disappearing from. Euphoria might be a popular strip club, but it is still just that—a strip club. The records that Wizz sent over show it's making over a million a month. At first, I assumed it was from when Chaos was funneling drugs through there. People came for a little blow and a little *blow*. The girls were not meant to be turning tricks, and I'm not naïve enough to think that shit doesn't happen occasionally, but that's not what this is. In fact, looking at the spreadsheets, the drugs side of things seems to have been tied up neatly, maybe a little too neatly as every penny seemed to be accounted for. But why?

Aside from all that, if Euphoria really is making one million a month then where the fuck is it? Because according to these records, barely a thousand is being banked.

CHAPTER NINE

Megan

I discreetly enter the code for the alarm before Kaz takes the keys from my hand, leaving me to sip my coffee and take him in. He's tall, tatted, and built like a tank with an air of menace hiding underneath his messy blond hair and easy smile. I don't remember Chaos ever having prospects like the few I've seen loitering around. They all seem to look older, stronger, and a fuck of a lot smarter than the ones that came before them.

Kaz pushes through the door, and a little flash of light signals his arrival, bringing a smile to my lips. Most people get a little bell or something but thanks to the lack of hearing, I need something more visual.

The soothing scents of jasmine and lavender invade my

senses, making me feel right at home. This place is my sanctuary and even Stokey's attempts at destroying it have failed.

Kaz leaves me with Grim, who stands so close I can feel his body heat against my back, while he checks out the rest of the shop. It's unlikely we'll be attacked by an errant candle or a rogue set of aromatherapy oils but after the month I've had, I suppose it's better not to take any chances.

I look around at the pale lilac walls lined floor to ceiling with chrome shelving. Each wall is littered with sense-stimulating products ranging from mellow to invigorating. Soothing candles, sumptuous cashmere throws, and seductive silk pashminas are just a few of the items designed to either smell, feel, taste or look captivating.

Having one of my senses taken from me made me realize just how important the remaining ones are. Sure, my items might run on the more expensive end of the price scale, but they're worth it. I only sell the best of the best and people come from miles around to buy them, among other more exclusive items.

The large bay window storefront lets a shitload of natural light in the room creating an inviting atmosphere. The dark cherry wood flooring gives the room an elegant and expensive feel. Not bad for a girl who at one point had nothing.

A nudge to the shoulder has me looking up at Grim who is now standing beside me with a frown on his face.

"Are my balls going to shrivel up and drop off? This place

screams 'I am female, hear me roar.' It kind of makes my dick want to tuck itself up inside me and hide."

I burst out laughing, not expecting that to come out of his mouth. He quirks a smile at me that he tries to hide by taking a sip of his own coffee.

"Don't worry, Grim, your cock and balls will be just fine. And if not, I'm bound to have some cream around here to make them feel better." He mock scowls at me but carries on drinking as Kaz reappears.

"Place is clear." He nods at Grim before walking outside and taking up a guarding stance by the door.

"Lord give me strength," I mutter to myself. Following him out, I grab him by his sleeve and yank him back inside. He doesn't resist, which I appreciate. We both know I only managed to move him because he let me.

"You can't stand out there looking like a lone member of a kill squad. You'll scare off all my customers," I tell him, stomping my foot a little like the mature adult I am.

He smiles at me. "Kill squad?"

"Customers?" Grim adds, making me frown at him.

"Yes, customers." I walk to the door and flip the closed sign over to tell the world we're open.

"I have someone who has been filling orders while I've been gone and he let my regulars know I was taking some time off. They'll be glad I'm back," I explain to Grim.

I turn back to Kaz and wave my arm up and down to encompass the colossal size of his body. "Yes, kill squad. You might have the kind of face that mamas love but your body screams lethal predator, the kind that has daddies reaching for their shotguns. Well, unless it's my father. He'd either try to steal your gun or offer me up in exchange for it."

When Kaz looks like he's going to interject, I wave him off, refusing to give in to the bitterness that comes from thinking about either of the men that once held that title.

"You can go sit in the back and leave me here with Grim. I swear I will release the biggest, girliest squeal if someone untoward comes in. Or I can grab you a chair and you can sit by the door, but on this side of the glass. Once people are inside, they'll stay for the products, especially as you look like you might fuck them up if they don't."

"Untoward? Seriously?" He laughs, looking up at Grim who appears equally amused. "I thought she didn't speak?" Kaz smiles, stopping only when he notices I've frozen stock still. "Hey, what's wrong?" he asks, making Grim look down at me with a frown before understanding dawns.

"She doesn't usually. I guess that means she likes you." Grim frowns at the last part and, dare I say, looks a little jealous.

Kaz smiles down at me softly and I can't help it, I smile back. Grim's right, there is something about Kaz that my subconscious decided to trust before the rest of my brain could catch up.

"Well, I'm going to take that as a compliment. And your instincts are correct. If you need anything and you can't reach Viper, Zero, or Grim here, find me, okay?"

I nod, still a little surprised at how easily I gave him my

voice, the voice I hid from even my best friend for the longest time. "Okay, Kaz," I agree, hoping my voice sounds as grateful as I feel.

"Right, I'll grab a chair and sit over there by the door. You and Grim go do what you gotta do." He turns and heads back behind the counter.

A hand on my jaw has me looking up to face Grim who is staring down at me with a little more clarity in his eyes as the alcohol in his system starts to work its way out.

"I haven't spoken more than a handful of words in years to outsiders and only when absolutely necessary. And now I'm just having conversations with random people willy-nilly. I... I guess I surprised myself," I tell him truthfully.

"You seem to be surprising a lot of us lately, Megan." The look in his eyes is intense like he's trying to figure out all of my secrets, but I don't turn away, scared to break this odd moment between us.

"It's not hard to surprise people when they have a tendency to underestimate you. I guess, in a way, it's better than being placed upon a pedestal. I've always been viewed as the lowest of the low, so I had no expectations placed on me, except my ability to fail. With nowhere to fall from, the only option I had was to go up. That suited me just fine because I climbed out of the pit they pushed me into and when I got up there, I waved down at the fuckers from my castle in the sky."

He laughs at my analogy but I know he gets where I'm coming from. He's already seen some of it. I've been labeled the unwanted princess, the traitor's daughter, and the Carnage bitch, but the only title that matters now is that I'm the president and VP's old lady, which, in the club's hierarchy, makes me a much more formidable foe than before.

The light above the door flashes just as Kaz comes strolling back with a chair in his hand. Jack, a regular of mine, stands frozen in the doorway with his mouth hanging open just a little as he takes in the tall and delicious males I'm surrounded by. He wipes his mouth with the back of his hand in an exaggerated fashion, making me laugh.

I do so love your new accessories, Megan. Where can I get some? he signs to me.

You have more men than I have pairs of socks, Jack. I really don't think you need any more, I sign back with a smile, heading behind the counter as Kaz takes up sentry duty by the door and Grim stands to the side, watching us interact.

Nonsense. I have one for every day of the week but sometimes it's nice to have a few spares. One on one is fabulous but two on one is even better. He winks, making me blush and give myself away.

He laughs. *Oh, you naughty girl.*

Behave, I sign, not sure he even knows the meaning of the word. Jack has been coming here since I opened. Born deaf, he was ecstatic to find a fellow signer as he ambled around my shop, declaring he needed one of everything before spreading my name around the deaf community. Thanks to Jack and his word of mouth recommendations, I built quite a following far quicker than the average new shop owner, and I've never looked back.

What are you looking for today? Anything specific or you just in the mood for something new? I ask.

I need some of that cucumber salve and some more coconut oil. Also, those aphrodisiac candles or fuck sticks, as I'm now calling them. I'll take whatever you have left of those. I don't know what's in them but I swear, they make me feel like I've dropped an E or something. I can fuck for hours and I never lose my hard-on, he tells me, making me shake my head. There is no filter with Jack, making me glad that Kaz and Grim have no idea what he's saying.

I only have four left in-store but I know I have another two dozen at the warehouse. I'll get Wyatt to courier them over to you.

Hmm... Wyatt. He can hand-deliver them if he likes, Jack tells me with a wink.

You can leave my assistant out of this. I can't afford for you to chase him off. Besides, you know he doesn't like people, which is why the warehouse suits him. He's hated every second of being in charge while I've been away. I laugh softly, thinking about him. Most people don't even know I have an assistant and that's the way Wyatt likes to keep it. He's hostile to everyone but me and our friend Viddy. To us, he's a teddy bear.

Fine. Jack pouts as I ring up his purchases and place them in a pretty purple paper bag with my shop's logo printed on the side.

I'll get him to text you. Take care. I smile and wave, handing over his bag of goodies and watch him sashay out the door with a jaunty wave of his own.

Both Grim's and Kaz's eyes are glued to me, looking amused.

"Are we safe here? I mean, I was under the impression that I was meant to be looking out for you, but I didn't know Kaz and I would be in danger. I'm pretty sure that dude just stripped me naked and did very dirty things to me," Grim points out with a sparkle in his eyes.

"Hey, it's not my fault you look so damn pretty."

He scoffs. "I'm not pretty. I'm all man, baby," he tells me with a wink, making Kaz and me laugh.

"Oh, I know that." I let my eyes travel over his body slowly, watching him swallow hard.

"Just a really pretty one." I give him a wink of my own before heading into the back. I reach up to grab some candles to fill the space where the others were when Grim appears and tosses me over his shoulder. I squeal in surprise and grip him for dear life when he starts moving through the back of the shop and up the stairs to my apartment above it.

We pause for a moment, I guess so he can fumble with the keys, before he swings the door wide and lowers me inside my home.

"What the heck are you doing?" I slap his chest but he grabs my hand before I can pull it back, effectively trapping it against his heart.

"I'm going to show you how unpretty I am." He nudges me farther into the room and closes the door behind him. He takes off his cut and hangs it on the hook near the door. Without looking away from me, he pulls his T-shirt over his head, leaving his impressive six-pack and tan skin on display.

He waves to get my attention, making me realize I had zoned out staring at the v that peeks out of his low-slung jeans. Jesus, is it hot in here? Maybe that's why he's taking his clothes off.

He runs his fingers over his left side. "Shrapnel." His fingers trail up to his shoulder. "Bullet graze." He keeps moving his fingers around his body, mapping out the scars etched into his skin.

I walk forward and place both of my hands on his chest, halting his movements. "If you think these scars make you any less pretty, you are out of your damn mind. Scars don't take anything away from how attractive you look, they add to your appeal. All they do is show that you are stronger than whatever tried to kill you."

His chest moves up and down rapidly, the heat of his skin seeping into my palms, reminding me that I have a half-naked man in my apartment. One I'm not sure I even like. Retreat, Megan, throw the guy his T-shirt and back the fuck away.

Do I do that? No, I let my vagina do the thinking and climb him like a tree. Seriously, one minute I'm looking up into his gorgeous chocolate eyes, and the next my legs are around his waist and my tongue is in his mouth.

He walks us over to the kitchen counter and sits me on the cool tile before pulling his lips from mine.

"We shouldn't be doing this," he pants before kissing me again.

"Agreed," I answer, pulling away. "It's a terrible idea." I lean forward and trace his lips with my tongue, feeling his growl vibrate against me

"I'm not going to fuck you," he tells me. "But…"

"Oh, I like but…" I breathe, panting as he looks me up and down.

"But I have to taste you." He doesn't give me time to protest, not that I was going to. I'm not the kind of girl that turns down free orgasms.

He presses against my chest until I'm lying flat on my back before making deft work of the button and zipper on my jeans. I lift my hips and let him drag them down over my ass until they get stuck around my ankles, thanks to my boots. Instead of pulling them off, he focuses on my exposed pussy with a look of rapture on his face. Oops, I forgot that I had gone commando. My underwear is still drying, hanging from the shower rail in the bathroom. He lifts my legs and bends my knees, pressing my thighs against my stomach. Locking my ankles together he holds them with one hand while he rubs his calloused fingers over my exposed ass.

And boy, am I exposed. The position he has got me twisted in leaves nothing to the imagination. I don't have time to be embarrassed though before he dips his head and drags his tongue through my slick folds.

"Oh, Jesus," I gasp.

He mumbles something against my pussy. I have no idea

what he says but lord, he can talk all he wants because the vibrations are sensational.

He flicks his tongue over my clit, circling it until it's hard and aching, then he dips inside me, lapping away at my juices. He feasts on me like a starving man, making me lose all sense of time. I don't care that Kaz is downstairs alone or that I have a damn shop to run. All that matters is the magical spell Grim has woven around us. When he slides two fingers inside me and sucks hard on my clit, I scream harshly enough to hurt my throat.

"Lord have mercy," tumbles from my lips. Vibrations ripple over my skin from him laughing against me, before he gently lowers my shaky legs. He looks pretty damn pleased with himself and he should, dammit.

"I feel like I should thank every girl that came before me, literally, because that tongue right there is the fucking shit. I guess practice really does make perfect."

He grins at me like the cat that got the cream and I guess in a way he is.

"All right, we'd better get back downstairs before Kaz sends out a search party," he tells me.

CHAPTER TEN

Grim

"This girl is going to be the death of me," I mutter to myself as I follow that delectable heart-shaped ass back down the stairs to the shop.

Kaz tosses me a knowing look when I meet his eyes, making me flip the fucker off. I made myself a promise to stay away but then Viper went and made her our old lady and now... Well, now I can't seem to think of anything other than her legs wrapped around my waist as I fuck her hard or her toned thighs squeezing my face as I lick her pretty little pussy.

I groan and adjust myself, ignoring the laughing asshole by the door.

"Laugh it up, dickhead, and I'll have you scrubbing the toilets later," I tell him, making him flip me off this time.

The light flashes above the door before a tall guy who looks like he belongs on the cover of Forbes magazine with his expensive suit and Italian loafers walks in. Something about him is vaguely familiar but I can't place where I know him from.

Megan doesn't seem to have that problem, though. She looks over and squeals when she sees him before running around the counter and launching herself at him. I clench my fists to stop myself from ripping her out of his arms before I snap them off and beat him with them.

He, unlike the guy before him, looks like he can handle himself. In fact, there's something about him that screams darkness, making me wonder if Megan is aware that this guy is not all he appears to be.

"I missed you," she tells him, and I frown again. Well, whoever he is, she obviously trusts him enough to speak to him. I don't like that, not one little bit.

"So, you wanna put my girl down now or do I have to make you?" I ask, letting the menace seep into my voice.

He dismisses me with a smirk before pressing a kiss to her forehead, sliding her down his front far slower than necessary.

"She was my girl first," he informs me with a smile, but I don't miss the hint of longing beneath his words. Interesting. I stomp over to them and snatch her up, causing her to squeal in the process, and wrap my arm around her shoulders, pulling her close to my side.

"Well, she's my girl now, so keep your fucking hands to yourself." I hold her tight making her squeak, before I loosen my grip a little. "You like this asshole enough to speak to him?" I question, looking down at her, but I sound like an idiot. Of course, she speaks to him if he's an ex of hers.

"Well, how else was I going scream out my safe word?" she sasses me as plans start running through my mind of retribution that involves this guy bleeding from a gunshot wound and my girl's ass being blistered red.

The dickhead in front of us throws his head back and laughs, making me want to punch the motherfucker in his exposed throat.

"Megan, Megan, Megan. Always full of surprises," he tells her with a charming smile when he finally gets himself under control.

"I've just come for my usual, and to see if you can order me some more of these." He hands her a piece of paper, which she reads and nods along to.

"Yeah, Jax, that won't be a problem. I'll message Wyatt and see if we have any of the silks in stock, but the rest of it I know I'm out of. I'll order them and get it sent straight to the club if you like."

"That would be appreciated, darlin'. Put it on my tab and let me know when to expect a delivery," he winks at her before walking over to give her a kiss on the cheek. His lips linger just long enough for me to want to rip them off.

"No worries, Jax, you know I will."

"When are you going to come by for a play? You can bring your friend." He looks me up and down and clearly finds me lacking.

"Don't be an ass, Jax. Besides, I'm not sure it's their scene."

"Their?" he questions. I look down at her, expecting her to blush or backtrack, but not this girl. She has more balls than most guys I know, at least when it comes to her sexuality.

"Viper, Zero, and the big unmovable statue here. They decided to make me their old lady, so what's a girl to do other than demand hot and sweaty sex for the rest of her life?"

"Excellent point. The offer still stands. You know, you are always welcome back," he coaxes, and I know damn well he means that in every way. Back in his bed, back in his heart—this fucker has a death wish.

"I know, Jax," she answers, waving him off as he leaves. I glare down at her, which she ignores, pressing a soft kiss against the scruff of my jaw before heading back behind the counter, I'm assuming to text this Wyatt person.

Kaz taps her arm.

"How the fuck do you know Jax?" he asks her, a look of surprise on his face.

"He's my friend and my ex-boyfriend," she replies with a shrug before ignoring us and sending a text.

"Who is this Jax guy and how do you know him?" I ask Kaz, who's still looking at Megan like she just performed a really cool trick.

"Jax owns Sinners in the next town over. It's an exclusive, by invite only, sex club." I whip my head around to stare at my girl. My sweet, young, innocent girl, and then back to Kaz.

"A sex club, seriously? How the fuck did he end up tangled with Megan?" I ponder, thinking he must have come in here for something and met her that way.

"That would be after I pulled off his mask the first night he fucked me." The soft voice has me looking up even as my vision flashes red.

"Don't talk about me like I'm not here, Grim, especially if it's about me. If you want to know something, then just ask me."

I stalk over to her, our bodies separated by the glass counter between us, and yell, even though I know she can't hear a word I'm saying.

"You went to a sex club? You had sex with a stranger? You were in a relationship with this guy?" I keep firing out questions, not giving her time to answer even as her eyes flash with anger.

"You stupid fuck," Kaz mutters behind me, making me stop and take a breath.

"First of all, you giant douche canoe, what I do with my body is up to me. If I want to walk down the street naked and bend over for the first guy I come across, well, that's up to me. Second of all, I was in a safe place where everyone had been vetted and all of us had been tested. Fuck, I had to go through so much red tape you'd have thought I was going to be fucking the president. It was ridiculous, but I can assure you, it was all consensual and I loved every second of it." Her chest is heaving up and down now as her temper rides her hard.

"I had nightmares every single day for a year after my attack. I couldn't bear to have anyone touch me for even longer than that. Nobody, man, woman, or child. It literally made me feel like bugs were crawling under my skin.

"After I got safe and bought this place, I started working on me. One of those steps was to teach myself how to not be afraid of touch, and the most effective way to do that was to change my perception of it. I always associated touch with pain but over time, I learned that touching someone or being touched by someone can also bring you unimaginable pleasure. You don't get to fucking make me feel bad for that. You were not in my life back then. You were not fucking me, feeding me, or providing for me financially, so you have no goddamn right to an opinion on the subject." She turns and storms off upstairs again.

"Well, fuck."

"You dick," Kaz snaps at me.

"Watch it, prospect," I warn, knowing he's right

"Fuck you, Grim. You were way out of line and I'm thinking any headway you made with that girl has now been erased. Nice job."

"Oh, and I suppose you wouldn't have a problem with your girl visiting a sex club?"

"Why the hell would I? She wasn't your girl back then,

Grim. Can you stand there and tell me you've been an angel waiting for her? No, of course, you can't. Don't be a fucking hypocrite. Have you even looked at it from the flip side? Your girl is confident and sexy. She knows exactly what she likes and she's willing to explore it. Lucky for you, I'd say, or I would sincerely doubt she would have given the idea of a relationship with three guys a shot. You have the perfect woman there. Sweet in the streets and a freak in the sheets."

He turns and heads back to his spot by the door, muttering under his breath, leaving me to my own chaotic thoughts. I know I was a dick. But I can't shake the image of Megan in a sex club out of my mind. It's like watching a lamb getting circled by a group of hungry wolves. I bet they had a field day with her. Is that why she has taken to Viper, Zero, and me so easily? Has it been conditioned into her? I like her, more than I should, given the colossal fuck up I am, but I'm not going to take advantage of her. I pull out my phone and dial Viper.

"Yeah," he barks out distractedly when he answers.

"Did you know Megan was a frequent flyer over at Sinners?"

"Sinners? The sex club?" he questions.

"Yep, it seems our old lady is into that whole scene." He's quiet for a while, so much so I check my phone, thinking the call's dropped.

"Viper?"

"Hmm... that girl is just full of surprises." He sounds intrigued.

"It doesn't piss you off imagining a dozen hands all over her or a dozen dicks inside her?" I ask, shocked.

"Jesus, Grim. She's been to a sex club. It doesn't suddenly make her the gangbang queen of the US. Have you ever even been to a sex club? Fucking hell, it's not like some giant orgy you are imagining it to be. From what I've seen, Jax runs a pretty tight ship."

"Wait, you know Jax?" I growl.

"I've met him, sure. I'm not exactly bosom buddies with the fucking dude but he meets everyone he gives a membership to."

"You're a member?" I question. "Why the fuck would you go there when you can get all the pussy you want at the clubhouse?"

"Not that it's any of your fucking business, Grim, but there is more to fucking life than club girls. They serve their purpose and most of them are respectful but sometimes I want to be able to fuck someone that hasn't also been dicked by every other brother in the clubhouse. Now we have Megan, it isn't an issue," he tacks on the end.

"I can't see what has you so riled up, Grim. Do I like the thought of Megan being with someone else? Of course not, but she has to deal with the fact that we've been with the club bunnies, so how is this any different? Just don't go off on one before you've had the chance to think clearly about it. The last thing we want is to push her away."

I don't say anything, which reveals my guilt.

"Grim, tell me you kept your mouth shut!" he warns, making me sigh.

"He had his fucking hands all over her! I reacted, so fucking sue me. I had her coming on my tongue and five minutes later she's in her ex's arms," I bite back.

"Ex?" His voice has gone dangerously quiet, letting me know I just tossed a grenade into the conversation.

"Yeah. Jax is Megan's ex, and from what I can see, they still care about each other, far more than I'm comfortable with."

"I'm on my way." He hangs up, leaving me glaring at my phone.

I turn to Kaz and find him looking at me like I've lost my damn mind.

"I'd love to know who fucked you over."

"What?"

"You just threw Megan to the wolves. He wasn't reacting to the sex club info like you thought he should, so you threw in the bit about her ex, knowing it would get a rise out of him. You played on his trust issues with his ex and then pointed him straight at Megan."

"What?" I repeat, genuinely confused.

"Real men act as a shield for their women. You just picked her up and placed her in the firing line. Dick move, Grim." Kaz storms outside, leaving me questioning his words and replaying what just happened.

"Fuck!" I dial Zero's number and wait for him to answer,

knowing he's at the garage today, which isn't too far from here.

"Yo!"

"I fucked up," I tell him straight out.

"Of course you did, it's a day ending in y. What happened?"

I ignore his sarcasm and fill him in, leaving him to curse me out.

"Goddamnit, Grim. I'll be there in five." He hangs up on me too, leaving me standing there with my dick in my hand. See, this right here is why I don't do relationships. I'm no fucking good at them and I fuck everything up.

"Fucking, fucking shit," I grumble and make my way upstairs to her apartment, hoping she doesn't throw anything at me when I walk in. I swing the door wide and step to the side just in case, but nothing comes whizzing by, so I sigh in relief.

When I step inside and see her on the floor sitting cross-legged looking sad and dejected, I kind of wish she had launched something at me.

I sit down in front of her, mimicking her position. Sliding my finger under her chin, I lift her head so she has to look at me.

"I'm not good at relationships. I've never seen a healthy one to emulate. I've never really aspired to be in one and like everything else I lay my hand on lately, I'm failing spectacularly."

"We're not even really in a relationship, Grim, at least not yet, so you haven't failed at anything. Did you ever think that we just might be incompatible? I'm not ever going to be one of those girls that will change who she is to fit the mold you're trying to squeeze me into. I've spent too long growing strong to let someone make me feel small again."

"I don't want to change you or make you feel small. It guts me that I made you think that. I'm a dick, Megan, I'm sorry," I tell her, wishing she could hear the sincerity in my voice.

She appears shocked for a second like she never imagined I would apologize. She's right, I'm not the kind of guy that says sorry. I don't believe it changes anything, it's just a way of easing your guilt, but looking into her startling blue eyes, I realize I am truly sorry I hurt her.

"You guys are having a party and fail to invite me? I'm wounded." I glance up and see Zero staring down at us. His words are casual but I don't miss the tick of his jaw as he takes in Megan's demeanor. He sits beside us and looks at me before focusing on Megan.

"So, what did I miss?" he asks her.

"Grim was just telling me how much of a dick he is," she quips, making him laugh at my expense.

"Well, at least he's honest. Grim's the biggest dick I know." I shove the fucker, making him topple over. He moves to shove me back but we both freeze when Megan's light laughter catches our attention.

"He did apologize though, so I guess he's not as big of a dick as he thinks he is," she says, making something warm in my chest.

"Did he now?" he questions, looking at me. I'm about to answer when the door slams open, banging against the wall, making Zero and me whip around to find an angry Viper storming over to us.

"You let him touch you?" he yells at her, making the bubble of guilt that had begun to shrink explode all over me.

She looks at him, startled by his appearance and confused by his words.

"What? You said you, Zero, and Grim. You said that." She thinks he's talking about me and her in the kitchen earlier. But when she turns to look at me, she must see the guilt on my face. She looks back up at Viper. He barks down at her.

"You let that motherfucker Jax put his hands on you? You are our old lady. Nobody touches you but us. Do you understand me, Megan? Stay away from him."

She looks at me, her face filled with hurt and anger and perhaps, worst of all, disappointment. She climbs to her feet, ignoring Viper and his outburst, and walks off towards the bedroom. Viper starts to follow her but Zero grips his arm.

"That's enough, Vipe," he tells him, his voice firm.

Viper seethes. "She let her ex-boyfriend, Jax-fucking-Lewis, of all people, touch her."

"She gave him a hug. She didn't drop to her knees and suck his fucking cock. You two are so fucked in the head that you can't see past your own shit. You keep pushing your issues onto her when she has done nothing to deserve it. We will lose her before we've even been given a real shot if you guys can't get your shit together," Zero snaps, losing his patience.

"She's not going anywhere," Viper growls. Zero's words are not penetrating Viper's cloak of anger, but they get through to me.

"There are more ways to lose someone than physically. If you carry on, you'll snuff out the fun-loving, vivacious girl she tries to hide inside herself, leaving you with the quiet, withdrawn, sad little girl from years ago. If that's what you want, then I'll send her back to Carnage myself because I refuse to be a part of it," Zero bites out.

Whatever Viper's response was going to be is cut off by the reappearance of Megan stomping towards us with a large shoebox in her hands.

"You want to know why I talk to Jax? Why I let him put his hands on me? Well, let's start at the beginning, huh?"

Slipping her hand inside the box, she grabs item after item and throws them one by one at Viper.

"Here's a picture of my mother and me. The only one I have before she sacrificed herself to save me just like she did every day of my life. Here's the address of the foster home I was placed in when I got booted from Chaos. It's also the address I ran from when the father tried to get handsy with me. Here's a flyer for the bakery I used to frequent. Not the inside though, the dumpster behind it, looking for discarded food because I was so hungry my body was eating itself from the inside out. Oh, here." She throws a bottle of pills at him. They bounce off his chest and scatter across the floor. "These are the same kind of pills I swallowed when I finally decided this life just wasn't worth living anymore." The tears are streaming down her face now, her pain and words lancing wounds into my skin that will never heal.

"Here's the hospital ID bracelet I wore when Jax sat beside me every single day until I was mentally strong enough to leave. I'm here because that stubborn ass refused to let me quit. He gave me the tools to help me build myself back up after a lifetime of being torn down, and I won't give him up for any of you. I have given up everything, over and over again. Yet, despite it all, I built a life for myself. Do you really hate me so much that you want to come in here like a wrecking ball and destroy that?"

Viper storms over to her, ignoring Zero calling his name. She backs up, placing the shoebox on the chair beside her, preparing to run, but Viper is faster. He wraps his arms around her and holds tight as she thrashes. He walks to the sofa and drags her onto his lap, holding her in place until she stops struggling. Zero and I crowd around them. I crouch down and tuck her hair behind her ear. She watches me warily and it breaks my heart.

"You're right. You are absolutely right. These are our issues, not yours. We'll work on it, I promise. Don't give up on us just yet, okay? This is all new to us and, well, we're men." I shrug, hoping for a laugh but sigh when I don't get one.

Viper loosens his hold, letting her sit up, but stops her from leaving his lap. A little frustrated sigh escapes her lips, which sounds adorable. I don't tell her that though. I like my dick attached to my body, thank you very much.

"My ex fucked around with anything that had a pulse while I was deployed. I thought we were happy, but the girl she pretended to be in her letters was far from who she really was. I found that out when I came back and turned up at her place unannounced. Turns out I'm the one that got surprised. She was heavily pregnant with a kid that obviously wasn't mine and had two more with her under five. She didn't even look ashamed, admitted straight up that she kept me on a string because of the money I sent her. I swore off relationships after that. Until you."

We all watch her silently while she absorbs his words before I speak again, breaking the silence.

"That was a lot of information you just threw at us there, Megan. Care to elaborate?" I ask her.

She shakes her head but Viper tightens his hold again, making her curse.

"You won't let me leave until I tell you, will you?" She sounds resigned.

"I'll never let you go, Megan," Viper tells her, sounding like the psychotic stalker he is.

"Fine, whatever." She shakes her head and starts talking.

CHAPTER ELEVEN

Megan

This seems to be the theme of my life at the moment. Wake up, everything is good, then bam! The day takes a major nosedive. They want the nitty-gritty details, fine. I'm not ashamed that I hit rock bottom. Quite the opposite, actually. I clawed myself out of hell one bloody fingernail at a time. How many people can say that they faced their demons and survived?

"After the attack, I woke up in the hospital with no hearing and a matching set of dead parents. I was sixteen years old and despite the fact I had aged overnight, in the eyes of the law, I was a minor. Chaos didn't want me—Rock made that clear when he dropped off a box of my mother's things. I got placed in a foster home with an older couple.

The wife, Jan, wanted the extra cash. The husband wanted a teenage girl under his roof and under his control. I was so fucking sick of overzealous men thinking they could just take whatever they wanted. He snuck into my room the first night I got there. Luckily enough, the wife disturbed him before he could take it too far. I ran before I had to fight him off a second night.

"Life on the streets is hard on anyone. But for an underweight, scared, deaf girl who couldn't bear to be touched, it was a fucking nightmare. For two years I dodged gangs and thugs while trying to find enough food to keep me alive."

Grim sweeps the hair from my face. "Jesus Christ, baby. Why didn't you tell Rock what was going on? Or your fucking brothers? Where the fuck were they when you needed them?" Grim asks, pulling his own hair in frustration.

"My brothers didn't know I existed until the day Stokey showed up here. The first time I laid eyes on Logan—I mean Orion—I was locked in the cells below the Carnage clubhouse."

Zero taps my leg to get my attention. "So you don't even know them?" he asks, shocked.

"Not really. And then you guys took me so I might never get that chance."

Viper tips my head up to look at him. "We'll figure that out, Megan, I swear. It will just take some time," he vows. I hope that's a promise he can keep. "Why didn't you tell Rock? He could have done something."

I give him a sad smile before continuing. "With no phone? I couldn't go back to Chaos, that had been made clear. Besides, it didn't matter in the end," I huff with a shake of my head.

"It does fucking matter. He could have helped, he could have—"

I cut off Viper's rant with my own words. "He knew. I didn't realize it at the time, but he knew. The day I turned eighteen, he found me asleep in an old warehouse I sometimes stayed at and told me I was now old enough to access my trust fund."

"That doesn't mean he knew—"

I shake my head. "He told me he had been keeping an eye on me but now I would have enough money to disappear."

Nudging my thigh with his elbow Grim asks, "Keeping an eye on you? Is he for real?"

Zero snags my attention as he jumps up and starts pacing, before turning to face me with his hands on his hips. "Fucking hell! Anything could have happened to you, fucking anything, and he stood by and did nothing," he yells, making my face soften at his words.

"Chaos forbade it. It was voted on, apparently," I remind him in what I hope is a soothing tone.

Viper turns my head back to face him once more. "He was the president. He had the power to change that. But even taking

Chaos out of the equation, as a man, a man who watched you grow and was well aware of what happened to you, he should have damn fucking well made sure at the very least you had somewhere safe to lay your head at night. I'll be dealing with him my fucking self." He gives me a stern look, letting me know it's pointless to argue with him so I sigh in defeat.

"Anyway, I took the money and bought this place outright. I had a safe place to live, a place to work, and food whenever I wanted it. That's when I decided to work on me. I... I was lonely," I admit, feeling silly, dipping my head to hide my embarrassment.

"Don't do that," Viper tells me after lifting my chin once more so I have no choice but to look into his eyes. "You don't have one single thing to feel embarrassed about."

I give him a nod and carry on, twisting my fingers in my lap. "I made two friends who I met on the streets, but they were battling their own demons and I didn't want to add to their problems so I just told them I was okay. And I was, for the most part.

"I tried to make more friends but I just couldn't handle being touched. I felt so stupid but then this woman came in here and mentioned Sinners. She said they were all about anonymity and they could cater to most wishes.

"I figured I had nothing left to lose and signed up. I jumped through the hoops needed, did all the testing they required, and sat through the interviews. Funnily enough, that should have been where I would have first met Jax but he was out of the country that week. Anyway, long story short, my first time there, I freaked, had a full-blown panic attack, and Jax appeared out of nowhere and coaxed me through it. I don't know why but I told him everything, just leaving anything Chaos related out of it, and he decided he was going to help me.

"And he did. It was a slow process though, and loneliness can be a cruel bitch. One Christmas morning, I found myself alone once more and decided I just didn't want to do this anymore. I was a shell of a person and figured nobody would miss me if I was gone and then maybe, just maybe, the pain would stop." Nobody speaks as I reveal the utter despair that haunted me and nearly took me away from them before we ever got the chance to know each other.

"Jax turned up out of the blue when he found out that Wyatt and Viddy couldn't make it and I'd be alone on Christmas. He found my address on file and decided to check on me. He saved my life, then spent an awful long time reminding me it was worth living."

Grim's hand falls heavily on my shoulder, gaining my attention.

"You became friends, then lovers, then more?" he asks, making me nod with a fond smile. "So, what happened? How come you aren't together anymore?" he questions.

"I couldn't give him what he needed and I didn't want him to try and change who he is for me. We would both end up miserable. I loved him enough to let him go but he will always be one of my best friends."

Viper slides his hand under my jaw so I look at him

before asking the question that I'm sure is on the tip of all their tongues. "What did he need?"

"Someone submissive, not just in the bedroom, but in general. He needs to be able to take care of someone, to anticipate their needs before they even know themselves what they want. I guess with how I was when he first met me, it seemed I might have some submissive traits, but as I got stronger and healthier mentally, it became clear that the only place I could be submissive was in the bedroom. Even then, it's hit or miss. I can be bossy as fuck too."

Viper laughs and a quick scan of the other two shows them grinning too, making me smile again, despite the heavy subject matter.

"Anyway, if you're worried there is some kind of competition between you guys and him, don't. He might tease you—no, he *will* tease you, it's just who he is, but Jax and I will never be anything more than friends. I haven't asked you for anything since you took me from my family and brought me back here." Viper flinches at my words even though there is no accusation in them.

"So I'm asking you now for just one thing." I focus on Viper, staring at his handsome face.

"What?" he asks.

"I'm asking you to trust me. I'm here with you three. I'm willing to see how this thing between us unfolds but I need you to have a little faith in me or we're doomed before we've even begun.

"I'm not your ex," I tell Viper. "Or your mother," I add,

looking at Zero before turning to Grim. "And I'm not your sister. I'm just Megan. I've made mistakes, for sure, but I won't pay for someone else's or for yours."

They don't speak as they think over what I've said, but I'm right. I know it, and I can see that they do too.

"Okay, Raven. We'll work on it," Viper pledges when he's sure he has my attention again.

"So, I'm Raven again now, huh?" I tease.

"You are when you get those claws out for sure," he snarks with a smile, making me elbow him in the ribs.

"Be nice or I'll claw those pretty little eyes out of your face," I sass, sticking my tongue out at him which, of course, he takes advantage of by slamming his lips down over mine.

How we can go from fighting to fucking is beyond me, but as his hands snake their way under my top, I realize I'm perfectly okay with it.

Unfortunately, he pulls away and looks towards the door, making me turn in his arms to spot Kaz standing in the doorway.

"Sorry, guys, but, Megan, you have a couple of customers down there looking for you." I wilt in frustration. Just when we were getting to the good stuff, dammit.

"Okay, I'm coming. Thanks, Kaz." He nods and heads back downstairs as I try to crawl off Viper's lap but his hold on me is unrelenting.

"Viper?" I question, looking up at him.

"You just told Kaz you were coming. Let's make that happen so you can get downstairs." He grins at me lasciviously, making me squirm before the meaning behind his words makes sense. By then it's too late, he's already summoned Zero and Grim with nothing more than a nod of the head.

It's about that time I realize these are no ordinary bikers. No, these guys must have some kind of superpower. It's the only way I can explain how I blinked and, boom, my clothes disappeared. Now I'm standing before them naked as they circle me like some virgin sacrifice that's ready for defiling.

"Do you have any idea just how fucking spectacular you are, Megan?" Viper asks, moving his eyes from my face down to my breasts.

"Um... yes. No. Maybe," I babble. "I don't know." I throw up my hands. "But you should definitely, absofuckinglutely show me. Just not while I have a shop full of customers," I protest, backing away. I soon find myself up against a wall of muscle.

Being as I can see Viper and Zero, I know its Grim's hands that pull my arms behind my back, making my chest stick out in a silent offering.

"Better let us get to work then, Raven, or everyone will wonder what's keeping you," Zero suggests, stepping forward and cupping my right breast with his rough hands.

"Hmm... so pink and rosy. Like little berries begging to be devoured." He dips his head and sucks my nipple into his mouth, eliciting a moan as my resistance starts to slip away.

I feel fingers sliding between the lips of my pussy, making my eyes, which had slipped shut, snap open again. Viper looks at me with a grin on his face that lets me know he's thinking of doing very dirty things to me.

A rush of wetness escapes me, coating his fingers. Once they are slick enough, he pushes two inside me.

"Fuck, you're squeezing my fingers so tight." He slides them in and out until I know my juices have soaked his hand.

Grim leans down and drags his nose across my shoulder blade before running it up behind my ear and nibbling on the skin there. I feel like there's a current running through my body and I'm a live wire zapping with untapped energy that's making every inch of my skin hum and sing until, finally, the pressure is too much to contain and it explodes out of me.

I don't know what I scream but whatever it was leaves my throat feeling hoarse. Oh lord, how I wish for all deaf customers.

"You guys are trying to kill me." Grim holds me upright so I don't slip to the floor, my post-orgasmic haze insisting that I should sleep but my brain knows damn well it's not an option.

"Okay, guys, form an orderly line," I manage to gargle out. Zero looks at me oddly before he bursts out laughing.

"This was just for you, Megan," he tells me with a shake of his head.

"Is this all part of your master plan? Every time you guys fuck up you're going to say sorry with orgasms?" I look to the ceiling and place my palms together in a praying motion.

"Thank you, Lord, for bad boys who break the rules." I

squeal when Viper tosses me over his shoulder and drags me into the bathroom. He turns on the shower and lowers me inside when the water warms up before placing a surprisingly soft kiss on my lips. He stares down at me and even though he doesn't do sorry, I can see the apology in his eyes.

"Get out of here before I trip and land on your dick," I grumble, turning my back on him as I hurry to clean myself up.

When I'm done, I lean my head against the cool tile for a moment and close my eyes as the water slides over me.

When I agreed to come to Chaos again, I knew I might have to fight to protect myself. It just never dawned on me that I might need to fight to protect my heart. And yet, here I stand, my heart warring with my head. I know that starting any kind of relationship under the circumstances that we did is like trying to build a house on the sand. It may look pretty and function for a while but without solid foundations, it's still doomed to sink and end up abandoned.

But this heart, fuck, it wants things I told myself were only for other girls. I just never realized how much I wanted to be one of those girls until now.

CHAPTER TWELVE

Viper

Mind still spinning over the information Megan dumped on us, I head back to the club, leaving the others back at Megan's shop. My plan is to find Rock and find out what the fuck he had been thinking. Pulling inside the gates, I'm surprised to find he's made it easy for me by standing out the front of the diner by the bikes, having what looks to be a heated argument with none other than Wanda. Fuck, I forgot to talk to her. I climb off my bike already in a bad mood, knowing it's about to get a whole lot worse.

Wanda turns when she hears me approach and swings around with her hands on her hips, scowling at me.

"Careful, Wanda, it looks to me like you might be

forgetting your place," I warn her before she can start with her bullshit.

"Is it true? You made that whore your old lady? Are you fucking insane? She's the reason your uncle and my boys are dead, and you make her yours?" she yells in disbelief.

My hand is around her neck, cutting her off before she carries on.

"Listen to me right now. John is nothing to me. I'm ashamed I ever called him uncle. You do not want me to get started on your boys. You're hurting, Wanda. I get it, I do, but you will do as I fucking ask, which is to be respectful and to keep your fucking mouth shut."

I release her and she steps back with a gasp even though I wasn't holding her tight enough to hurt her.

"And what do I tell Conner when he comes home tomorrow? Sorry, your whole family is dead, oh, and the bitch responsible is going to be here day in, day out, rubbing it in your face?" she screams.

I nod for the two prospects hovering nearby watching and wait for them to approach.

"I didn't see you worrying about Conner when you shipped him off to school," I point out.

"He needed to get away from here and the memories."

I roll my eyes at her. "He's only six years old. What he needed was his mother." Her eyes flash at my words but she doesn't say anything as I turn to the prospects. "Get her out of here," I order them as she tries to shake them off.

"You can fight all you want, Wanda, but I call the shots

around here so consider this your last warning. I let you stay by my good graces but you are burning through them rapidly." I turn my back on her and ignore her shouts as the prospects drag her away.

"Viper—" Rock gets out but it's all I allow him to say before I ram my fist into his face.

"I have never been ashamed of where I came from until right now. John wasn't my uncle by blood, not like you. I thought you were a better man than him, turns out I was wrong." I shake out my hand, relishing the sting of the split skin where my knuckles connected with his teeth.

"You knew where she was. You knew the kind of danger she was in, and you turned your fucking back on her!" I roar, drawing an audience.

"I was the fucking president!" he yells back, wiping the blood from his mouth. "I had the club to look after. It was in utter turmoil after John's and Crogan's deaths. I made a choice for the greater good and I stand by it now." He puffs out his chest.

"Thank god you're not the president anymore. If you couldn't provide safekeeping for one measly girl, how the fuck would you provide it for everyone else? You use this club as an excuse but it's your job to set the example. I guess, in a way, you did. You made it perfectly acceptable to make a sixteen-year-old deaf girl, who had just lost everyone she ever had, homeless and broke. You didn't even bother explaining the truth of what happened all those years ago to anyone. You didn't step up, you turned your back on her!"

"I had Wanda and then Conner to consider too. She had just lost her old man and kid!" His explanation makes me even madder.

I step up to him toe to toe, letting my face show my disgust for a man I spent my whole life looking up to.

"Megan had lost everything and she was a goddamn child."

"All right, guys that's enough." Flow steps between us. "Now isn't the time nor place."

I look up at him, ready to rip him a new asshole when I spot all the people staring at us like a fucked up version of Jerry Springer.

Fuck this shit. I turn to face the crowd and cross my arms over my chest in an I-don't-give–a-single-fuck manor. I'm done with this shit. It's time for some hard truths.

"As you're all here, it bears repeating that Megan is off-limits. She is under mine, Grim's, and Zero's protection and we will kill anyone who messes with her, as is our right according to the bylaws. You'd do well to read up on them because I can see some of you still seem to be confused. You all look at her like she wronged you in some way but we're the ones that wronged her."

"Her mother killed our old pres. It's only natural that there would be bad blood there," one of the guys calls from the back of the crowd.

"Sins of the father, or in this case the mother, right?" I ask. When a murmur of agreement ripples through the crowd, I laugh sardonically, surprising them.

"Well, fuck, why didn't you say so? If we're all to be held accountable for our parents' actions, then what does that say about all of you? But then, I guess you were too busy pointing your fingers and judging Megan to notice that you were standing on the skeletons that fell from your own damn closet."

I point to a few individuals in the crowd who I know for damn sure had a less than stellar upbringing.

"Murderer, thief, whore, drunk, addict, wife beater. Shall I go on? Are you telling me that I should wash my hands of you because of the choices your parents made?" There is no murmuring now, just uncomfortable silence as they shuffle, not liking the tables being turned one little bit.

"Want to know the best part? Melinda was only doing what any of you would have done—"

Boner cuts me off. He thinks being an old-timer gives him free rein to use his smart mouth and bad attitude.

"She shot and killed two brothers in cold blood because she was a jealous whore. She knew nothing about loyalty so don't lump her in with the rest of us," he shouts indignantly.

"You fucking fool," I spit at him. "She was more loyal than any of us." I turn to Rock who is still standing beside me and bark at him. "Tell them the real story."

"Jesus, Viper, it was a long time ago. Just let sleeping dogs lie." He shakes his head, making my disappointment in the man continue to grow.

"You tell them or I will strip you of your patch and you'll never set foot on Chaos soil again. If Megan can handle it out there without the club at her back, I'm sure you can."

"Well, someone tell us, for fuck's sake," Cougar, the ladies' man, yells with frustration.

"Melly was not here by choice. John and Joker made a deal and Melly sweetened the pot. She went grocery shopping one day, leaving her boys with her sitter. They snatched her up and brought her here." Rock shakes his head, as if trying to wipe the knowledge of what happened from his brain. He might not have been here when it happened but he knew after the fact and still did nothing.

"She was kept locked up until she became pregnant with Megan." I see the look of anger on Cougar's face but this time, it's not at Megan. I'm guessing it's because he understands completely how a prisoner gets pregnant.

"Fucking hell, are you serious?" Trip, a tall lean brother with brown hair that is showing signs of silver at the edges, asks from beside him.

"Yeah, I am. She was given her freedom to wander the compound after that so that she could service the men. It was made perfectly clear that if she denied anyone, spoke out of turn, or tried to run, he would kick the baby out of her body. So she did as he asked. Day after day, year after year, she endured so that Megan was kept safe. But then Crogan started sniffing around Megan. She wasn't interested, hell, she was barely into her teens, but that didn't matter to him. He didn't care what she wanted. The day she turned sixteen, he went to John and asked for permission to make her his old lady," Rock tells them, his face etched with sadness.

"I walked around with blinders on for the most part. It's how it is in our world but I couldn't support this. I vetoed it, knowing it would open the floodgates to everyone's daughters, making them fair game. For once, John agreed with me." Rock looks to me and swallows. "Do you really think she would want them to know the rest?"

Probably not, but this shit needs sorting now.

"Just say it," I spit out through gritted teeth.

"Crogan decided if he got her pregnant, John would be forced to change his mind."

Trip's old lady, Honey, gasps from beside him. I watch as he reaches up and tucks her into his side.

"He attacked her in the middle of the night and tried to rape her. Her screams finally got John's attention but by then Crogan had beat her so badly that she wouldn't wake up until days later without the ability to hear."

"Wait, Crogan did that? We thought that happened when she left? What the fuck? Why was this kept from us?" Cougar yells.

Ignoring him, Rock carries on with his story, looking more and more defeated.

"John gave him a beating and told him to stay away from Megan when she got discharged, but that was never going to happen. Crogan went straight to Melly, figuring if he couldn't have the daughter, he'd take the mother for the night."

"Oh, god, I'm going to be sick." Honey turns and heads

back towards the diner but the others are focusing on Rock's words.

"She knew what would happen to her daughter if Crogan got his hands on her so she shot him and then tracked down John and shot him too, knowing he would hurt Megan as punishment for what she had done."

"I don't understand. Why didn't she just take Megan and run? She was finally free!" Flow asks.

"She would never be free. She knew Chaos would hunt her to the ends of the earth looking for retribution and Megan was in no state to leave the hospital." Rock shrugs nonchalantly, making me want to punch the fucker again.

"So she shot herself, freeing Megan, and I guess herself, in a way. She either didn't realize Chaos would blame Megan and shun her or was just flat out of options. Either way, Megan got bounced into the system and ended up on the streets for a couple of years."

Some of the crowd slinks off now, either ashamed by their actions or trying to hide that they don't give a fuck. That would be a mistake because I will stand by my word and annihilate anyone who causes her any issues.

"Don't get me wrong. What happened was shitty but that's not why you and Rock are fighting in front of the diner," Flow points out, sparking up a cigarette and taking a deep drag.

"Rock here knew all of this. He was the one who went to the hospital to tell her that her mother was dead and she was being booted out. No, what has me seeing red is the fact that he knew Megan was on the streets and half-starving, fighting off predators without any assistance from the man she always thought of as her uncle." I glare at him.

Flow freezes with the cigarette in his mouth, eyeing Rock just like Cougar and Trip are.

"You knew where she was and didn't slip her some cash or food or shit?" Trip asks incredulously.

"She was exiled!" Rock tells them, getting agitated.

"You could have changed that by telling us what happened. Why keep it a secret?" Trip questions.

"I told you, Wanda and Conner—"

"Bullshit," Trip spits out. Rock, seeing he isn't winning this round, storms off, kicking up dust as he stomps away.

"We really didn't know any of this, boss," Flow tells me, dropping his cigarette butt to the ground and stamping it out.

"Yeah, well, it's all new info to me too." I wipe my hand over my face in frustration. This week has been a bitch. The only highlight has been sliding my dick into Megan's tight pussy.

"He was wrong, Viper, we all were. I have no beef with you and yours." Trip holds his hand out for me to shake, which I do, nodding to the others before heading back to my office for painkillers and a whiskey chaser.

I ignore the looks I get, knowing if I stop, I'll only end up ripping someone's head off their shoulders for looking at me. When I finally get to my sanctuary, I'm surprised to find the door unlocked.

I know I rushed out of here after Grim's phone call

earlier, but locking up is second nature to me. I pull my gun and slam the door open, pointing it at the person sitting naked in my chair with her feet kicked up on my desk.

"What the fuck are you doing in here, Betty?" I ask the sweet butt twirling her badly dyed red hair between her fingers. She pouts at me in a practiced move meant to make her look innocent but she's forgetting I've seen her lips wrapped around more cocks than I care to remember. And after the stunt she pulled in the diner, I'm shocked as shit she's showing her face again.

"I came to help you relax. You've been so stressed lately and I miss the way you taste," she purrs, her voice high and breathy, adopting a babyish sound that makes me cringe and my balls shrivel up like raisins.

"I thought I made it clear that you weren't welcome here anymore. Now I'll ask you one more time, Betty, how'd you get in here? And don't make me ask you a third time. I'm not in the fucking mood to deal with your bullshit. You have two minutes to tell me, then get your fucking ass out of my club."

"But Papi—" I cut her off, uninterested in what she has to say, lifting the gun once more and aiming it at her head.

"I've been meaning to decorate this office," I tell her with a snarl. She jumps to her feet and hurries to slip past me but I grab her arm.

"If I ever find out you've stepped foot on Chaos property again, I'll shoot first and ask questions later." I let her go and she scurries out.

I kick the door shut behind her and walk around my

desk. All the drawers are still locked. Not that it matters—I would never leave important shit lying around. I open up the top one and grab the half empty bottle of whiskey and the painkillers beneath them, popping two of them in my mouth and swallowing them down with the lukewarm whiskey.

Picking up my phone I call Scope, another prospect who is on gate duty. He answers after the first ring.

"Hey, Viper."

"Scope, keep an eye out for Betty. I just found her in my office, naked. Could be she was just looking for a quick fuck but that doesn't explain how she got in here when it was locked. Make sure she leaves and let everyone know she is now banned from Chaos indefinitely."

"On it, Pres. I'm working down at Elusive tonight. Want me to spread the word there too? She's been known to pick up shifts there, on top of what she does at the diner."

Finally someone willing to take some initiative.

"Yeah, do it. That reminds me. Megan will be joining us at the party here on Friday. No doubt all fucking eyes will be on her," I grumble, making him chuckle. "Work the schedule so that a couple of the girls can get the night off and come here. The boys will need something other than my girl to look at, especially if they want to keep their teeth in their heads. We're down to only three club bunnies at the moment so the more the merrier."

"You got it." He hangs up, leaving me at least content in the knowledge that something is running smoothly. Now back to those fucking books.

I pour over them until there's a knock at the door.

"Yeah?" I yell. The door opens, revealing Megan and making me glance at my watch. Five o'clock. Fuck, I've been doing this shit for hours.

"Hey, Viper, I came to see if you wanted something to eat," she asks me with a smile.

I trail my eyes over her body and lick my lips. Even in a pair of skinny jeans and a plain black long-sleeve T-shirt, she's still hands down the most beautiful woman I have ever seen.

"I could eat," I tell her with a leer.

She throws her head back and laughs. "Food, you perv."

I wink and shut down my laptop, locking it in the safe, before grabbing my cut from the back of the chair and slipping it on.

"I'm starving. Let's go. Where is everyone else?" I ask her with a frown, not liking her wandering around here by herself. Which reminds me, I need to get her a cut made, declaring her ours for the world to see.

"Grim walked me to your door and waited for you to yell before heading over to the diner to place our order," she explains as we walk down the corridor towards the entrance.

I tug her hand, making her look up at me. "And he couldn't just phone it in?"

"Apparently he's going to stand and watch the fuckers—his words, not mine—make them so we don't end up with any hidden extras." Her face twists into a grimace at the remembered pancakes. Yeah, can't say I blame Grim one little bit.

"Pres." Trip nods his head in greeting as he walks towards us with his arm wrapped around Honey's shoulder.

"Megan." He nods his head in respect to her, making her stop in shock. "This is my old lady, Honey." He introduces them, reminding me there are a few new faces here that joined after Megan left.

Megan offers them a quick wave and a wobbly smile in response, her voice locked back inside her. I slip my hand around her and rest it on her hip, giving it a little squeeze.

"Gotta run, I need to feed my girl," I tell them before dipping my head and placing a kiss against her lips when she looks up to see what I'm saying. I'm aware enough to hear Trip and Honey say their goodbyes, but it's not enough to keep me from deepening the kiss, sliding my tongue between her lips and letting the unique taste that is all Megan tantalize my taste buds.

It isn't until I hear her stomach rumble that I pull back with a sigh.

"Cockblocked yet again." She snorts at that but takes my hand and drags me towards the door, following the scent of burgers and onions that hit us when we step outside.

The diner is busy but at this time it's to be expected. We head towards the back, to the booth that's always reserved for us, and ignore the eyes that seem to be dissecting each of our movements.

Zero is already there, playing with his phone, but he

looks up when we approach. Being the sneaky bastard he is, he snags Megan's hand and yanks her onto his lap, planting a wet one on her like he hadn't seen her for days, not hours. She has us both eating out of the palm of her hand.

"Hey, Raven, get any more men to fall at your feet while I was gone?" he asks her. Grim had been keeping us both up to date throughout the day. It would appear that her customers seem to love her. Especially the male ones.

"Not yet, but the day is still young," she murmurs, conscious of everyone around us. It's a little louder than a whisper, but nobody seems to have heard her.

Carla, the waitress, plops down a couple of plates loaded with burgers, fries, and onion rings before taking the remaining plates from Grim, who's standing behind her watching her every move.

Zero steals a fry from the plate closest to him and shoves it in his mouth.

"Well, fuck, that is one ugly waitress." Carla looks up with a frown until she realizes Zero is looking at Grim. She walks away with the empty trays, leaving space for Grim to slide in opposite us. All the plates are the same, so we divide them up between us and eat.

We take our time talking about inconsequential shit, keeping the mood light but I stop when I notice that Megan has cleared her plate and is now stealing Zero's fries.

"Damn, where the hell do you put it all?" I ask her, impressed and a little turned on. There is nothing sexy about a girl who orders a salad and just pushes it around her plate.

"I'm just glad you like it. I ordered the usual, then worried you might be a vegetarian or some shit," Grim admits, finishing up the last of his own burger.

"Pretty sure you guys know I eat meat by now," she points out but freezes with wide eyes when she realizes how it sounds. "I was talking about the pizza you gave me the other night, for god's sake." She waves her fry at me.

"Hey, I didn't say anything!" I lift my hands in mock surrender before leaning closer. "But you can show me how much you like eating meat later," I tell her before biting down on the fry in her hand with a smug smile.

CHAPTER THIRTEEN

Megan

Asshole. I go back to eating the rest of Zero's fries and he doesn't complain. He seems happy to just have me sitting in his lap so he can twirl my hair around his fingers. I don't even bring it up now, finding it strangely comforting.

Zero is talking to Grim about the bike he's working on at the garage when Viper pulls his phone from his pocket and places it next to his ear, making our eyes cut to him.

I can't see his mouth clearly enough to see what he's saying but whatever it is steals the happy mood from him, making me sigh. He hangs up before nodding to Grim and Zero then looking at me.

"Carnage are at the gates. They have your phone and

some other shit for you," he tells me, but something about his words feels like a warning.

Maybe I'm reading too much into it but that's the thing about being deprived of one of your senses. It heightens the others, making me pick up on things like facial tics and micro-movements that others don't always catch.

I stand up with a nod and reach for his hand, letting him know that I understand we need to present ourselves as a united front. More so to Chaos, who will be judging my actions and questioning my loyalty, than Carnage. He gives my hand a squeeze and pulls me towards the door. The heat of Zero and Grim at my back let me know they will be following us out. Viper pulls me toward him, lifting my chin with his finger.

"Prospects are letting them in the gates now. You can't go home with them though, Megan, so don't ask," he tells me, making me roll my eyes.

"Don't be a dick, Viper. I know that. Did we not just talk about you trusting me?"

"How the fuck does your smart mouth manage to piss me off and turn me on at the same time?"

"It's a skill. Bet you wish you hadn't made me use my voice now, huh?" I grin and turn, which Viper takes as an invitation to slap my ass. I flip him off and walk into Zero's arms for protection against the big bad president, making him smile.

"Viper's being mean to me," I pout at Zero before pulling back and looking up into his mischievous green eyes.

"Want me to kick his ass?"

I have a vision of them topless wrestling each other in motor oil and get so lost in the moment I don't even notice we've made it to the gate until Zero stops me. Viper stands on the other side of me and grips my hand while Grim takes up center at my back. Good lord, what do they think Carnage are going to do, kidnap me back? I catch sight of my brother Diesel standing by his bike talking to—

"Parker." His name escapes my lips before I can stop it, making him look up and see me. He stands taller, the look on his face is so intense, it almost brings me to my knees. Instead, I shake off Viper's hand and run flat out towards him. When I'm a few steps away, I launch myself at him and wrap myself around him when he catches me, before bursting into tears. I grip him for dear life as my tears soak us both and take in his smell and the rapid beating of his pulse against my cheek. A pulse that last time I held him was so slow, I thought he would die in my arms.

I find myself being pulled from his embrace and even though I want to protest, I don't, knowing that I've already fucked up. I just couldn't help it.

I look up into Viper's angry eyes and apologize. "I'm sorry."

"Who is he to you?"

I don't get to answer before I'm pulled into Diesel's arms, making a fresh round of tears slip over my cheeks. I turn my head so I can see my guys and my stomach flips at the look of disappointment in their eyes. I've let them down. Even knowing that, I can't say I would have done anything differently.

I pull away and brush away my tears, pushing my shoulders back, and take a deep breath.

"How come I'm only just now hearing that pretty voice of yours?" Diesel asks me, ignoring the hostile looks I'm getting from everyone.

"Yeah, I guess I spent so long not using it, it just became easier." I shrug. It's probably best if I don't go into how Viper forced the issue.

Parker steps up beside me so I have him on one side and my brother on the other flanking me like I was when I walked over here. Only now I have Carnage at my back, Chaos at my front, and a blinding headache as I feel myself being torn between the two.

I look at my guys. Beneath the layer of anger, I see hurt too. That was never my intention. I step away from my brother and from the man who took a bullet to protect me and I take a chance. I step across the invisible line that's been drawn and turn so my back is pressed against Zero's arm. I reach down to grab Viper's fingers, lacing mine through his.

"Guys, you remember my brother Diesel, and this is Parker. Parker got shot when Stokey—" I look at Parker "— aka Weasel attacked my shop." Zero gives my shoulder a squeeze, whether it's in warning or for comfort, I don't know.

"It's Lucky now, Megan. Got my patch last week. I'm not sure luck has anything to do with it though. We both know the only reason I'm standing here is because of you."

Viper nudges me, making me look up at him.

"What's he talking about?"

"Stokey came to my shop when Luna was there. He shot the prospect outside and killed him. We thought he was there for Luna at first. She was the reason Carnage kicked him to the curb but he was actually there for me."

"Hold on, what do you mean he was there for you? I thought Chaos had cut you out completely?" Viper grits out. I nod in confirmation because they did, but not without their rules.

"Apparently, I still had to abide by a code of conduct. I broke that by having Luna at my shop. In my defense, I was working with and became friends with her long before she ever got involved with Carnage. Parker—Lucky here—was on prospect duty when Stokey opened fire. He made us hide behind the counter before getting shot in the neck."

"Shit!" Zero sums it up nicely.

"I'm not going to lie, I thought that was it. Game over, but then Megan was there with her fingers literally inside my neck until help arrived. This is the first time we've seen each other since then," Lucky explains before turning to me.

"I never got the chance to say this before, but I'm saying it now. Thank you, from the bottom of my heart. You saved my life. There is nothing I can do to repay you for that. Just know that if you need me, for anything, just ask."

I smile and nod my head. "Seeing you here and in one piece is all the thanks I need. I'm glad you're okay, Lucky."

I look over at my brother and see him frown. "Are you okay?" he questions.

I nod and offer him a small smile.

"How they treating you?" he asks as Zero's hand slips down to grip my hip in a move that just screams of possession.

"I know we haven't had nearly enough time for us to get to know each other and I'm really sorry about that. I can tell you this, I will never let a man treat me like shit, put me down in front of others, or hurt me. I had a lifetime of watching my mother get treated like she didn't matter. Well, she fucking mattered. She mattered to me and to honor that I swore to her I would never settle for anything less than I deserve and I deserve the best," I tell him emphatically. Whatever happens between Zero, Viper, Grim, and I is frankly none of Diesel's business. I can't go running to my brothers every time one of my men pisses me off without starting a turf war. Jesus, and people think they have family problems.

He looks over at Grim, who is standing quietly behind me, just taking it all in. I forgot how awkward this was going to be for him.

"I hope you know what you're doing, Megan. Not everyone can be trusted. We found that out the hard way." I notice Grim wince, but only because of how close I am to him. Well done, brother, you just scored a direct hit. I shake free from Viper and Zero and turn towards Grim, offering him a small smile before reaching up and placing a soft kiss at the edge of his mouth. I turn back to Diesel, who doesn't look happy, and speak before he says anything else.

"I grew up around bad and untrustworthy males so believe me, Diesel, when I tell you I can spot the difference between a bad man and a good man who did a bad thing. Unless your halo gleams brightly above you, you have zero room to judge. I know he lied to you all. He let you down, I get it, I really do. I'm not even saying you shouldn't be angry or that you should forgive him but at least take the time to find out why he did what he did."

"There isn't a reason good enough to excuse ever betraying your brothers." Anger coats his features as he says the word "brothers."

"As your sister," I spit the word "sister" out, emulating him, "I'm sorry you feel that way but at least I know where I stand on your list of priorities. Thanks for bringing me my things. You can see yourselves out."

I turn and walk away, not surprised when Grim slings his arm over my shoulder a second later and tucks me into his side.

I don't get far before I feel a tug on my elbow, making Grim and me turn to find Diesel watching me, measuring his words, no doubt.

"I just don't want to see you get hurt, Megan."

"All I know is hurt. For once, I just want to feel something other than pain, fear, and loneliness. They give me that and so much more." I place my hands on either side of his face and tip his head down to mine.

"I know you're trying to figure out how to be a good brother as well as a good VP for your club—"

He cuts me off with a shake of his head. "Our club, Megan, you're Carnage now too," he tells me. I offer him a smile but it's a sad one filled with what-ifs.

"Carnage is in my heart, but Chaos is in my blood. You're a good man and I know you'll be a great brother, but some battles I'm just going to have to fight myself."

"But why? If I can stop—"

It's my turn now to cut him off. "I have been through more than you know about. I might not be a skilled fighter like Luna but I know a thing or two about survival."

He sighs in defeat. I know it's hard for him. It seems my brothers are natural-born protectors. They are going to be a fantastic father and uncle combo. "Okay. Any message you want to give Orion and Luna?" he asks.

"I'll video call them tonight but I have a feeling if Luna doesn't see my face in person soon she'll come stomping down here herself armed to the gills." I roll my eyes as he laughs.

"You are not kidding. She wanted to come today but Orion forbade it with her being pregnant. He knew she would sneak over the second he turned his back."

"She's okay though, right? The baby?" I ask, hating that I'm missing out on all of this.

"They are both fine, Megan. She had an appointment yesterday and everything looks good but I'll let her tell you all about it when you call her later. Oh, and you better use your words. Your voice is far too pretty to hide it from them."

He takes a step back and looks up at Grim, doing nothing to hide his disdain. I don't intervene this time. Grim earned that when he betrayed them. As shitty as it is, it's a reminder that all actions have consequences.

Diesel steps aside, making space for Lucky to give me a quick hug. When Lucky pulls back, I swear I see a look of longing on his face but he quickly masks it. Hopefully, it went undetected by the others. Or maybe I just imagined it.

"Take care, Megan. And remember what I said. If you need anything, call me," Lucky orders ignoring everyone else as he steps over to join Diesel. I wave goodbye as they climb on their bikes and pull away. The two prospects manning the gate let them through before locking them out and me once again inside.

We stand there quietly as they drive away, leaving a plume of dust, smoke, and recriminations in their wake that I'm not really in the mood to hear.

I turn to face the guys and wait for them to reprimand me, well aware of the twitching apartment curtains and prying eyes.

They stand there staring me down but I refuse to cower before them. I square my shoulders, hold my head up high, and wait for them to speak. If this is some kind of power play to get me to speak first, then they are going to be disappointed. I've made an art out of not speaking, they better show me what they've got.

I see Zero's lips twitch but he tries to hide it from me.

"Are you always going to be a pain in my ass?" Viper asks, looking exasperated.

"There is a high probability, yes."

"I figured as much." He sighs before hauling me against him and kissing me in a way that's meant for the bedroom, not for a bunch of onlookers. Saying that, for a compound of bikers, I guess it's not too shocking to see someone with a tongue shoved down their throat instead of a cock.

He pulls away, leaving me feeling breathless and needy.

"The things you do to me," he mutters before I find myself being yanked away and lifted into Zero's arms. I wrap my legs around his waist when he hoists me up, his warm hands on my ass making me groan. I ready myself for his kiss but he surprises the fuck out of me when he takes off running.

I squeal and grip him tighter, tucking my head against his neck, wondering what the fuck is happening. I look over his shoulder and see Grim and Viper looking shocked for a second before chasing after us. I look around but can't see anything out of the ordinary. I feel Zero fumble with a door behind us before I'm hit with the blissful coolness of the air conditioning and then tossed onto a bed. I register the fact that I'm in our apartment and try to get up to see what's happening when Zero's body crawls over mine and pins me down.

"What is it? What's happening?" Wondering if he can

hear the panic in my voice. For all I know, bullets could be flying and I wouldn't know. Oh god, Viper, Grim.

"I need to fuck you," he groans out, kissing the edge of my jaw, his words making me freeze.

"You need to fuck me?" I question. I grip his hair and yank his head back hard so I can see his face.

"Goddamnit, Zero. I thought we were being attacked or invaded by aliens from the way you took off," I scold.

"Oh, you're going to be invaded in a minute, trust me," he promises turning his head and kissing the inside of my wrist, making me shiver in anticipation.

"You're an ass," I inform him as the others crash through the door.

"You like my ass," he sasses before dipping his head and kissing me, effectively stealing my ability to argue, speak, or think. Damn him.

I shut out the room and everyone in it, focusing on the slide of his tongue against mine and his rough hands snaking their way under my T-shirt.

He sits up abruptly and pulls me up with him but only enough to whip my T-shirt over my head and to free my breasts from my bra.

I look for the other two and find them gone.

"Where are Grim and Viper?" I ask before gasping as he sucks one of my nipples into his mouth before popping it free and pushing me back down on the bed.

"Don't know, don't care." He yanks off my boots and

tosses them aside before tugging my jeans and panties down my thighs.

"The compound could be on fucking fire and I wouldn't give a fuck."

He throws my disregarded clothing behind him then spreads me wide.

"I am one lucky fucker."

He frees his dick and leans down over me, rubbing his cockhead up and down my slit, coating it in my wetness.

"There will be times when I will want to lavish you, Megan. Sucking, biting, tasting," he lists off, still sliding his throbbing cock through my folds, making me squirm with need.

"I'll bring you to the edge over and over but won't let you come until I say so."

"Please," I beg, his words driving me crazy.

"But there are times when I'll just want to fuck you so hard you won't know where I end and you begin."

"What..." I gasp as he bumps over my clit. "What do you want now?" I ask because I'll take whatever he's offering. His grin turns downright sinister and damn if I don't feel myself gush because of it.

"Ready those claws, Raven," he warns me a second before he surges inside me.

I scream as a heady mix of pleasure and pain wash over my body and my eyes lock on to his lust-filled ones, before dropping back to his lips.

"Fuck yeah, scream for me." He slides almost all the way

out before thrusting back in even harder than before, making me grant his request by screaming his name.

He pauses for a second, making sure I'm okay, but I don't want him to stop. I tighten my pelvic muscles around his cock, squeezing him as hard as I can and get rewarded with a groan that vibrates across my collar bone.

Suddenly it's too much and yet not enough. I pull at his T-shirt, wanting it off, needing to feel his slick skin against mine.

He figures out what I'm trying to do and reaches up to pull it over his head in that sexy way that only guys seem to be able to do. Pressing his body against mine again, he snags my lip between his teeth, biting down before swiping over it with his oh so talented tongue. I wrap my legs around his hips as he fucks me into submission. There's no fight for control. I willingly give myself over to him.

"More!" I cry, using my legs to pull him onto me, the edge of pain at him being so deep pushes me over the edge of the wave of pleasure I had been riding. I rake my nails down the skin of his back as my body draws up as tight as a bow before folding in on itself.

Zero pulls free from my body and finishes himself off with his hand, shooting his cum over my navel and chest as I lie there panting and taking in the erotic sight before me.

He leans over me, kissing me softly, the demon riding him before having been sated.

Sliding his fingers through his cum, he paints my skin

with his essence, branding me. Marking his territory in the most animalistic way.

"I like my mark on you," he rumbles with a wink before climbing off me and heading to the bathroom. When I catch the view of his back, I gasp out loud, drawing his attention.

"What?" I can't see his back now, but it doesn't matter, I can still picture the scratch marks, some bleeding a little where I broke the skin. I squirm a little as heat pools low in my belly. He takes in my face with a frown, disappearing into the bathroom for a second, before returning moments later with a smug look of contentment on his face.

"I think you like marking me too." He picks me up bridal style and carries me to the shower, climbing in with me still in his arms.

"I don't remember ever losing control like that before," I admit as he stands me on the shower floor in front of him. He soaps up my back before turning me around to face him and washing my front.

"Bleeding for you makes me hard as a rock," he states, making me laugh out loud but when I look down and see his cock hard again, I can see he's telling the truth.

I guess bikers really do, do it better.

"I thought I was prepared for anything when I came here," I muse, reaching for his cock with my hand.

"What I wasn't prepared for was you."

CHAPTER FOURTEEN

Grim

"Remind me again why I'm here with your ugly ass when I could have my dick in Megan?" I grumble at the man who I thought was my friend until he yanked me out of our apartment earlier.

"We all need time alone with Megan as well as time together if we are going to learn to trust each other. I mean, fuck, we hardly know each other at all and let's be honest, we can be an overbearing bunch of assholes."

"Speak for yourself, Viper," I tell him with a smirk, collapsing in the chair opposite his desk.

"When she threw herself at that Lucky guy, I was this close to losing my shit. It was like a red haze descended and all I wanted to do was rip her away from him and lay into her for showing that her loyalties lie with the wrong club."

I nod in agreement, accepting the glass of whiskey he slides my way.

"I would have done it out there in front of everyone, not giving a flying fuck who witnessed it because she fucked up and made us look like limp dicks."

I stare at him, waiting for him to continue. It's not that I don't know where he's coming from, but she stood by me and defended me to her brother even though he was right to be pissed. There is never a good excuse to betray your brothers.

"But I would have been wrong. For starters, I keep reacting as if Carnage is the enemy when the whole point of this fiasco is to build an alliance with them. If we punish Megan every time she shows loyalty to her brothers' club, we can kiss this truce goodbye. What would you do if it was your sister?" he asks before a look of remorse crosses his features. "Fuck, Grim, I wasn't thinking."

The familiar feeling of sorrow and bone-breaking guilt swamps me but I force it down and swallow the whiskey in my glass, tipping it toward Viper for a refill.

"I think we can both agree I'm the wrong person to ask in this scenario. Even so, like fuck would I have let my sister go with an enemy MC, especially given the torrid history between us."

"We didn't give them much of a choice, Grim. Their sister or their old lady," he reminds me as I swallow the contents of my refilled glass.

"Not a choice to make in my book. Their answer should have been to shoot us in the back of the head before we even left their compound."

"And what? Start a war that leaves every man, woman, and child in danger? Remember, Luna is pregnant. No, I actually think that deep down they trust us not to hurt their sister."

I shake my head.

"Who knows? But that was a risky as fuck gamble to take with someone's life." I think back to her reaction to seeing them, the joy on her face, and marvel that there is no animosity from her towards them.

"She hardly knows them and yet she shows them love and loyalty. Can that possibly be genuine?" I wonder out loud.

"I sure as fuck hope so because that's exactly what we're asking from her."

We sit quietly for a moment thinking about the captivating woman who unexpectedly went from a pawn to a game-changer.

"Speaking of sisters," I broach the subject that can bring me to my knees.

"Without Carnage, what is our next step to finding this Gemini fucker?" The only name that had come up in connection with my sister's disappearance had been Gemini, the elusive arms dealer who provided Carnage with their weapons before he ghosted them. I had been playing prospect and finally scored a meet with the guy before everything went tits up.

"From what I've heard, Gecko had set you up. He knew he had to take you out as you were the only person left who could point out his duplicity within the club. There was never a meet, it was just a way to get you alone and take you out. Gemini had disappeared on Carnage weeks before. Why? Well, they still don't know, but whatever the reason, it more than likely died with Joker."

"So I was never any closer to finding her," I deduce. Part of me wishes that fucker had taken me out and finally put me out of my misery.

"You can wipe that look off your face right fucking now," Viper tells me. The asshole has always been good at reading people, it's what made him such a good leader.

"We won't stop until we find her, Grim. I give you my word." I know he means it. Men like Viper build their reputations on their promises. Not like me. I couldn't even keep my promise that I'd keep my kid sister safe.

"Maybe," I concede. "But what, exactly, will we find, Viper? That's what fucking haunts me the most," I admit, standing up and leaving the office without another word knowing if I stay, I'll lose it.

I make my way to my bike and climb on, ignoring everyone else around me. Not that many people go out of their way to speak to me anymore. Nobody wants to get their heads ripped off just for saying hello.

The prospect who lets me out, Wizz, is actually a friend of mine. We were soldiers together and when we came home, he agreed to help Viper out by joining the club. The bonds forged in a war zone are bonds that stay intact for life. Nobody will ever understand what it's like dragging your buddy, who is bleeding out at your feet, across five miles of sand and dust, then another buddy dragging him out by his other arm.

It's what's missing from Chaos. Trust and loyalty, which Viper is determined to bring back to a club I'm not sure had it to begin with.

I drive for the next couple of hours with no destination in mind, letting the wind blow the memories through my mind like cobwebs.

I thought I was doing the right thing enlisting when I turned eighteen. There were no other prospects for a boy like me, from where I came. It was either sign up or get locked up. I chose the former, not realizing it would be the worst mistake I would ever make, and lord knows I've made a few.

I left behind my mother and kid sister with promises of visits and letters but I hadn't been prepared for the war zone I would find myself in. In an effort to keep them from finding out what kind of man I had become, I stayed away, figuring they would be better off without me. If I had kept my word and come home, I would have known they were fighting a war of their own.

Instead, when I did finally return, it was to find my mother dead and my sister missing. The worst thing is, I don't even know when she disappeared. It was almost like she never existed at all and part of me wonders if that was the plan all along.

I hold on to the guilt. It's what I deserve but I let the memories drift and fade until I can breathe without feeling like my soul is being torn from my body.

Eventually, the skies start to darken so I turn my bike around and head home with thoughts of Megan on my mind. After everything she endured, and I have a feeling we only know a fraction of it, she is still here, fighting tooth and nail to carve out a life for herself despite how many times it gets derailed.

If she can survive and somehow find her way back to her brothers, it makes me wonder if my sister is out there, somehow trying to find her way back to me.

Pulling up at the gates, I can hear the music blasting from inside but I'm not in the mood for it tonight. I park the bike and head back to the apartment. It's dark inside, letting me know the guys are elsewhere. I take a shower and crawl into bed in the backroom I'm claiming as mine and pass out as soon as my head hits the pillow.

I'm blissfully oblivious to everything until sometime during the early hours I become aware that I'm no longer alone. I don't need to open my eyes to know it's Megan. I'd recognize her unique fragrance anywhere. I just wonder why she ended up in bed with me. Unless Viper and Zero had her dropped home by a prospect and they are still not back yet. That would make better sense, after all, of the three of us, I'm the poor man's choice.

I'm a selfish fuck though and will take whatever she's offering. As much as I wanted to push her away, there is a part of her that thaws the frozen numbness inside me.

I wrap my arm around her waist and pull her close until I can rest my head upon hers and feel her warm breath against my skin.

When one of her hands slides over my ribs and holds on to me, I feel something inside me click into place. I don't know what's going to happen down the line, but this woman is starting to mean something to me in a way I could never have predicted and there is a small part of me that can't help but think I'm sadly unprepared.

* * * * *

It's the feel of a finger drawing a figure eight repeatedly over the skin of my back that has me slowly opening my eyes.

I look down and see Megan's startling blue ones staring back at me.

"Hey," my voice rumbles out, blowing across her face, making her grimace and raise her hand to cover her nose.

"Your breath smells like ass," she tells me, making me bark out a surprised bout of laughter.

"If I go brush my teeth will you let me play with your ass?" I tease her.

"I'll let you play with my ass even if you don't brush your teeth, but your mouth isn't getting anywhere near mine until you do." I tickle her ribs, making her squeal. When she puts her hands up to protect herself, I lick up the side of her face.

"Eww...biker cooties!" She pulls away and launches herself off the bed, running into the bathroom and closing the door. I lie there and smile, feeling lighter than usual. My smile only grows when I realize she hasn't locked the door.

I climb from the bed and walk over to the bathroom in exactly the same way I went to bed, naked. Only this time, I'm so hard I could hammer nails with this thing. Well, there is one thing I want to nail for sure.

I push open the door and see she has washed her face and the little wisps of hair around the side of her face are damp. She looks at me with a mock glare in the mirror as she brushes her teeth, but most of my attention has slid to her long-ass legs. She is wearing one of my T-shirts, which is huge on her slim frame, but when she leans over the counter to spit out her the toothpaste, I catch a glimpse of the bottom of her very naked asscheeks and home in on them like a missile seeking out heat.

I stalk towards her as she rinses her mouth and places her toothbrush on the counter next to my electric one.

I press up against her back, stopping her from being able to move away as I stretch over her and grab a new head for my toothbrush from the shelf above the mirror. I pin her hips against the counter with mine as I reach around her body for my toothbrush. She follows my movements with a frown as I put toothpaste on it without changing the head and brush my teeth behind her. I keep my eyes on hers as I lean around her and spit. Then I switch the tap from cold to hot and run the whole brush under the water, scrubbing it until it's clean. I grab the towel from the rail and dry it before pulling the head off and tossing it in the bin beside the counter and slipping the new one on in its place.

She looks puzzled for a moment but doesn't say anything. When I place it next to hers she looks at me expectantly, waiting for me to move back, I'm sure, but I have other ideas.

I snag the hem of the shirt she's wearing and before she can protest, pull it over her head, watching her black hair tumble down in a riot of curls as I pull the shirt free and toss it aside.

I press my chest against hers again only, this time, I can feel the sleek smoothness of her skin against mine. I reach around and cup her breasts in my large, rough hands, loving the dichotomy of my rough to her smooth. We watch each other in the mirror, her eyes boring into mine with unleashed desire.

"I love your hands on me. They're so large and strong, they make me feel safe and protected," she tells me, softening my jagged edges even more, but I can't have her thinking I'm some kind of hero because I couldn't be further from it.

I pinch her nipples hard, making her gasp and push back against me.

"Don't build me up into something I'm not, Megan. I'm not a good man, far from it."

"Be who you need to be. As long as you're good to me, I

couldn't care less if you're the devil himself." My eyes narrow at her words, not sure I should believe her or not. All women tell you what they think you want to hear but then spend the rest of their time trying to change you.

"Oh, I'll always be good for you." I smirk at her before pushing her down over the counter, making her gasp when the cold tile presses against her pebbled nipples.

I get on my knees behind her, ignoring my painfully hard dick in favor of the pretty pink pussy that's now at eye level.

I nibble on her ass cheek, making her squirm before running my thumbs up the seam of her sex, spreading her lips wide as my fingers grip her thighs to keep her in place. I can see how wet she is as her folds glisten in the harsh bathroom lighting.

I slide both thumbs inside her, making her curse out my name even as a rush of wetness greets me. I pull her open again and study her. If I'm making her uncomfortable, she doesn't show it.

"Such a good girl," I mutter, remembering belatedly that she can't hear me. Well, that's okay, there are other ways for me to share my appreciation.

I slip my tongue inside her, my thumbs keeping her wide open for me to delve in and enjoy every drop of nectar that each lick and stroke of my tongue tastes. I push in deeper, fucking in and out of her with my tongue rapidly like a tiny cock before slipping down a little further and swiping my tongue over her clit. I flick over the bundle of nerves harder and harder with each pass until her legs are shaking and my face is soaked in her juices. Just when I have her poised on the edge of release, I stand up, ignoring her mewl of disappointment, and turn her around before lifting her up and settling her on the edge of the counter, facing me.

I spread her legs wide, stepping between them, and devour her mouth, letting her taste herself on my lips. My hard dick stands proud between us, wanting nothing more than to be buried within her velvet pussy, but I'm not done teasing her yet.

"So, you like my hands on you, huh?" I question her, making sure her eyes are on my face.

"Yes, god, yes!" she answers when I dip my head and suck one of her hard nipples into my mouth for a second before releasing it with a loud pop.

"And my mouth? You like my lips, teeth, and tongue on you?" I question, already knowing the answer but I love driving her crazy.

"Yes," she whimpers, her body in desperate need of release.

"What about my cock, Megan? You like that?" I ask her as I grip it at the base and drag it slowly through her folds.

"Please," she begs, making my cock throb and leak in response.

"Please what, Megan? What do you want?" I tease, still holding back, making her delirious with want and need.

"I just want you, Grim, please fuck me," she implores. The grin that stretches across my face must look as devilish as it feels because a tremor runs through her and a small frown mars her brow.

"All in good time, my little Raven. First, we play." I slip one hand down and push two fingers into her, hard.

"Hmm... so wet. So responsive." I use the other hand to reach behind her and grab my toothbrush and switch it on. The vibrations seem overly loud in the small room.

"Grim," her voice croaks out with a mix of worry and need.

"Shh... don't think, just feel," I tell her, then bring the rotating bristle down on one of her nipples.

"Ahhh..." she screams, but it's not in pain. Oh no, as I piston my fingers in and out of her, I feel her coat my hand in her arousal.

I move the brush to the other nipple and suck the now sensitive one into my mouth again.

"Fuck, fuck. Grim!" she sobs as I tease back and forth over them both until I know she can't handle anymore. That's when I start to trail the toothbrush lower.

"Ohmygodohmygodohmygod," comes out all garbled, making me laugh, then groan as my dick brushes up against her overheated core.

I flick the switch and the toothbrush turns off but I don't pull it away. I keep moving it lower as her eyes watch its descent with trepidation.

Sliding my fingers from inside her, I tease her entrance with the bristles of the brush before sliding it up over her clit to the very top edge of it. Using my free hand, I line my cock up with her entrance and surge inside her just as I flip the switch and the toothbrush whirls to life.

She screams and squeezes my dick so hard when she comes, I have to fight not to explode from one stoke.

I hammer into her as she rides out the wave of what has to be the most intense orgasm I've ever witnessed.

"Too much," she begs with tears in her eyes so I slow my movements and turn the toothbrush off, pulling it away from her pussy and popping it in my mouth with a smile at the scandalized look on her face.

I toss the toothbrush in the sink and grip her hips hard.

"Hold on tight," is the only warning I give her as I fuck her into the middle of next week. Instead of shying away from my aggression, she leans forward and wraps one arm around my neck and the other grips my hair. She pulls my hair back hard, making me groan, then her mouth is on mine, her tongue demanding entrance, and she isn't taking no for an answer. I feel a tingle at the base of my dick but I try to fight it, wanting to stay inside her forever. But then the little minx bites the side of my neck hard and I erupt, painting the entrance to her cervix.

We don't move for a second, both of us panting hard but eventually, she pulls back enough to place a soft kiss on my lips that's so at odds with the crazy fucking from moments ago that I feel another chink appear in my armor.

"You are a pervert," she tells me but she has a smile on her beautifully flushed face. "And I fucking loved it," she murmurs against my lips.

I hum in pleasure and gently pull my aching cock from its new favorite place.

"I wasn't too rough?" I question, knowing she will at the very least have fingerprint shaped bruises on her hips tomorrow.

"It was perfect. There is just one thing..." she says, me chewing her lip.

I grab the washcloth and hold it over her dripping pussy and look up, waiting for her to finish.

"What's that?"

"We are so getting you a new toothbrush."

CHAPTER FIFTEEN

Megan

Friday rolls around bringing with it a nervous kind of anticipation. Over the last few days, the hostile stares have eased, at least for the most part. People even spoke to me in a friendly manner. I don't know why I found that harder to deal with than all the animosity. Maybe it's because hostility was what I was used to and sometimes there is comfort in the familiar, even if the familiar is bad for you.

When people greet me and smile or ask about my day, there is always that moment of doubt that's waiting for the other shoe to drop. Like that scene in the Stephen King movie *Carrie*, where she gets tricked and ends up with blood all over her on prom night and a roomful of people laughing at her, that's what I've been waiting for. So far, so good, no blood showers as of yet.

As I slip a silver hoop into my ear, I take a step back, check my reflection in the mirror, and smirk. The guys left an hour ago for church but I imagine they're done now. When they see what I'm wearing, they're likely going to kill me.

In my defense, they dumped this party information on my head at lunchtime. When I tried to back out, they informed me that as their old lady it was mandatory that I go. Of course, that's utter bullshit. I swear they forget I grew up with bikers.

Sure, old ladies are welcome to most of the parties but they don't have to go. Most women don't want to sit around watching aging bikers getting their dicks sucked by the club girls. And then there are the brothers that prefer to leave their old ladies at home so they can fuck whoever they want.

In that sense, I'm glad they want me to go. It shows they aren't interested in the other girls but I want to be there tonight about as much as I want to get a Pap test.

Well, if they are going to force me to go even though I will be uncomfortable as fuck, then I'm determined to even the score and make them uncomfortable too. If this outfit doesn't make them hard, nothing will.

The white sleeveless T-shirt with the slash neck was a steal at a few dollars, but what's the point in spending more when I was going to cut most of it away? And that's what I did. The T-shirt now stops just below my boobs. In fact, it's so short that if I lift my arms, you can see the bottom of my white lace bra underneath.

I teamed it with a pair of dark denim shorts. They aren't short enough to get a flash of the money shot but they are short enough to leave little to the imagination. They are so tight, they look like they've been sprayed on.

On my feet, I'm rocking six-inch stiletto thigh-high black leather boots, which make my legs look endlessly long and give my look a sexy, edgy vibe.

I'm showing a lot of skin but at the same time not revealing anything I shouldn't be. It's all about the tease tonight.

I tousled my hair in large beachy waves, giving me a just fucked look, and slapped on a coat of mascara before finishing with fire engine red lipstick.

Jax once told me that red-stained lips cause a short circuit in a man's brain because men are hardwired to think of those red lips wrapped around their cocks. Well, tonight I will be testing his theory.

I slip the key card in my back pocket, glad that Viper had these locks updated since I was a kid. The old locks were a joke. A blindfolded amputee would have been able to pick it in seconds.

I open the door, knowing Kaz is out there waiting for me. He seems to have become my unofficial bodyguard when my guys aren't around.

For all Viper's talk about turning this club around, he doesn't seem to trust everyone in it.

Kaz turns to face me when he hears the door open, then stands staring with his mouth wide open.

"Holy fucking shit!"

I smile at his words. That is exactly the kind of reaction I was going for.

He grabs his phone and sends a text before looking me up and down again. He doesn't give off a skeevy vibe, more analytical. It doesn't make me cringe but it does make me wonder what he's thinking.

"I hope you know what you're doing, Raven." Ah, I see the name is catching on.

"I don't know what you are talking about," I deny, fighting back a smile as we head towards the compound.

"You okay walking in those?" he asks, looking down at my heels.

"I can run and do a roundhouse kick in these babies," I tell him, making him laugh. "Wanna see?"

"I'll just take your word for it."

I shrug. "Suit yourself."

"So, what did they do to piss you off this time?"

"They're making me come to this thing tonight. Isn't that enough?"

"We're not all bad, Megan. You just have to give us a chance," he says reproachfully, as I feel a strong bass beat out of the clubhouse when someone opens the door.

"You mean like the chance everyone gave me?" I bite back but then sigh. "You're right, sorry, I shouldn't have snapped. I'm just on edge and I don't even know why. I feel like something is going on. I don't know what, call it a sixth sense or a woman's intuition or whatever. I don't care, but something feels off." I shake my head, knowing I'm not really making any sense. The pounding beat softens as the door closes.

"I trust Viper, Zero, Grim, and you. Right now it's enough, but I promise to make more of an effort, okay? Thanks for the TED talk." I nudge him with my elbow as he reaches for the door and indicates for me to go in ahead of him.

Even after six years of silence, it's still a bizarre thing to step into a room full of people and hear nothing. I can see people laughing, fighting, hell, there's a guy fucking a club girl up against the wall, and yet it's all done with the absence of sound. It's easy to feel disconnected from everyone and just another reason why I don't want to be here.

Kaz indicates the far corner where I spot Grim and Zero laughing about something. Turning back to Kaz, I frown.

"Where's Viper?" I ask before I feel hands on my hips. I don't flinch. Even if Kaz's smile didn't give it away, I'd recognize those hands anywhere.

Kaz disappears into the crowd when I turn to face Viper. I look up and find his heated eyes burning through my clothes, leaving me standing bare before him.

"I'm going to spank the shit out of you later," he tells me, making me smile.

"Promise?" I give him a wink as I pull away and head over towards the guys in the corner. I feel Viper's eyes on my ass so I make sure I put just enough sway in my hips to drive him mad.

Grim sees me first. His shock gives way to anger, then lust then, as he scans the room, to jealousy.

Zero turns to see what's caught his attention and spits his drink out.

"Fuck me!" he says in awe, making me feel like a goddess.

"Well, it wouldn't be the first time I've fucked in front of a room full of people," I muse, deliberately winding him up. Of course, he had taken a second swig of his beer as I said that and ends up choking on it.

"Zero, Zero, Zero," I tease, stepping up to him and bending down to whisper in his ear, knowing Viper is getting quite the view of my ass.

"You're supposed to swallow, not spit. Tsk, tsk." I shake my head then let out a little squeal when I find myself picked up and plonked down on Viper's lap. Or should I say, on Viper's very hard cock. If I didn't think I would look like a complete idiot, I would pat myself on the back. Mission complete, Megan.

An hour later, I realize there is a reason you shouldn't play games with bikers because they play dirty.

They've each insisted on a hug. I use the term loosely because it was more an excuse to grope me and get me all hot and bothered more than anything else.

A pretty girl wearing a red halter top and a pair of Daisy Dukes far shorter than mine approaches the table with a tray of drinks for us. They each snag a beer while I go for a bottle of water, feeling the heat in more ways than one.

"Thanks, Legs," Viper tells the pretty blonde. She smiles at him and then at me too as I'm perched on the end of his knee. It's a refreshing change from the other girls that look at me like I'm either competition or a threat. I wink at her, making her blush, before leaning back against Viper's chest.

"If I had been flirting with her, you would have cut my balls off," Grim quips before taking a sip of his beer.

"I gave her a wink, not an orgasm, Grim. Just saying, out of the four of us, I'm probably the only one who hasn't had my fingers inside her, so I wouldn't go there if I were you." I pick up my water and take a sip, moaning as the icy cool liquid slips down my throat.

No wonder these girls wear hardly any clothes, it's like a fucking sauna in here.

I look up and find Zero and Grim staring at me. A quick look over my shoulder shows Viper is staring at me too.

"What?" I ask, confused.

"You know we've been with the club girls," Zero tells me, making me frown. Where the heck is he going with this?

"Yeah... what's your point?" I question, looking over at Grim for an answer.

"I think we're waiting for the kicking and screaming," he points out.

"It's called trust, Grim. Who came before me is irrelevant. I wasn't a virgin when I arrived, so it would be a little hypocritical to judge you for your actions before I walked into your lives. Now that I'm here, I trust you not to dip your wick anywhere else while you have a candle burning for you at home." I shrug, what's not to get?

"Are you—" Grim's words stop abruptly. I turn to see Viper on his phone and whatever they are saying to him has his face morphing from disbelief to homicidal rage. Oh boy.

He hangs up and eases me to my feet before stepping in front of me and addressing Zero and Grim. His words have the same effect on them that the phone call had on him.

I tug on his arm, making him look down at me.

"What's going on?" I ask, worried by their abrupt change of behavior.

"Club business," he tells me, turning back to the guys as my shoulders drop. Right, of course.

He finishes telling them whatever he needs to then turns back to me as Zero disappears.

"Zero, Grim, and I need to head out for a while. We wouldn't leave you if it wasn't urgent, but it is. I want you to stay here—" I interrupt him, not wanting to stay here without them.

"I'll just go back to our apartment and wait there. I'm kind of tired anyway," I admit but he shakes his head.

"I need you to stay here. Something is going on and I need to know you'll be protected." I'm ready to argue again but he throws me a look saying I won't win this battle. He's not Viper right now, he's President of the Chaos Demons so I nod my head and agree.

"Good. I want you to sit at the bar and have a drink or

two. Kaz will be watching you. Don't go anywhere without him, not even to the bathroom, all right? You don't have your patch yet and even though the guys know the score, I'm not willing to take any unnecessary risks with you."

That's kind of sweet in a how-fucked-up-is-it-that-I-can't-go-to-the-bathroom-alone kind of way.

I sigh and nod as he plants a kiss on my mouth and then he's gone. Grim follows suit, after a quick kiss, he trails Viper through the crowd, leaving me still none the wiser as to what the fuck is going on.

I sit at the bar alone for the next hour, nursing the same drink Kaz gave me before he was called over by one of the other guys. It's more for show anyway. I won't be getting drunk around these guys anytime soon. I look at the mirrored paneling behind the bar which offers me an unobstructed view of the room behind me. I hate having my back to people I don't trust, but the mirror acts as a second set of eyes.

It's starting to quiet down a little as people drift back to their rooms for the fucking portion of the evening but being here alone is still making me feel a touch antsy. I'd rather wait for the guys back in our room but when they ran out of here on club business, I gave in, not wanting to fight with Viper when he was needed elsewhere. I know I have Kaz and another prospect watching over me until they get back but it's not the same.

For the most part, people have left me alone, some throwing me a look of curiosity, some throwing a little shade, and some are just downright hostile now that my guys aren't here to beat them bloody for it. It takes some serious skill to piss off so many people without actually doing a thing to earn it. I feel like I should at least get a trophy or a crown or something.

I catch Boner behind me and keep my eye on him in case he approaches. I never liked him as a kid, going out of my way to avoid the man who always looked at me just a little too long. I can see his creep factor hasn't diminished over the years I've been absent.

He's arguing with one of the girls who served us earlier. I can't see what he's saying as his back is facing me, but whatever it is has her shaking her head adamantly. When she tries to walk off, he grabs her arm and spins her around, finally putting his face and, more importantly, his mouth in view of the mirror. As I watch him, my skin heats, making me so fucking thankful I can read lips.

"You will do it, Legs, or I'll have you sold off and shipped out before you can blink."

I see her glance over at me before she answers. "Please don't make me do this."

I can't hear her tone but I can tell by her face she's begging him to reconsider.

She winces as his grip gets harder. I refuse to sit here and let this shit happen when I see him slip something into the front pocket of her tiny Daisy Dukes. The move was so smooth that if I wasn't watching them so closely, I would have missed it.

"Slip it in her drink. It will loosen her up and have the little slut showing her real colors," he tells her, shocking me. When will I learn that this place is filled with snakes?

"Viper will kill you if you lay a hand on her," Legs warns him, still trying to talk him out of his foolhardy plan. What a fucking idiot. He's talking about drugging an old lady, for fuck's sake. Not just any old lady, but the president's.

"Oh, he might want to go a few rounds in the ring with me but he's a pussy and I can take him. Besides, what's he gonna do? Take on everyone that runs a train on her? Because that's what's going to happen. You're going to get her ready, then I'm going to get a little taste of the Carnage whore before tossing her to the boys. Viper can do what he wants. The important thing is that he'll be done with her. Nobody wants used up pussy for an old lady," he informs her, making her flush. What a fucking tool. Okay, game face on, Megan. I see Kaz over in the corner talking to one of the other prospects. He does a scan of the room, eyes taking me in before continuing on. I can't afford to react right now and give anything away, so I carry on twirling the straw in my drink and wait.

I don't have to wait long before Legs approaches me and sits on the empty barstool next to mine. I wait until Boner gets distracted with one of his club brothers before taking a risk and turning towards her.

"We don't have much time so listen carefully."

"You can talk?" She blushes, I guess thinking she's being rude but that shit really doesn't matter right now.

"Only to people I trust. I know what he wants you to do and I know you don't want to do it. We need to play along so you are going to have to go along with whatever I do, okay?" She nods, not bothering to deny anything, making me respect her even more.

"Pretend to slip me the drug and I'll drink it down. We will ham it up a little before heading over to Kaz so I can fill him in. You need to take the lead with Boner, tell him you'll warm me up or something, and to meet us at the cabin away from the brothers that are supportive of Viper. Shit—" I stop talking as Boner looks over before turning back to whoever calls his name.

"Gotta do this now. Please trust me, Legs, I won't let him hurt you," I promise. She looks at me for a second before offering me a slow nod, then slips into her role of distracting me for effect. She points over my shoulder, making me turn but I can see in the mirror that she is pretending to slip that shit in my drink. Most importantly, I see Boner clock the movement in the mirror too and watch an evil smile curl up his face.

I turn back and adopt a confused face before shrugging. I toss the straw aside and drink down the full glass of rum and coke. It burns going down, making my eyes water a little. I never was much of a drinker to begin with and that shit is going to go straight to my head, but at least that will lend to my credibility.

We make idle chit chat for a little while until she gives me another nod, letting me know that I would have been feeling the effects by now. Thanks to Boner's earlier comments, I know it's meant to loosen me up and get me feeling frisky. Well, here goes nothing. I lean over and fake laugh at her like she said something funny and tuck her hair behind her ear. Her face flushes from the contact. It dawns on me that I might not be into girls but that doesn't mean Legs isn't. I look down and see that her nipples have pebbled and her breathing has picked up a little. A little rush of power runs through me.

I'm not gonna lie. It's a heady feeling having this effect on someone and my body doesn't seem to care if that person has a dick or a pair of boobs.

I take her hand in mine and drag her over to the little dance floor, which puts us a little closer to Kaz. I slide my hands to her hips and she lifts her arms over my shoulders, entwining her fingers behind my neck. We dance and grind against one another, me following her movements as she can hear the beat. I see her eyes flick behind us and her steps falter for a second, making me assume Boner is there. I don't think about my next move, I just react and slide my fingers into her hair and tug her lips down to mine. The shock makes her freeze for a second before she responds, surprising me this time by sliding her tongue between my lips and playfully tangling it with mine. It's not my first time kissing a girl. Even if I generally prefer the throw-down-smack-your-ass roughness of a man, there is something sensual and seductive about a woman's touch. After all, nobody knows a woman's body better than a woman herself.

Her lips pull from mine as she's tugged slightly by Boner. I can't see what he's saying from this angle so I can only hope she keeps her cool and tells him what I told her to.

He scowls at her but eventually nods and walks back to the two guys he was talking to before.

She turns back to me and gives me a playful wink, letting me know she did her part and now it's my turn. I spot Kaz frowning at me. I pull on Legs's hand, leading her over to him with an exaggerated sway of my hips. I know everyone's eyes are on us so we have to play this part and do it well. I stop in front of Kaz and look up at him. Legs steps behind me and grips my hips before dipping her head and kissing my neck, her hair blocking the view of my face from everyone else. Clever girl.

"What the fuck are you doing, Megan?" he asks, confused and with just a hint of arousal on his face. Well, crap. I wiggle my finger at him in a come-hither motion, making him bend down. As soon as he is close enough, I place my lips against his ear and tell him what's going on as quickly as I can.

His body becomes more and more tense. By the time I'm finished, he's literally vibrating with rage.

"I'm going to fucking kill him." Seething, he tries to take a step around me but I yank on his leather cut and halt his movements.

"No, don't do that. I need you to let us take the lead here. Too many people won't believe the deaf girl who could have been mistaken and the club whore who has no power inside this club against a brother. Aside from that, Boner kept saying 'we.' Not I. I would really like to know who the 'we' is. If I can find out that would be great."

He frowns at me, not happy at all. "Don't ask me to let you put yourself in danger. That is not going to happen. I'm going to call your men and let them deal with your ass."

"Please, Kaz." I reach for his arm again and give it a squeeze. "It's important, and you know it. Viper needs to know who he can trust. His own brothers are plotting against him, he needs to know who. I'm okay. I have the upper hand here. All I need you to do is storm out after we leave so they don't try and stop us. Make a scene or yell that the pres can deal with my slutty ass, whatever you think will work, but come straight to our apartment because I guarantee Boner won't be far behind. I need you, Kaz. Please trust that I can do this. I won't let myself get hurt, I swear."

He looks at me hard. I know what I'm asking goes against everything he believes in. Kaz is one of the good guys. He has more integrity than most of the men here. I sigh in relief when he gives me a small nod.

"Okay, do it now, Megan. I don't think I can hold myself back much longer."

I lean up, kiss his cheek and thank him before grabbing Legs's hand again and with a giggle, we run towards the entrance. Nobody tries to stop us but I feel every pair of eyes in that room on me as I leave. Some give a gentle caress, a look of appreciation, but some definitely have a malevolent vibe so strong I feel it pushing down against my shoulders, making me feel violated just being in the same space.

We burst through the doors and keep running in case anyone tries to stop us. I suck in lungfuls of air, trying to fight off the dizziness that wants to take over as the adrenaline rushes over me.

I fumble with my key card and let us in. I flick on the lamp, knowing it will cast a glow through the thin curtains. I open my mouth to speak when Legs steps forward and kisses me again, hard, her tongue dueling against mine as she rubs herself against my thigh. I kiss her back briefly before pulling away with a sigh and sitting her on the bed.

"Okay, talk to me, Legs, and don't leave anything out.

"Boner is an asshole. He wants Viper out of here and fancies himself as the new president of Chaos. I don't know how or why because he isn't even next in line, but he can't see past his own ego. He thinks you make Viper weak and he is willing to exploit that to its full potential."

The door opens, making Legs jump. It's just Kaz, with a look of anger on his face.

"Boner is all riled up. He'll be here any minute so what the fuck is your play here?"

"Do you have another prospect or two nearby that you trust with your life or, more importantly, mine?"

He nods.

"Good. Text them and tell them to come here. Tell them to come in the back window and not make a sound. Any chance you can record what's about to go down?"

He finishes sending his texts before looking back up at me.

"Yeah, I can, but what the fuck exactly do you think I'm going to be recording, Megan? There is no fucking chance I'm letting that guy put his hands on you. I'll carve out his heart before that ever happens."

"You know, if I hadn't already reached my biker quota, I would add you to my boom-boom team in a heartbeat. You are the fucking bomb, Kaz. But no. When it comes to Boner making his move, you can take him down by any means necessary."

Kaz's grin turns feral. I spin to face Legs who is staring at Kaz like he just hung the moon.

"Go and open the window in the back bedroom on the left and then come back. It's time for the grand finale," I prompt her with a reassuring smile.

She takes a deep breath, straightens her shoulders, and does as I ask.

"You trust her?" Kaz asks me.

"Yeah. I think Boner has some kind of hold over her but she fought hard against him. I need to find out what's going on there but it's going to have to wait."

Legs comes out and three prospects fall in line behind her. Kaz gives them a quick rundown and they turn from curious to fuming in a nanosecond. Damn, I really like this new wave of prospects. These guys have all the makings to turn the Chaos Demons into a formidable club.

Kaz whips his head around, towards the window, so I know they heard something. Right, showtime. I wave the guys out of sight and whip my T-shirt over my head, leaving me in my shorts and lacy bra.

"Take some clothes off, lovely," I tell Legs in what I hope is a soothing voice. "We need to make this as convincing as possible." She doesn't need telling twice, stripping down to a tiny red G-string as I climb onto the bed and recline against the pillows.

"Straddle my waist." She does so without question, climbing onto the bed and sitting across my hips. I can feel the heat of her body seeping through the denim of my shorts and smell the scent of her arousal in the air.

"I'm sorry, it's just, you are so fucking sexy," she remarks, dipping her head to suck one of my nipples through the lace of my bra. My body arches up of its own accord just as I see the door open behind her. I close my eyes into slits and make my body go limp.

"Good girl, Legs. That shit always works like a dream," Boner praises, looking down at me. I suspect it isn't the first time he has done this to someone. I have to fight the urge to lash out at him on behalf of whoever he hurt but I can't give myself away right now.

"I don't want any part of this, Boner. I did what you wanted. Now let me get out of here. I won't say anything," Legs says, not looking away from me so I can see her speak.

"Oh, I know you won't. You see, I filmed you rubbing yourself all over her back at the bar. I even caught you slipping her the drug so I'll just let Viper know it was you who set her up. This worked out better than I thought." He pulls her off me, holding her arm tight so she can't go.

"You see, I have all I need to let Viper know that you set her up and had Carnage come in and gang fuck his girl. He'll have you labeled a traitor and start a war with those sorry assholes. I'll offer to take care of you for him so he can concentrate on getting rid of Carnage, then when his back is turned, I will burn his throne to the ground. Don't worry, I have a buyer all lined up for you." He licks her cheek, making her recoil.

"He will never believe that. Viper is far smarter than you, not to mention Carnage is her family. You might not know what loyalty is, but they do. They would never do that to their sister and you are a fucking fool if you think differently. I have nothing left to fear. If you're planning on selling me anyway, what's stopping me from walking out of here right now and coming clean to Viper?"

"You'll never make it past Fender and Mac." He grins but there is nothing funny about his words.

"They want to play with the Carnage bitch themselves but while they're waiting, they want a little appetizer. By the time they're finished with you, you won't be able to walk or speak."

His head turns towards the door with a frown. Keeping hold of Legs, he stomps towards it, yanking it open to show Fender and Mac with guns pointed at their heads by two of the prospects from the other room.

The prospects must have climbed back out of the window and snuck up on them.

"What the fuck?" Boner shoves Legs aside, ready to draw his own gun, but finds Kaz's pressed against the back of his skull.

The prospects move the others into the room as Legs struggles into her clothes.

"I'll have your prospect patch for this," Boner spits at Kaz before he catches me watching him from the corner of his eye.

When he turns to face me fully, I climb from the bed and saunter towards him.

"You set me up?" he asks, shocked.

"I know. Ironic, huh?"

He stares at me wide-eyed.

"Oh yeah, I speak too. I know all kinds of awesome tricks like that. See, that's your problem, Boner. All you see is a girl who, in your eyes, is the weaker species. Not only that, this one is defective, right? Did you forget I can read your lips?"

He curses, confirming that he had indeed forgotten.

"Tut, tut. You've been underestimating me for years, Boner, and look where it got us."

"What, with you held hostage as a biker sex toy?" he snaps at me.

I reach over and toss him the box of tissues off the nightstand.

"You have a little bullshit on your lip there, Boner. I've seen the way you watch me, how you adjust yourself whenever I walk by." I run my hands over my ribs and cup my lace covered breasts.

"You've been doing that shit long before I ever got these. No, you are jealous as fuck that the president you deem unworthy of the crown gets to slide his dick into something you can only dream about touching. How fucking pathetic do you have to be to drug a girl just to score some pussy?" I step up close to him, ignoring Kaz's protests, and suck my finger into my mouth, watching as Boner's pupils dilate. While he's watching my hand, he misses me lifting my leg until my knee connects with his dick.

"That was for Legs," I spit at him as he folds in on himself and collapses on the floor. I pull back my booted foot and kick him in the face as hard as I can, feeling a sick sense of pride when his nose explodes in a burst of red.

"And that one's for me. I can't let Viper, Zero, and Grim have all the fun now, can I?" As if summoned, my avenging angels in leather cuts slam open the room's door and stream in, guns pointed at the now prone figure on the floor.

"What the fuck is going on?" Viper asks, making me laugh.

"Hey, honey, welcome back. I got you a gift."

CHAPTER SIXTEEN

Viper

After dealing with a fire some asshole set at the garage, the last thing I expect is a text from Kaz telling me there was an emergency back home involving Megan.

Expected or not, Grim, Zero, and I tore out of there like the hounds of hell were chasing us.

Never in a million years did I think I would find Megan half-naked, surrounded by a bunch of club members, a stripper, and Boner bleeding on the bedroom floor.

"What the fuck is going on?" I yell.

"Hey, honey, welcome back. I got you a gift." I look from her near-naked chest to Legs sitting quietly on the bed behind her.

"What kind of present, exactly?" The words come out

deceptively calm as I struggle to bury my swirling rage. Every man tenses at my tone but of course it's wasted on Megan.

"Boner here decided he wanted a little taste of what his president has been sampling. Only thing is, I wasn't interested when I was twelve and I'm still not interested ten years later."

Knowing he had been after her when she was just a child signs his death warrant even if he hadn't pulled whatever this shit is tonight.

"And everyone else?" I gesture around the room at the bodies filling it. Kaz starts to speak but I raise my hand for him to shut up, keeping my eyes on Megan. She might not give me all the information when I want it but she never lies to me.

"Dumb and dumber over there wanted to be passengers on the train Boner decided to run on me."

Looks like Fender and Mac will need graves next to Boner.

"The prospects are here to make sure I'm safe. In fact, they have kept me safe all night. I like these guys," she tells me with a big smile on her face, completely calm standing there virtually topless with a splatter of blood across her toned stomach. I growl when they all look at her with a smile, except for Kaz who looks like he wants to strangle her too.

I'm so fucking pissed off that this went down in my club, I lash out without thinking. "Put some clothes on, for fuck's sake. Maybe if you covered up a little more people would be able to keep their fucking hands to themselves," I scream at her.

The smile slips from her face and in its place is a look that burns itself into my brain. A look of betrayal, disappointment, anger, and so much fucking pain.

I reach for her, but she steps back.

"If you touch me, I'll make what I did to Boner look like we had a pillow fight."

"Leave!" I bark at everyone. "Take those three to the basement."

"No, stay." Everyone freezes, not wanting to disrespect their president's orders, but not sure if they should ignore my old lady either.

She stares me down as she speaks. "I have something they all need to hear and if you make them leave, I'll leave too. Only, it won't be this room, it will be this compound and your lives for good," she vows, her chest heaving with the force of her words.

"You can threaten me all you want, Megan, but I won't let you go," I warn her.

"Maybe so, but I will never stop trying. Every single day you turn your back, I will try to escape until my hands are bloody and my legs won't hold me up. I will never stop," she says calmly, looking at me with sheer determination and fuck if it doesn't make me hard. Worse though, I know she's telling the truth.

"You have five minutes," I grit out as the guys turn back to her, guns still trained on each of the assholes who will die later. But Megan's anger isn't directed at them like it should be, it's all aimed at me.

She gives the three prospects a sad smile. "Sorry about this, boys," she apologizes to them a moment before she reaches around and unclips her bra and her magnificent breasts fall free.

"Megan," I snap, stepping forward, but she steps back again. I'm about to charge her but a hand on my arm stops me. I glance back and see Zero looking down at me, anger visible in the clenched jaw and the unreadable stare he throws my way.

"Let her speak." I can tell by his voice that he's barely hanging on to his own temper.

"You like what you see?" she asks Kaz, who doesn't answer her. She looks down at his dick, which even I can see from here is hardening through his jeans. Looks like I'm going to have to kill him too.

"Of course you do, I can tell. It's okay though because you might really like what you see but you won't touch me, will you?" she asks him, her voice flat and listless.

"Never," Kaz agrees adamantly.

Okay, fine, maybe he can live for a little while longer.

"And why is that, Kaz? I'm standing here showing an awful lot of skin. Why won't you touch me?" Anyone else and I would think her words were an invitation, but I can see the slight tremble of her hands at her side.

"Because you're not mine to touch," he answers. Simple

as that and I guess it is. With that comes the realization of what I said to her.

"Megan—"

She cuts me off, her eyes flashing with anger. "And what about you, Viper? In the eyes of the club, I'm your old lady. If I crawled into bed naked beside you and said not tonight, dear, I have a headache, would you pin me down and take what you wanted anyway?" she asks.

"Fuck no, of course not," I answer angrily. She should fucking know that already.

"Why is that?" she asks in that calm, almost robotic tone.

I don't answer her, done with this fucking night. Done with her standing here showing half the club what's mine.

"Why is that?" she repeats, this time letting her anger bleed into her words.

I still don't answer, staring at her, knowing I've fucked up, but I have no idea how to fix it.

Legs brushes her hand against Megan's leg to get her attention. "Because no should always mean no," Legs says in a soft voice.

Megan nods before facing us again. "Ding, ding. We have a winner. Isn't it funny how it took a woman to answer that question?" she asks in a tone suggesting that it is anything but funny.

"Look, I get it—"

She steps forward, growling, looking like a Valkyrie, every inch of Megan replaced by Raven.

"You get it? You know nothing. Not a fucking thing. We

are taught from an early age to either hide our bodies to avoid unwanted attention or to play up our assets in the hope of finding a husband. Thanks to Crogan and this club's misogynistic point of view, I grew up trying to hide my body under dark baggy clothes and trying to blend into the shadows. And what did that get me? A reputation for being an elusive freak and an easy target.

"Crogan didn't fucking care what I wore and neither do they because the problem isn't how much skin I show, but how their fucked-up brains are wired. You said it yourselves. You guys wouldn't force me to do anything even as I stand here half-naked because that is a normal response. It's how it should be. So why should I be reprimanded for something that is their problem, not mine?

"This is my body. It is my right to do with it what I want, which includes how I cover it. And it is absolutely my right to say no. Until you guys understand that, I hope to fuck you never have daughters." Her words cut me deeply and one look at the others tells me she scored a direct hit.

I nod to the prospects so they can get these pieces of shit out of here. They do as I ask without a backward glance.

"Erm... I'll just—"

I look at Legs and she shuts up and folds in on herself. I'm not sure what her role in all this was but I'm going to find out just as soon as I fix what I broke.

I step forward and when Megan doesn't step back, I take another step and another until my chest is against her heaving one.

"You are absolutely right. I fucked up. I was angry and lashed out without thinking. I'm sorry," I tell her and mean it. I never apologize but Megan has earned the right to one.

Her eyes well with tears as she stares into mine, searching for the truth, and I hate that I put that doubt there.

I pull her tightly to me, wrap my arms around her, and hold her while she cries quietly into my T-shirt before pulling back.

Wiping her cheeks, I kiss her forehead and turn her towards Grim and Zero, who I know are itching to get their hands on her too.

Grim has slipped his T-shirt off before putting his cut back on. He walks over and slips the shirt over Megan's head. She lets him before stepping into his arms. He holds her tight, staring at me with anger of his own in his eyes. Some I'm sure is aimed at me but I'm guessing this stirs up a lot of shit regarding his sister too.

Zero gets impatient and pulls Megan free from a reluctant Grim so he can hold her for a moment. It's almost like we need to actually touch her to verify she's here, safe and sound.

I turn to Legs, who is watching us warily.

"What's your involvement in all this?" I ask her, my voice still angry, my patience running thin.

"Boner wanted me to slip her something to make her more compliant," she tells me. I watch Megan pull free from Zero and walk back over to us.

"And did you?" I wonder if that might explain Megan's behavior tonight.

"I was going to," she admits softly.

White noise stops me from hearing anything else as my anger takes over. I reach to grab her by the neck but Megan steps in front of her, blocking my way.

"Move!" I growl. "This is club business." I try to move her, but she twists out of my hold.

Grim reaches over to grab Legs but Megan backs her up until she's in the corner and takes a protective stance in front of her like a tigress protecting her cubs.

"You won't touch her!" she grits out, willing to take me on if necessary.

The stupid girl can't win but she knows I won't risk hurting her.

"She told Boner no. She told him you would kill him. She said no. Can you guess what happened next, boss man?" Her sarcasm grates on me but I know she has more to spew.

"He told her he had a buyer all lined up to sell her. She said no, so he took her choice away from her. Sound familiar?" She turns her back on me, knowing at the very least I won't hurt her, and crouches down to a now crying Legs, who is sobbing with her face buried in her knees.

I look at Zero and Grim and see them watching the scene play out.

"This is so fucked up," Zero points out and he isn't fucking wrong.

"Legs, can you talk to me? I swear to you nobody is going

to hurt you. I'm guessing you don't have a lot of faith in the male species and that's okay, neither do I, but can you try to have a little faith in me? I won't let anything happen to you, I promise." She lifts her tear-stained face to Megan and takes a shuddering breath. She looks past Megan to me.

"What will you do with them?" she asks me.

"That's club business, Legs, you know that."

Megan turns to look at me with questions in her eyes.

"Can you keep her safe?" Something stirs within me at her words. After everything that happened here tonight, she still trusts me. I nod at her.

"They won't touch her again." I don't tell her they'll be dead but she's a smart girl. I can see in her eyes she knows exactly what kind of retribution will be dealt out.

"And Peter?" Legs asks me, making me frown.

"Peter? The manager of Elusive? What does he have to do with this?" I just spoke to the guy. He was the one who called and said the garage was on fire. He was waiting with the fire department when we got there.

"If he finds out I had a hand in this, he'll kill me."

"He won't touch you," I promise her.

She sighs but eventually starts talking. "Boner wanted me to slip a D in Megan's drink to make her horny, then he and his friends were going to run a train on her. He said you wouldn't want her then and even if you were pissed at him, he could take you, which was bullshit. Then when we got here, he said he was going to frame me as an accomplice and make it look like Carnage had raped Megan in some kind of payback. I don't know, it sounded to me like the worst fucking idea on the planet and I told him so but he just couldn't see the stupidity in it." She snorts, but I'm stick stuck on this D.

"A D? Do you mean an E?" I ask her, wondering how much she has had to drink tonight or if it's a case of the lights are on but nobody's home.

She looks at me, bewildered. "No, a D. Why do you look so confused?" she asks, making my head spin. It's like going around in fucking circles.

"Because there isn't a drug called D," Grim answers before I can.

"Sure, there is. You guys are the ones who make it." She reaches into her pocket and grabs a tiny pink pill, which I'm guessing is the one she was meant to spike Megan's drink with. Sure enough, there is a D printed on it.

"D for demons," I guess, handing the pill over to Zero. I'm so fucking pissed off, it's a surprise my head hasn't exploded.

"D because the guys think it's funny to slip a girl a D before slipping her the D," Legs says sarcastically and I don't doubt for a second she has heard that more than once.

"Legs, Chaos has only been dealing in weed since I took over." Megan looks surprised by my words. I guess I forgot to tell her that.

"Well, Pres, I hate to be the bearer of bad news, but I don't think the whole of your club is in agreement."

"These could be from an old batch," I tell her but she shakes her head.

"Boner likes to brag about how fucking smart he is and how dumb you are—his words, not mine—for pulling the wool over your eyes. He thinks he can take over and flood the streets with the stuff."

"Jesus fucking Christ." I grip my hair in my hands, feeling another headache coming on.

"I guess this explains why the club is doing so well. It must be the draw of the drugs."

"It's the draw of the girls," she tells me sadly.

"It's a strip club, Legs, no offense, but strippers are a dime a dozen. The kind of money that place is making isn't because people are coming for a flash of gash."

Megan sucks in a sharp breath, making me look at her thinking I've pissed her off again, but she isn't looking at me, she's staring at Legs with a dawning look of horror on her face.

"What? What the fuck am I missing?" A tear runs down Legs's cheek but she swipes it away angrily.

"They get to try out the new wonder drug on a girl of their choice. A try-it-before-you-buy-it kind of sample, if you like. Trust me, they do, they always buy."

"Fuck!" Grim shouts. Zero looks like he's going to be sick.

"Are you telling me girls are getting drugged and raped in my club?" My words are so vicious I'm surprised she isn't bleeding, but my anger isn't at her.

She nods.

"But that's not what I meant when I said it's the draw of the girls. Pres, these guys don't just come to buy drugs, they come to buy girls who, thanks to D, are moldable into the perfect sex slave. Didn't you ever wonder why the club had such a high turnover?"

I never cared. Strippers come and go, it's the nature of the beast. I just had no fucking clue my club was selling girls. I'm so ashamed I can hardly meet her eyes.

I pick up the thing closest to me, which just happens to be a lamp, and launch it at the wall before grabbing the vanity table and flipping it over. I'm acutely aware of screaming but I can't stop.

The rage is boiling me from the inside and if I don't get it out, I'm going to burn this place to the ground.

I'm oblivious to everyone else as I systematically destroy the room, shrugging off hands that try to restrain me until a pair of small, shaking palms press against my chest, freezing me in place. I look down and see big blue eyes brimming with tears looking up at me with sadness and a hint of fear.

"Come back to me, Viper," she implores, pressing her head against my chest before wrapping her arms around me tightly.

I stand there with my chest heaving, looking around the room I just destroyed, and take in Zero and Grim who have taken a protective stance in front of Legs, who is cowering in the corner. Zero has a split lip and Grim has the beginnings of a bruise blooming under his eye.

I look down at Megan and wrap my arms around her, using her smell and touch to calm me.

She peers up at me and offers me a small smile.

"They're trafficking girls." I shake my head in disbelief. I look up at Grim and Zero again.

"Burn it to the fucking ground."

Megan stops me. "Wait. You stopped dealing in hard drugs?"

"Yeah," I grunt out. "I wanted to focus more on the legitimate businesses. We'll never be squeaky clean but I don't want to be looking over my shoulder for the rest of my life. I'm getting too fucking old for this shit."

"Let me have it," she suggests, surprising the fuck out of me.

"What the fuck do you want a strip club for?"

"I don't want a strip club. I want to gut it and turn it into another legal business for you," she offers with a shrug. "I know what I'm doing, I do run a pretty successful business of my own."

"One small shop doesn't make you an entrepreneur," I tell her with a smile.

"Remind me to show you my books sometime," she quips back. I stare at her. She's serious. I look at Grim and Zero, who are helping Legs to her feet.

"Two seconds ago you wanted it burned to the ground, so what have you got to lose?" Zero answers my unspoken question. Grim nods in agreement.

"Fine, it's yours," I tell her.

"How far does your trust in me run?" she asks out of the blue, making me suspicious for a moment but then I realize that I do trust her.

"My trust is absolute. Why, are you planning on abusing it?" I ask, only half-joking.

"Maybe just a little bit." She pinches her fingers together in demonstration.

"I'm going to regret this, I know it. Tell me what you need."

CHAPTER SEVENTEEN

Megan

I stand next to Zero and a prospect called Wizz outside Euphoria, waiting for my guests to arrive.

"I can't believe you talked Viper into this." Zero shakes his head at me.

"Honestly, neither can I but I'm not one to look a gift horse in the mouth."

A large truck pulls into the parking lot, making me smile. As soon as it stops, a tiny blonde angelic-looking woman climbs out sporting a cute little baby bump.

"Luna," I breathe out before taking off in her direction and wrapping my arms around her.

She pulls away and signs to me, *I have a truck full of guys on their way over. Who do you need me to kill?*

Most people would laugh in her face but not me. I know exactly how deadly this woman can be.

"Nobody yet, but give it time. The day is still young." Her eyes light up, partly from hearing my voice, which I never really used until recently over Skype, and partly from the thought of killing people.

A large arm drops on my shoulder, making me turn to the familiar scent of Zig.

"Hey, big guy."

He looks down at me with a thousand questions swirling in his eyes but settles on "Hey, Megs."

"Out of the way, fuck face." Oz shoves him aside, picking me up and spinning me around before placing me back on my feet.

"I always knew you'd have a sexy voice. It makes me want to do very dirty things to you."

I see Zero approach from behind him and wince.

"You wanna get your hands off my old lady before I peel your skin from your bones?" Oh shit. Abort. Abort.

I step up to Zero and stand in front of him protectively as Wizz steps up beside us.

"What did he say?" Zig asks, eyes flashing to mine.

"Erm, that he wants to skin Oz alive. In fairness, don't most people that meet him?" I ask.

"Old lady?" Oz questions, not smiling anymore.

"Yeah, did I forget to mention that part? Oops?"

"They kidnapped you," Zig points out.

"More like borrowed. Plus it's a biker thing. Isn't that what Orion, Gage, and Halo did to Luna?"

"Luna can handle herself," Oz grates out.

"So can I," I tell them softly. I know they have seen me at my worst and are super protective of me but, Lord above, they are not my parents.

"Hey, perv," Luna greets Zero.

I look behind me and watch him greet her with a smile, not the least bit bothered by the title.

"Watch anyone in the shower lately?" she asks.

"Only Megan," he answers casually.

"Wait, you watch me shower?" I ask.

"Babe, I watch you everywhere," he admits unapologetically.

"That's both creepy and hot," I mumble, forgetting the audience we have.

"You like my eyes on you," he answers me with conviction.

"Stop turning me on, Zero, we have things to do dammit." I turn back around and watch Oz gagging as Luna smiles at me. She walks forward and links her arm through mine, looking at me as she herds us towards the club.

"He's a mechanic, right? Hmm... they do like to get their hands dirty."

I laugh, giving her a squeeze. "Damn, I missed you."

"Back at ya, Megan. Now tell me what you need."

I'VE GATHERED ALL the girls that work here together. They are sitting at one of the large tables in the middle. All the guys are across the room watching but giving me enough space to talk to them without them feeling intimidated.

Luna stands beside me and, after having been filled in, she's as pissed off as me.

"Okay, ladies as you know, Euphoria is now closed for business." I look at the girls in jeans and T-shirts, yoga pants and hoodies, and see what the guys who come to watch them shake their tails don't. The real them.

"How many of you are here willingly?" I ask softly. Nobody answers but a few shuffle in their seats.

"Hey, you will get no judgment from me. We all do what we have to do to survive," I reassure them when a pretty redhead snaps at me.

"What do you know about survival?"

"My mother was forced to become a club whore to keep me safe. It didn't stop them though. It never does. I was attacked when I was sixteen. I lost my hearing, my family, my home. I ended up on the streets for a couple of years." I feel Luna jolt beside me at this, but she doesn't say anything. "Trust me when I say I understand what it's like. I'm asking you this so I can figure out what to do with you all. I'm going to turn this place into a bar/restaurant that will cater to the local MCs but act as neutral ground. If you ladies have seen enough bikers to last you a lifetime, I will happily let you leave and help you find somewhere else to work. For those who might want to stay, it will be in a waitress/bar staff only capacity with a little bar dancing where the clothes stay on. Think *Coyote Ugly*, but biker style."

A young girl in the back with hair as dark as mine raises her hand. "Will we have to have sex with them?" she asks, her voice shaking.

I walk over towards her, my heart in my throat when I realize just how young she is. I squat down in front of the chair she is sitting on and don't take my eyes away from hers.

"Never. If a girl decides she wants a hot night with a biker, she does it on her own time. You ladies will be paid to wait tables and that's it. I will have the best security available and if someone attempts to touch you, I will have their fingers broken. Understand?" She nods, a tear slipping free, her relief palpable.

"What's your name?" I question her.

"Jenna."

"How old are you, Jenna?" I ask but I already have a suspicion she is young.

"Sixteen." She jumps and looks over to the corner, frightened. I look and see that Zero has punched a hole in the wall.

I turn back to her and hold her hand.

"He isn't mad at you, sweetheart. He's mad at the people who put you here." I turn back to Zero and yell, "Hey, Zero, stop messing up my goddamn club." He plops down in his chair and the girls laugh a little at the big badass biker getting told off by little old me.

I look down at Jenna again and squeeze her hand.

"You can't work here, sweetheart, you are too young." She squeezes my hand so tightly, I wonder if she'll break a finger. Her face goes white as she tries to get her words out.

"Are you going to sell me now?"

"Nobody is getting sold, ever again. You see those guys in the corner? The hot geeky one is a genius on the computer. With the help of you ladies, he's going to try and locate the girls that got sold. The blond giants next to him are going to bring home the ones we find." I look her up and down and notice that her clothes are clean but threadbare.

"Where do you live?"

She chews on her lip. I don't think she is going to answer me but eventually, she opens her mouth and forces out her words. "Peter lets me sleep in the storage room if I—" She shuts up, but I know exactly what Peter took in return.

"Do you have a family?" She starts shaking violently.

"No, don't send me back please, please don't send me back." I try to calm her down when Luna crouches beside me with a small knife in her hand. She holds it out to Jenna, the handle facing towards her. Jenna looks at the knife, then to Luna, then to me in question.

"Take it. Anyone comes near you again who makes you feel uncomfortable, you stab them with this. They'll think twice about coming near you again." I roll my eyes at my psychotic friend but she's not wrong.

"I'm not sending you home, but sweetheart, you are far too young to work here. I have a better place for you. Let me just text my friend and I will get everything sorted out, okay?" She looks unsure and why wouldn't she? She knows it's usually a mistake to trust anyone.

"I own a little boutique in town. Anything girly you can think of, I sell it. I could use another set of hands to work there. I also have an apartment upstairs. I'm not using it at the moment, so you are welcome to stay there, but I don't want you staying alone. My friend Wyatt looks like a scary ass motherfucker, but he's a teddy bear. He will keep you safe, sweetheart, I promise. He has kept me safe many times over."

She looks at me, studying my face for any signs of deceit but when she doesn't find any she nods slowly. "Okay."

I smile. "Good girl."

I walk away and leave Luna chatting with her while I send a message to Wyatt explaining what I need and to meet me here.

I face the group of ladies who are now looking at me with a mix of gratitude and respect.

"This place will need to be closed for renovations for about a month. You will be getting paid while we are closed. It's the fucking least we can do. There will be a no drugs policy. A little bit of weed off the clock is fine but anything harder and you'll be gone." I watch as they all nod.

"Good, now the guys are going to come over and ask you some questions. Tell them everything you can think of no matter how insignificant it might seem to you. I'll be just over here."

When nobody objects, I head over to the table of guys.

"They're ready for you but take it easy on them. It's a lot to take in."

"Don't worry, we've got this," Zig assures me, squeezing my shoulder as he, Oz, and Wizz make their way over to the girls.

"What a clusterfuck," I grumble at Zero, collapsing into the chair beside him.

"I know, but Viper and Grim have managed to get some information from the traitors. Your girls over there were not the ones being traded. They genuinely did need people here to just dance, strip, and suck dick." He holds his hands up at my glare.

"Not my words, Megan. Anyway, these girls kept their mouths shut with the threat of being sold and yeah, some were sold anyway. For the most part, the girls that were trafficked were stolen to order. If someone wanted a short dark-haired girl-next-door type, then that was who they got. And some poor drunk co-ed stumbling home after a frat party would have her life irrevocably changed forever.

"The only girl from Elusive named on the list Viper got was Jenna. She was sold by her father to Peter. Peter sold her to someone else as she fits the requirements he wanted, but we shut shit down before he could collect her. She'll need to be watched until we can track down the buyer and take that fucker out."

"She will be," I promise, maternal instincts flaring when I turn to look at her smiling softly at something Luna says to her.

"The construction crew will be here tomorrow. Once they're done, you guys can set your security shit up."

"I still think we should have our own guys working here."

I shake my head. "Oz and Zig have handpicked a team. You know why I'm doing this. Those girls need to know their safety is a priority, even over club brothers. They have had enough of being treated as expendable. I want a team of men who don't give a flying fuck about the MCs. Their sole job is to protect all female staff. Without exception. Plus, like I said to the girls, I want this spot to be neutral territory. A place where Chaos and Carnage can meet, for example, without the threat of death."

He stares at me for a second before lifting me out of my chair and sitting me on his lap.

"How is it we keep throwing all these balls at you and you keep on hitting them out of the park?"

"I guess I just have amazing ball skills," I snark, making him laugh.

"I shall require a demonstration."

"I'm sure that can be arranged, Sir."

Ooh, his nose flares at my use of the word "sir" before his eyes narrow with lust.

"I'm also looking at purchasing a new toothbrush. I was wondering if I could get a demonstration on how you use yours?" My eyes open impossibly wide at his words and I feel red creep over my face as I press my hand over his mouth.

"That asshole," I grumble. "Mention it again and I'll

show you exactly what I can do with a toothbrush," I warn him, making him laugh behind my hand.

His eyes leave mine for a second as something at the door catches his attention. He is on his feet with his gun trained at the beast walking through the door before I can even open my mouth.

One quick look shows that each of the guys has followed suit and all are now standing with their guns aimed at his head.

I stand up and smile, catching the beast's eye. He spots me and heads straight over, not fazed in the slightest.

"Who the fuck are you?" Zero barks at him, all traces of the fun-loving guy from before gone in the blink of an eye.

The beast ignores him and runs his eyes over my body in an assessing way, but he's not checking me out sexually, he's making sure I'm in one piece and unharmed.

"Wyatt." I walk over to him and wrap my arms around his waist and wait for him to reciprocate, which he does. Wyatt's arms are huge, strong, and lethal when needed.

I met him on the streets when someone grabbed me from behind and tried to fuck me in a dirty alley. Wyatt had been asleep next to the dumpster. All I remember from those moments was one minute the abrasive brick wall was cutting into my face as I was pushed against it and then I was being held in these arms that felt like an impenetrable force field.

He pulled me out of the gutter that day and I returned the favor a year later when I got my inheritance. I may have blood brothers now but Wyatt is the brother of my heart.

Stepping back, I look up at him with a smile before I'm yanked backward, colliding with a hard chest and a familiar arm is wrapped tightly around me.

"Lord spare me from alpha males," I mutter.

"Wyatt, the guy behind me with the gun is Zero. He's a little protective." I turn my head to face Zero, who is glaring at Wyatt.

"Zero, meet Wyatt, the guy you have to thank for me standing in your arms safe and sound." Zero's arms loosen at my words, but he doesn't take his eyes away from him.

"Zero, he's my brother, maybe not by blood, but in every other sense of the word. You should know what that's like."

His jaw clenches but he finally nods and puts the gun away. I notice the others follow suit.

Luna strides over, full of grace and sass in her floor length floral print maxi dress and flip flops. I imagine her flip flops making a staccato slap, slap, slap sound against the wooden floor, echoing loudly around the room for everyone but me.

"Hey, Wyatt." She offers him a genuine smile. He offers her a nod in return. She doesn't take offense. She has only met Wyatt once before when he dropped off supplies at my shop, but she knew then that he wasn't a talker.

I pull free from Zero and he begrudgingly lets go but follows behind me as I walk towards the girls and indicate for Wyatt to join me.

When we get there, Jenna stands up and twists her hands in front of her.

"Jenna, this is Wyatt. He is one of my favorite humans on the planet and if you give him a shot, I guarantee he will become one of yours too. I'm willing to share him with you on a joint custody kind of basis. What do you say?"

She looks away from me to Wyatt, tipping her head back so she can stare into his deep dark eyes before looking back at me, clarity showing behind her eyes and reminding me she might have the body of a sixteen-year-old, but her tortured soul has aged her beyond her years.

"There's someone looking for me, isn't there?" I didn't mention anything before because I didn't know if she knew she had been sold, but if I have any chance of building a relationship with this girl, I can't start lying to her now.

"Yes. You were sold, but we shut shit down before you could be collected. The Chaos Demons will not stop until we find him and wipe him from the face of the earth. Until we do, Wyatt will keep you safe."

She looks up at Wyatt. "What happens if he finds me?" she asks him.

"Then I'll rip out his heart and give it to you. Every time you see it, you'll be reminded that I'll kill anyone who tries to hurt you." He holds his giant hand out to her. She looks down at it before looking back up to his face, searching. She takes a hesitant step forward and slides her small hand into his. A flash of déjà vu washes over me as he leads her away, everyone watching them go in silence.

Oz nudges my arm. "I like him," he tells me, making me laugh.

"Me too, Oz, me too."

Zero steps in front of me. "I thought you said you didn't like to be touched before you started—" he stumbles over his words for a second "—dating Jax."

"And it was true of everyone but Wyatt and Viddy. I think maybe it was because they had both saved me at one time or another that I instinctively knew I could trust them."

"Viddy?" Zero questions.

"Another street kid," I answer him, not wanting to go into it with an audience.

"Wyatt, Viddy, Jax. It scares me, baby, how many times someone had to save you or that you were in danger to begin with."

"What can I say? I'm a trouble magnet. How the fuck do you think I ended up with you, Viper, and Grim as my boyfriends?" I question, making him laugh.

"Besides, you're only seeing half the picture," I remark, walking back to the table we sat at before.

"How so?" he asks, sitting in front of me.

"I wasn't the only one with issues. They might have saved me first, but I saved them right back. That's why we have an unbreakable bond between us now. We had nobody when we met but then in each other we found a family."

"Where's Viddy now?" he queries, making me smile. Viddy makes Luna look well adjusted. Actually, Viddy makes Ted Bundy look well adjusted.

"Busy causing trouble as per usual." Which is really an understatement. Viddy has had shit go down that needs dealing with so barring the odd email, our contact has been lacking lately.

"How come they didn't flip their shit when they found out what happened to you?"

"What happened to me? Zero, honey, you are going to have to be far more specific than that." I laugh but cut him some slack.

"I didn't tell them anything more than the basics. So instead of 'hey guys, my shop got shot up and I got shoved in a cell at the Carnage clubhouse.' I went with 'hey guys, I found my long lost brothers so I'm spending a little quality time with them. Oh, and the shop is being fumigated so it will be closed for a few days.'"

"And they believed that?" he asks incredulously.

"Sure, I've never lied to them before."

"So why start now?"

I look at him like he's dumb which, honestly, at the moment, he kind of is.

"If they knew the truth, both clubhouses would have been blown to smithereens with everyone inside it. They have no loyalty to anyone but me."

He looks at me to see if I'm joking, but I'm not. If anything, I'm downplaying what would happen.

"Wyatt is more than capable of holding his own, I could tell that straight away but even with him and this Viddy person, I doubt they would win up against MCs," he points out, making me snort.

"Wyatt married his high school sweetheart when they both turned eighteen. They had a little girl a year later. His life was perfect until one day his wife was driving home and she was carjacked. She was shot in the face point blank at a green light. They tossed her in the road and drove off in the car that was a secondhand Honda and worth fuck all. What they didn't realize until later was that there was a kid in the back fast asleep. See, his daughter was born deaf, that's how he knows how to sign. Anyway, obviously, she didn't hear the gunshots. When they spotted her, they pulled over and tossed her from a bridge into the freezing water below."

"Jesus fuck!"

I nod in agreement. My heart bleeds for Wyatt every time I think about everything he went through.

"He found out it was some kind of fucked up gang initiation thing so Wyatt returned the favor and killed those responsible for the deaths of his wife and daughter."

"And the gang didn't retaliate when he killed two of their own?"

"Oh, you misunderstood me. He didn't just kill the two guys who stole the car, he wiped out the entire gang. All two hundred and seventeen people."

He stares at me, trying to process the information I gave him so I figure I might as well give him the rest while I'm here.

"As for Viddy, Viddy makes Wyatt look like a Care Bear." His mouth snaps shut at that.

"Grim was right to give you the name Raven. You really are a death omen. One wrong move and we will all be meeting our makers."

"You have no idea." I wink at him.

CHAPTER EIGHTEEN

Grim

I pull my hand back and shake out my knuckles as Boner's head flops forward when he passes out yet a-fucking-gain, the pussy.

I turn to look at Viper, wiping my hand on my jeans with a smirk as he picks up the pruning shears from the counter. I focus my attention on the back wall where Fender and Mac are hanging from meat hooks screwed into the fortified ceiling.

Gagged and naked, they don't make a sound even as they kick and swing.

"Who's first?"

"Mmm... I call Mac. You can have Fender," Viper answers, staring hard at Mac as he approaches him. Mac's eyes widen in fear, renewing his struggles but his body is out of shape and he tires easily.

"No point in fighting the inevitable, Mac. We both know you won't be walking out of this room. I guess the question is how quickly will I kill you?" He grips Mac's chin with his hand and squeezes hard.

"You will tell me everything I want to know or I will dismantle your body piece by piece. Then I'll bag all the little pieces and send them to your sister. Hell, she won't even know it's you unless she puts all the bits back together. Kind of like a human jigsaw puzzle. Hmm... maybe I should record this for her, like a teaser of what's to come."

I stand and watch Viper work as he reaches down and without hesitation snips off one of Mac's toes. I follow the fallen digit with my eyes as it drops to the ground.

Mac's screams are muffled by the gag and sweat drips down his face but Viper just moves on to the next toe. When he finally removes the last one from Mac's left foot, he looks at him.

"Still not gonna talk huh?" Viper moves to the next foot before smacking his hand against his forehead. "Oops, I forgot to take the gag out. My bad."

Reaching up, he rips the gag free. "Now, what do you have to tell me?" His voice sounds every bit as lethal as he is.

"Please—" Mac is cut off as the gag is shoved roughly back into his mouth.

"Nothing? Well okay then." He starts removing the toes on Mac's other foot all while singing "this little piggy went to market." I grin at the crazy motherfucker and grab the blowtorch from the counter, stalking over to Fender because I'm done letting Viper have all the fun.

Fender starts fighting in earnest now as Viper looks back at me and grins sadistically when he spots the blowtorch in my hand.

"Now, how did I know you would pick that out? I mean, I get the appeal, but the smell of burned flesh lingers for days afterward."

I shrug, not caring. "He was going to rape our old lady. That shit would have branded her soul. She has enough scars inside her to last a lifetime. I refuse to let this traitorous punk-ass leave his mark on the outside too. I figure I'll just do to him what he wanted to do to her, but tenfold."

I pick up the six-inch piece of steel piping from the floor that Viper had used earlier to break Mac's nose and begin heating the end of it.

"He was going to fuck her, tear her up, and make her bleed. Let's see how he likes it." I drop the blowtorch and yank the gag from his mouth.

"Feel free to scream as loud as you want. You know nobody other than Viper and I will hear you. Gotta love soundproofing. But then, if I'm being totally honest, I don't think one person inside or outside this clubhouse will miss you."

I walk behind him and press the heated pipe against his back and drag it lower so he knows exactly where I'm going to shove this pipe.

"Stop, please," he screams. "I'll tell you everything you want to know." I pause and look at Viper.

Viper stands and removes Mac's gag again. "Guess we won't be needing you then, Mac." He slaps his face hard.

"Fender doesn't know shit. He just wants to be put out of his misery."

"Fuck you, Mac," Fender snarls.

"Boner was double-crossing you. You were just too blind to see it. He didn't want you as his second because he knew you'd eventually take his crown. You were just a means to an end," Fender spits at Mac.

They could be words spoken in desperation and anger but Mac believes him. I can tell by the look of defeat on his face when he realizes all this was for nothing. The man was destined to die either way.

"My mother is on life support. She doesn't have long left but I'm the one who pays her bills. Keep her safe and I'll tell you everything."

"Done. But know this Mac, if I find out you are lying, I will do to her what I would have done to you. Then I will eradicate every single person from your bloodline." Mac nods his head. He doesn't need to know that's not Viper's style.

"Sorry, Fender. Looks like your input isn't needed anymore."

"No, please, no," he cries.

"What a fucking pussy," I spit with disgust, stepping back when he pisses himself.

"Would you have stopped if Megan begged you to? No, I don't fucking think so. However, it must be your lucky day because I want to get back to my girl. Spending any more time with a pathetic creature like you makes me want to toss myself out the fucking window so I'm gonna make it quick," I say from behind him, drawing both my knife and my gun. I push the gun to his temple, making him whimper as I walk around him so I can look him dead in the eyes when I send him to hell.

I click off the safety as he closes his eyes and takes a deep breath. That's when I shove my knife into his abdomen and draw it up through his stomach. His eyes shoot open with fear and pain, making me smile like the devil himself.

"I said I'd make it quick. I didn't say I'd make it painless," I tell him as the life drains from his eyes.

"Now, speak!" Viper commands Mac. He does, telling us everything he knows including where he hid the ledger he had been secretly keeping.

"That everything?" Viper asks, slapping Mac as he starts to lose consciousness once again.

"Yeah, everything I know, at least. I know you're going to kill me now. I just want to say something first." He stops to cough, bloody spittle flying from his mouth. "I was wrong and I'm sorry. I thought you were too soft and you would lead this club into ruin. I underestimated you and I deserve to pay the price for it."

"You would have made a better VP than Fender. Your mistake was giving your loyalty to a man that didn't deserve it," Viper informs him before pulling his gun and rapidly firing two bullets—one into Mac's heart and one through his skull.

Groaning draws our attention back to Boner, who has unfortunately been unconscious for all the good stuff.

"Text Zero and let him know what Mac said. If that kid is there, she will be a target. Don't let on to Boner what we know. I want to see what we can get out of him first," Viper orders. I pull out my phone and do as he asks, knowing time is of the essence.

"Boner, Boner, Boner," Viper mocks, walking back toward him. "Nice of you to join us. You missed all the fun."

He spins the chair Boner is strapped to so Boner can see what's left of his so-called brothers. The rest of the color drains from his already pale face before he looks up at Viper with pure hate in his eyes.

"Suck my dick," Boner manages to choke out.

"I'm gonna pass but that does give me an excellent idea."

I cringe at Viper's words, knowing exactly what's going to happen next. I can almost feel my balls retreating inside me.

"Grim, hold him still for me. I would hate to nick myself," he orders, picking up a wicked-looking serrated hunting knife from the table.

"Anything you want to say before you choke on your own dick?"

Boner struggles in my arms but he can't move at all. "Yeah, take that knife and shove it up your ass. I'm not afraid of you," he screams but his anger isn't enough to coat the fear oozing from him.

"Now, you're just giving me ideas, Boner." Viper laughs, leaning down and grabbing the base of Boner's limp dick, carving straight through it as Boner's high-pitched screams echo off the walls. He passes out once again but that doesn't stop Viper from squeezing his mouth open and shoving his dick inside it.

I'm thankful I have a strong stomach. It might not be the first time I've seen Viper in action but this shit always makes me want to hurl.

"You done? I doubt he's gonna tell us anything else. He knows he's going to die. He'd rather take what he knows to the grave with him. More out of spite than bravery is my guess."

Viper sighs, tossing the knife back on the table. "I know. I'm bored with this shit anyway. I want to get back to Megan and see if the spell the little witch has woven over me has worn off."

"Spell?" I snort, washing the blood from my hands in the sink in the corner.

"How the fuck else did she manage to get me to agree to her bringing in a team of mercenaries? And not just any mercenaries but ones with direct links to Carnage?"

"Magic pussy," I agree, seeing his point.

"The sad thing is, I trust Carnage with Megan more than my own club. She made a good call and it can only help solidify the truce between us. Having Megan as a go-between for both clubs can't hurt right now."

He's quiet, thinking over my words as he washes blood from his own skin. "Let's just hope it doesn't come back to bite us in the ass. Besides, as she pointed out the team might have links to Carnage but they don't work for them. I guess time will tell. At some point, one of us is going to have to take a leap of faith. I mean, isn't that what we're expecting of Megan?" he asks.

I nod. I guess he's right but after what I did, I will never be welcome or trusted by Carnage.

"Hungry?" Viper questions, heading up the stairs like he isn't walking away from three dead bodies that we just finished torturing.

"Sure, I could eat."

* * * * *

EIGHT SLICES of pizza later Megan strolls into the diner with Zero behind her, his hands on her hips as he guides her towards our booth.

"How'd it go?" I ask her when she sits down beside me and steals a slice for herself.

"Pretty good. Most of the girls are planning on staying on in a waitress capacity once the bar opens. Two of them want to go back home so I offered them a severance package until they can get themselves back on their feet. I had a talk with Legs before I went and she's interested in the manager position. I've told her to enroll herself in some part-time courses, which we'll pay for, and the job's hers, pending a probation period."

"What about the kid?" Viper asks from across from me as he signals to the waitress for another round of drinks.

"Jenna? She's staying at the apartment above my shop with Wyatt."

"Wyatt?" I ask. "Isn't that the guy who does your packing and shipping?" I frown, picturing a lean hipster type in skinny jeans and tie-dye helping out so he can get a staff discount on candles and girly shit.

"I'll put a couple of prospects on her," Viper offers Megan, but Zero shakes his head.

"That's not necessary. Wyatt can take care of himself. If you want to have prospects keeping an eye on the store that's fine but I don't want a bunch of bikers following her around."

"Not your call to make, Megan," Viper reprimands her gently.

"Oh, I'm sorry I must not have received my copy of the what to do when your club crosses you and traffics girls handbook."

"Megan," Viper growls angrily.

She sighs in frustration. "Wyatt can handle it, trust me."

Viper and I look to Zero for his opinion.

"I'm pretty sure Wyatt could bench press the three of us together with one hand tied behind his back while eating a cheeseburger," he tells us straight-faced.

"No shit?" I look at Megan who shakes her head.

"Don't be silly. Nobody eats cheeseburgers while working out," she finishes, taking a large bite of her pizza.

"I don't know why I'm constantly surprised by the company you keep," I say with a huff. Of course, the dude isn't a skinny hipster. This is Megan we're talking about.

"I should be offended by this but... well there may be some truth in that."

I laugh, shaking my head.

"Bikers," I tick off one finger.

"Mercenaries," Zero holds up a finger too.

"Jax-fucking-I-own-a-chain-of-sex-clubs-Lewis," Viper chimes in.

"And now this Wyatt dude who is probably a fucking ninja or something," I add.

"Oh no, it's better than that. Good old Wyatt is a vigilante," Zero informs us, making Viper and me stare Megan down as she happily ignores us in favor of her pizza.

"Of course, he is." Viper sighs, wiping his fingers on a napkin before tossing it down on the table.

"I spent the first eighteen years of my life being raised in a one-percenter motorcycle club and on the streets. I really don't know why you are so surprised."

"I have a feeling, Megan, you'll never stop surprising us," I tell her before leaning down to breathe her in.

"I'm glad you feel that way," she whispers before reaching her hand up to my chest and twisting one of my nipples hard.

"Motherfucker!" I roar, making the few diners turn their heads to look.

"What the fuck was that for?" I grimace, rubbing where she pinched me.

Zero is laughing his ass off across the table and even Viper is grinning. Fucking assholes.

"You told Zero about the toothbrush thing. Snitches get stitches so you're lucky I'm feeling generous today." I laugh, I can't help it. I said the exact same words earlier while stabbing a guy to death.

"I didn't tell him shit. Asshat over there likes to watch. I bet he stood on the other side of the door jacking himself off while we put on the mother of all shows for him."

"Toothbrush?" Viper questions.

Her eyes blaze for a second before she slowly turns to face a smug, unrepentant Zero, who is happily sipping his beer.

"You let me blame Grim for that? I could have really hurt him," she shouts indignantly, making me smile. It was a nipple twist, not a bullet wound.

Zero shrugs, not bothered in the slightest, until she launches her slice of pizza at him. It smacks him right in the forehead before it slides down and lands on his white T-shirt. We all stare frozen in stunned shock for a second before Viper and I lose it.

Zero gapes at Megan with his mouth open like a fish.

She pouts. "And now you made me waste my pizza. You are off my sex list."

"Sex list?" I choke out.

"Toothbrush?" Viper questions again.

"You know what? You can all just—" Her words cut off as something catches her eye outside.

"Oh my god!" she gasps, making us all turn to see what has garnered her attention.

Looking out the large window, I see Wanda yelling at a young boy who I'm assuming is Conner. I don't know though, as I've never met the kid.

"What? What is it?" I ask her again. Her face is so pale, I'm worried she might pass out.

"Wanda won't say dick to you if that's what you're worried about," Viper tells her with a frown on his face. I mean, I get it, this is the first time she has seen the woman since she's been back but her reaction is a touch extreme.

She stands up and bolts out of the booth. Shit. Definitely extreme.

We all jump up and head after her as she tears out of the diner, heading straight for Wanda.

"You fucking bitch!" Megan yells when she reaches her before punching Wanda full force in the face.

"Oh shit."

CHAPTER NINETEEN

Megan

She drops to the ground, leaving me enough space to take a protective stance in front of the boy.

"You!" she screeches, climbing unsteadily to her feet with blood running from her nose onto her chest.

"Give me one good reason why I shouldn't kill you where you stand?" I scream at her, using every ounce of restraint to hold myself back from wrapping my hands around her throat and choking the life out of her.

"Megan!" Viper steps in front of me and grabs my shoulders, giving me a little shake. "Snap the fuck out of it and tell me what the hell is going on? You can't just come out here and attack her in front of her son."

He's mad, I can tell, but he has nothing on the rage

coursing through my veins. "He's not her son," I spit out through gritted teeth.

"What? Megan, that's Conner, Wanda and John's six-year-old kid. He's been away at school but I can assure you he's her son."

He tries to pull me away but I back up and luckily the kid goes with me, his little hands gripping the fabric of my jeans.

"Megan." Zero lifts his hands in a calming gesture but I turn my back on him and drop to my knees and face the little boy who captured my attention through the window.

"You have pretty hair," he tells me, ensuring he also captures my heart.

"Thank you. I like yours too," I say with a smile, fighting back my tears.

"We match," he points out, touching a strand of mine and a strand of his. His big blue eyes blink up at me.

"That we do, baby," I say softly, not knowing how I manage to force the words out around the lump in my throat.

A hand on my shoulder has me swinging my fist out at Grim but he catches my hand and holds it tightly. Old habits die hard, I guess, when I'm feeling cornered.

"What's going on, Megan?" He searches my eyes, knowing I'm seconds away from a meltdown.

"You spent a lot of time with Diesel and Orion when you were at Carnage right?" He nods slowly, unsure of where I'm going with this.

"And you know every inch of my face that you could

picture it with your eyes closed, huh?" I question, feeling my voice crack as he nods again.

"Look at Conner and tell me what you see when you look in his eyes." He stares at me for a moment before turning to face Conner. It takes him a few moments before his body jolts and he turns to face me with a look of shock on his face.

"He looks like—" he doesn't finish his sentence because I finish it for him.

"He looks like his mother. Just like Orion, Diesel and I do," I choke out.

"Holy fuck!" He turns to talk to the others but I focus on Conner, who is playing with the strand of my hair like Zero does.

"My name's Megan. It's really nice to meet you, Conner."

He holds his little hand out for me to shake, my lips tipping up into a smile, as I wrap my larger one around his.

"Nice to meet you, Megan."

Grim shuffles us back a bit, making me stand up and turn around to see Wanda screaming and shouting in Viper's arms as she tries to get to us.

I drop my head and try to separate my emotions from the equation. I hate this woman with every fiber of my being but she is fighting tooth and nail to get to Conner. If he loves her and she loves him back, will I be causing more damage by ripping them apart?

Conner steps closer to me and grips my hand tighter. I look down at his handsome little face, taking in his deep blue eyes that are so much like my own.

"Mother doesn't like me very much."

And *boom*, there goes the final nail in Wanda's coffin.

"Does she hurt you?" I ask him, rubbing soothing circles over the back of his hand with my thumb.

"She just yells a lot and calls me names then she sends me back to school. I don't like school but it's better than getting yelled at all the time."

"That's my favorite thing about being deaf, I don't have to listen to anyone being mean," I tell him with a wink.

"Will you stand with Grim for a second for me?" I ask him. He looks up at Grim, who is watching both of us interact. Conner nods, letting go of my hand before moving towards Grim and slipping his hand in Grim's huge one. Grim looks at him with awe for a moment before his protective instincts kick in. He nods to me to say "I got this," then walks Conner over towards the bikes and out of earshot.

I spin around and stalk toward Wanda, who is now being restrained by Kaz. Viper says something to her. I can't see what, as I can only see the back of him but he is clearly pissed as his whole body vibrates with fury.

I step up beside him and Wanda's ire transfers from Viper to me. I will never understand the depth of hatred I see swimming in the pools of her soulless black eyes. I never did anything to her but exist. Clearly, that was enough of an offense in her eyes.

"I don't know how you convinced my mother to conceal a pregnancy from everyone, but I imagine my life was used as a weapon once more. The difference between her and me is that I have nothing to lose. I used to think you were just a bitter woman who had been used up too many times by the men you let into your life. Now, I see what I should have seen all along. There is an evil inside you. You enjoy inflicting pain on others but your method is psychological bullshit instead of physical wounds. Both leave their scars but people ask questions when the scars are on the outside, don't they?"

She opens her mouth to speak but something else catches her attention. When she starts with the crocodile tears and yelling "my baby," I know she has spotted the crowd of people gathering and is playing to them.

I laugh at her. She can do and say what she wants but she doesn't scare me anymore. I turn to face the growing crowd and realize I'm not scared of them either.

To a young girl, these guys seemed like a scary-ass bunch of people to have hating you but now, after everything I've been through, it's easy to see them for what they are. Human. And humans are nothing if not flawed.

I don't speak, taking in the faces before me. I wait for their condemnation and judgment but mostly I see a sea of confused faces looking to Viper for an explanation.

He steps up beside me, showing the club exactly whose side he is on and addresses them, standing at a slight angle so I can read his lips.

"Go home," he tells them, crossing his arms over his chest.

"Erm... Viper," Trip speaks up. "You can't just take someone's kid away from them. Don't get me wrong, there is no love lost between Wanda and me but taking someone's kid doesn't sit right with me."

"And yet nobody seems bothered that Melinda had her kid taken away from her," he tells them, waiting for the penny to drop. When it does, Trip's eyes widen as people start talking animatedly among themselves.

"Conner is Melinda's?" he asks, looking for clarification.

Viper doesn't give him an inch. I said the kid is my brother and that is clearly good enough for him.

"How the fuck?" But Trip isn't looking at Viper, he's looking at Wanda.

"You fucking bitch. You had everything you wanted but it was never enough, was it? You disgust me." He turns to face me and a look of guilt and sadness covers his features.

He steps towards me, which makes Viper pull me into his side with his large arm wrapped around my shoulder.

"I'm sorry. It's not enough. I know that. You know that, but it's all I've got. I hope one day I can earn your forgiveness. I'm sorry we ever treated you like less. You were always the best of us. Welcome home, princess," he says sincerely, as a sob breaks free from inside me.

I pull away from Viper and step closer, watching a man who never did anything to hurt me, but he never offered me aid either.

There will always be an ember that burns inside me. A fire that fuels itself with my anger and regrets but I decided long ago not to let them consume me. If I did that, I would only end up like Wanda.

Trip watches me, waiting for me to tear him to shreds but instead, I close the space between us and wrap my arms around him.

I feel him take a shuddering breath as my forehead rests against his shoulder. He holds me tightly for a moment as I absorb his apology and my forgiveness absolves him.

Pulling back, he looks down at me with a genuine smile before I'm turned to face other members who want to say their sorrys. It seems, now that Trip has broken the seal, everyone is rushing to apologize. I doubt all of them are genuine but it's more than I expected. I nod and smile at them until Zero steals me away, sensing I'm getting a little overwhelmed.

People start drifting away as I face plant into Zero's chest, breathing in deep the comforting scent of leather and motor oil.

"What just happened?" I mutter to myself, confused about the whiplash of emotions I've gone through today.

Zero tips my chin up to look at him.

"Viper had already called everyone out on their bullshit. They all believed the lies they were fed. Most were horrified when confronted with the truth. The only reason people haven't approached you before now is that most of them are ashamed of the part they played in what happened to you. Today was a long time coming."

I feel stupid when my eyes start to water at his words.

"Don't you dare make me cry, mister. I'm trying to channel Luna and be badass here," I scold him.

"Megan, you don't need to channel anyone. You are our Raven, fearless, protective and brave. You are perfect exactly as you are."

And there go the tears.

"Fuck!" I face plant into his chest again, his words proving to be my undoing. I allow myself a little girly cry before pulling up my big girl panties and stepping back to wipe my face.

I glance up when an arm hooks me around the shoulder and offer a small smile at Viper, who looks like he wants to hulk out and smash something at the sight of my tears.

"We didn't know, Megan," he swears, his jaw hard and eyes flashing with anger.

"I know that, Viper. What's gonna happen now?" I ask apprehensively. I might flirt the line with what is and isn't okay within the MC rules but ultimately the decision falls to him and in some cases will be put to vote.

"She'll get her say when she calms the fuck down and I'll bring it before the officers. They'll vote on whether she can stay or if she should go."

My shoulders slump, knowing I was right. I know he must feel stuck between a rock and a hard place too because, despite everything, Wanda was effectively his pseudo aunt for a large chunk of his life.

"My vote will be to get her the fuck out of here," he promises me, causing my eyes to widen in surprise.

"Really?"

"She hurt you by keeping that little boy from you. She

blames you for shit that had nothing to do with you and she sure as hell didn't look out for you when you were a kid. I'm guessing there are a whole lot of interactions that have been less than stellar between you two over the years that you haven't told us about. I want you to be happy, Megan. If that means she needs to leave then so be it."

I wrap my arms around him and squeeze him tight before facing him again. "Part of me gets it. John would have taken Conner from my mom as a punishment like he did with me. That little boy would have become the next thing to keep her in line, but all that meant was that Wanda was yet again stuck raising a kid that wasn't hers but a woman's who her old man just couldn't give up."

Viper's head dips and rests on mine as he takes in my words. It's a fucked-up situation and I do feel for her, but she chose the life she led. Instead of rising above all the bullshit, she let it flow through her veins like poison.

"And that right there is what makes you special," Zero says pointedly.

"What?" I ask, surprised.

"Your ability to even be able to muster up a molecule of empathy for a woman who doesn't deserve it."

I think about his words and let them warm me. I could have let the life I've lived harden me. I could have withdrawn from the world like Wyatt or set out to burn it all to the ground like Viddy, but then I wouldn't be the daughter my mother so valiantly raised.

In the six weeks since that day, my relationship with my guys and most of the Chaos Demons has changed. Our bonds have been strengthened. Whether they be from friendship or love, I have finally carved out enough space here for it to start to feel like home again.

I hadn't been surprised when the vote went in Wanda's favor. After all, she had more ties to this place than I did but Viper let it slip that the vote was a lot closer than I might have thought.

Wanda had been allowed to stay. She still lived in the house I was raised in at the back of the lot near the woods so I rarely saw her, which suited me fine.

I spent most of my time getting the former Elusive, now aptly named Ravens, ready for its grand reopening next month. The girls turned out to be an amazing bunch of ladies who just needed someone to take a chance on them and Legs was proving her weight in gold.

Jenna and Wyatt were running my shop in my absence, much to Wyatt's disgust. Jenna had him wrapped around her little finger and he would do anything to make the girl who had become like a daughter to him smile.

The most important change perhaps, had been my relationship with my little brother. It had been a hard decision but ultimately we decided to let him finish out this term at school, giving him a chance to say his goodbyes in the process because when he came home today, he was staying.

What I hadn't done was tell my brothers or Luna about him. I hated hiding it but Conner needed time to adjust to all the changes and there would be no holding my brothers back when they found out.

There was also a part of me that worried it would be another mark against Chaos. That Carnage would decide the truce just wasn't worth it anymore and demand my return. That would mean I would be stuck choosing between my blood and my heart and I wasn't ready to make that impossible choice.

A finger on my chin tips my head up.

"Relax, its going to be fine," Zero assures me, breaking into my thoughts.

"Sorry." I laugh. "I was a million miles away."

Viper wraps his arm around my shoulder and places a kiss on my temple.

"You guys have Skyped every single day that he's been gone. He loves you already. You have nothing to worry about."

I stare at his lips as he speaks and smile at him nervously. "I'm being a big baby huh?" He laughs and I take a moment to appreciate all that masculine yumminess that I get to call mine when the sight of an SUV approaching catches my attention.

I feel Grim step up behind me and squeeze my shoulders in silent support. I take a deep breath and wait for the gates to open and the car to stop just in front of us. The back door opens and a black-haired bundle of adorableness jumps out and heads in my direction.

I drop to my knees and open my arms just in time for him to throw himself at me. I wrap my arms tightly around him, thankful to Grim for bracing our combined weight and stopping us from toppling backward.

I close my eyes and soak in the feelings of love for the little boy who I've come to adore and who is the last piece of my mother.

"I've missed you," I tell him, pulling back and smiling big when he does.

"I missed you too," he answers almost shyly.

Viper crouches down next to us staring at Conner with a smile on his face making my heart melt.

"Want to grab some lunch at the diner with us?" Viper asks him.

Conner looks up at the president with what looks like a little bit of hero-worship in his eyes and nods rapidly, making me laugh.

Zero reaches down to help me up as Viper ruffles Conner's hair. I smile my thanks at Zero, watching his lips move as I catch the end of his sentence to Conner.

"Come on then. I've had a craving for mac and cheese all day," Zero shares with him, making me smile. He's not even saying that to make Conner feel welcome, knowing it's his favorite. He really has been going on about it all damn day.

"That's my favorite," Conner informs him looking at me

for approval before, walking beside Zero and Grim, as I hang back for Viper and we follow them in.

People greet us with a smile and a wave at Conner, everyone pleased to see the little boy back where he belongs.

We all climb into our usual booth and place our orders. Mac and cheese for Conner and Zero, while Viper, Grim, and I opt for BLTs.

"So are you happy to be home?" Grim asks him after swallowing.

Conner nods quietly but he has a look of trepidation on his face too.

"What's up? Is it because you're going to miss your friends? I promise you can call them or Skype them whenever you want," I reassure him but it doesn't seem to help. I give him a moment, seeing that he is trying to figure out what to say, and sit and wait him out.

"Do I have to stay with Mother?" I want to snap at him that Wanda isn't his mother but that's my issue, not Conner's and I'll never make him uncomfortable if I can help it.

"Nope. You get to stay with us. Oh, and I haven't told you this but you have two brothers to meet yet," I inform him and sigh with relief when his smile stretches over his face.

"Awesome," he answers before we tuck back into our food.

I excuse myself to use the bathroom and when I head back, it's to find Grim, Viper, and Zero at the counter waiting to settle the bill.

I look for Conner and see him laughing in our booth

where Trip has sat in the seat next to him. He has shoved two straws up his nose and crossed his eyes, much to Conner's amusement.

Walking over to my guys, I lean against Viper, twisting my neck so I can watch my brother, loving how calm and relaxed he looks compared to the last time he was here.

"We should buy a house with a yard big enough for a large dog," I muse out loud. Viper goes solid beside me, making me look up to see what's wrong.

His look is fierce and filled with heat. I whip around to look at Zero and find a similar look in his eyes.

"What?" I question, thinking about what I was saying. "Oh… you don't want that? Do we have to live at the compound indefinitely?" Because that would suck donkey balls.

Nobody answers me, which makes me deflate.

"I didn't realize I had to stay at the clubhouse indefinitely. It's not the kind of place I wanted to raise kids. I mean I knew they would be here all the time but I wanted them to have a safe haven that was just theirs away from drunk men and half-naked club girls. Are you guys sure you want daughters living on-site? I mean there are some things little girls can't unsee, trust me."

Still, nobody speaks and it's making me nervous, especially as Grim looks down at me with an expression on his face I can't read.

"Why the hell are you guys looking at me like that?"

"House?" Viper finally comes unstuck.

"Dog?" Zero asks.

"Daughters?" Grim stares at me in awe and I realize that what I was feeling from them was shock.

"Well... yeah. I mean, we don't have to have them yet. We can wait, or do you not want kids? Shit. See this is what happens when you kidnap someone. You don't have time to figure out if you're compatible."

I'm about to give in and tell them it's fine, we don't have to have kids if they don't want them. But no, fuck that.

"I want kids," I admit softly. "I want to fill a house with them. I want a family and a place to call home. I... I'd give up everything for you guys but please don't ask me to give up on that," I finish, holding my ground and bracing for their reaction.

Grim's lips are on mine in the blink of an eye, making me jolt with shock. Grim is a demanding kisser, taking what he wants whatever the cost but right now his kiss is all about giving. I can feel it beating at me and taste it on my tongue. He wants that too.

He pulls back before I can hump his leg, which is just as well because I remember I have the kiddo just behind us. I look behind me and see him watching us, making a face like he sucked on a lemon, which makes me burst out laughing.

"You'll understand one day, Conner, I promise," Zero calls out to him as he steps up for a kiss of his own.

He doesn't push his luck like Grim, probably trying not to make Conner feel any worse. When he steps back, I look to

Viper, but he doesn't move. He just stares at me for so long I start to squirm.

"Guys, can you get Conner some desert? We'll be back in a minute," he asks them without looking away from me. My palms start to get sweaty, feeling like something's wrong.

"Hey Conner, you want ice cream?" Zero asks. I look over at him to see if he is okay but his smile is an answer in itself.

I wave goodbye as Viper leads me outside. I watch them interacting through the window and feel my heart and something much lower spasm. I want that. Little boys to look up to—

"Oof." A gasp of air rushes out of me as I find myself unceremoniously tossed over Viper's shoulder. I'm so stunned I don't even realize we're moving until I find myself back in an upright position pressed up against the wall of some kind of office.

"You want my babies?" It's moments like this I ache to be able to hear his words, wanting so desperately to feel the cadence of his voice as it trembles over my skin leaving goosebumps in its wake.

"Not right now but one day, of course," I tell him, knowing that at twenty-two I still have plenty of time to have them.

He swallows hard, looking at me, his next words stealing my breath.

"You're free to leave, you know?" I stare at his mouth for a moment, thinking maybe I read that wrong but one look in his eye tells me I didn't.

"What?" I whisper, feeling like he just ripped my heart out of my chest. All the warmth his kiss infused inside me turns to ice.

"I'm free to leave?" I question, shoving at his chest, wanting—no needing—him to put me down but he just tightens his hold on me.

"Get your fucking hands off me. Was this all a game to you, huh? Make the Carnage bitch fall in love with you so you could toss me back to them as damaged goods?" I shove him again but he refuses to loosen his hold so I rear back and slap him.

His body goes rigid but my anger is so acute everything but the fire inside me disappears.

"Newsflash. I was already damaged goods long before you came along."

Finally, he moves but only to free one of his hands holding me up. He uses it to wrap around my neck and pin me to the wall.

It doesn't hurt and despite everything, I know he won't lay a finger on me in anger. He just wants my attention.

"You are not damaged goods," he bites out, his face right in front of mine.

"Fuck you. Let me go."

He ignores me because doesn't he fucking always? I scream in frustration but he swallows it when his mouth presses against mine in a kiss that screams of possession. Not the actions of a man who wants to throw me away. He pulls back and squeezes my throat a little when I move to hit him again.

"You love me?"

I freeze in his arms, going back over the words I spewed in anger and shake my head. No, he doesn't get that from me. Not now.

"Say it," he commands but I refuse.

"Fuck you," I spit at him.

"That how you wanna play it, baby, then so be it," he answers, but I don't have any time to question his words because he slips his hand under my T-shirt, shoving the material up before pulling my breasts from the confines of my bra.

Before I can protest further, he sucks one of my nipples into his mouth, nibbling on it before swapping to the other. He walks me backward to a desk, sitting me on the edge of it before ripping my T-shirt over my head and resuming the task at hand, which I can only guess is to make me hate myself a little more as my body betrays my brain's protests. I grip his hair and keep him in place, my hold on him harder than usual as my lust wars with my anger.

Standing up he glares at me. "Say it."

"Kiss my ass," I say with gritted teeth. He can't make me do shit but when he pulls me up and spins me around, bending me over the desk, I realize maybe I was too quick to assume anything.

He reaches around me and yanks open my jeans before pulling them and my underwear down to my ankles. I feel his lips on my ass for a second, letting me know that he thinks he's funny by kissing my ass. His finger dips inside me, making me jolt, my humiliation complete when he finds me dripping. He grabs my hair in a ponytail and pulls, maneuvering me just enough that I can see his face over my shoulder. He uses his free hand to rub his cock, which I didn't even realize he had freed, over my slick folds.

"You want me to fuck you?" he questions, hitting my clit with his cock as he keeps gliding backward and forward. "Then say it."

I don't speak but only because my resolve is cracking.

"Fucking say it!" he commands.

"I love you," I sob as he thrusts inside me and glides in all the way to the hilt.

He pauses once he is all the way in, a look of complete satisfaction on his face as he stares down at me. He leans forward and places a chaste kiss on my lips before pulling back again.

"You want this?" he asks and I know that if I say no he'll stop.

"Fuck me," I answer, which is all he wanted to hear.

He lets go of my hair and grips my hips with both hands, fucking me with long deep strokes and filling me in the most delicious way but I don't want it like this, my anger refusing to dissipate.

"Harder," I tell him and feel his thrusts get harder, ramming my hips into the desk with just enough force to leave bruises.

"Harder," I demand once again. His movements falter for a second before he resumes the pace he already set.

"Harder," I grit out, needing that edge of pain, my heart still feeling hurt by his words and angry at the weakness I showed by giving in.

"Harder," I say again but this time I feel my voice crack.

He slows his movements. The brutal punishing fuck I wanted gets replaced with gentle touches and slow shallow thrusts that leave me panting and my body yearning for more. He reaches around and strums my clit while placing feather-light kisses along my spine.

I don't want to give in, I want to order myself to get a grip, to tell him to stop, but I have no control over my actions as Viper expertly plays with my body the way he played with my heart.

He doesn't speed up or slow down. He just continues sliding his cock in and out of me as if he has all the time in the world. In the end, it's impossible to fight. I gasp as an orgasm so intense rips through, it makes my legs buckle.

I feel him spill himself inside me as the tears I had been holding at bay run unchecked down my face and onto the scarred wooden desk below. When he pulls free from my still trembling core, I don't bother to look at him before I bend down and yank my underwear and jeans up my legs even as I feel him leak out of me.

I need to clean up but I need to get away from here first. Punching the Chaos Demon President in the face is a big no-no.

I walk over and grab my T-shirt from the brown corduroy sofa it was tossed onto and slip it over my head, not bothering with the bra, which I shove into my back pocket.

When I turn to leave, Viper has a big smug grin on his face until he catches sight of my tear-stained one. His smile dissolves only to be replaced with a look of utter horror.

CHAPTER TWENTY

Viper

"Megan," I say her name softly as I reach for her. The sight of her tears is my undoing. "Fuck, did I hurt you?"

She steps back before I can touch her and I watch as her faces blanks of all emotion. Something's wrong—very, very wrong.

"Megan, baby, talk to me." I reach for her again, but her words stop me dead.

"Why, so you can twist my words around to fit your own agenda and use them against me too? No thanks."

"What?" My confusion is warring with my anger. What the fuck is she talking about? She just told me she loves me and now she's acting like my touch repels her.

"Are you happy now? Will you have someone deliver me or do you expect me to walk back in there with your cum running down my leg? I mean, I guess that's the ultimate fuck you, right?" She swipes angrily as more tears spill over her cheeks in an unrelenting cascade.

"You got this all wrong, Megan. I don't know what's going on inside that head of yours but whatever it is, it isn't right."

She shakes her head at me in disgust. "So, I'm free to go now, right? You got what you wanted?"

I nod. I wanted her to tell me she loved me and she did.

"Glad I could be of service then," she replies caustically, heading for the door but I block her way.

"Megan, what the fuck?" I'm at a loss here. I try to grab her, but she swerves violently out of my way, shocking us both.

"Please, please just let me go. I can't handle anymore. It's enough Viper. You win." I step aside and let her go to the door even though everything inside me tells me to make her stay. One more look at her tear-stained face and I swallow whatever I was going to say.

"Goodbye, Viper. I hope it was worth it." She turns and heads out, slamming the door closed behind her, leaving me in a state of shock and confusion.

I sit in my chair and try to figure out what the fucking hell is going on. The anger takes root, so I yank the drawer to my desk open and grab the whiskey from the bottle and take a large swig. Swallowing it down, I realize it's not nearly enough to numb the growing sense of unease so I gulp another slug and another until over half a bottle is missing.

When the door opens without a knock, I lift my head with a smirk plastered on my face betting its Megan ready to get down on her knees and apologize. I mean, nothing says I'm sorry for being a raving bitch than a little head. The scowl is soon back in place when I see it's Grim and Zero instead. They were chatting about something when they came in but stop when they get a look at my face. Zero looks around my office with a frown.

"Where's Megan and Conner?"

"Who the fuck knows?" I wave my arm with the whiskey bottle in it, making it splash over the side of the bottle.

"What do you mean you don't know? We've been back to the apartment and nobody was there. We thought she had come back to find you after she picked up Conner over an hour ago," Zero questions, eyeing the bottle. "What's going on?"

"I have no fucking clue. One minute she was fine, the next she was crying and saying goodbye," I manage to mutter through my alcohol-filled daze.

"She was crying?" Grim yells, making me wince.

I wave for him to shut up before he starts spouting off at me. I already have the beginnings of a headache forming and I could do without his bullshit on top of it. Grim doesn't give me a second glance before he storms out yelling, probably to find Megan to figure out what's going on. Yeah, well, good luck with that buddy.

Zero sits in the chair opposite me and sighs. "What the fuck happened? I thought for sure you would have been bruising her hips not bruising her heart."

"Don't get all philosophical on me, Zero. I'm not in the mood." I take another swig before he reaches over and snatches the bottle from my hands and takes a huge swallow himself.

"You know, between you and Grim, I'm going to have my work cut out for me as the fucking peacekeeper."

"Nobody fucking asked—"

He glares at me. "Nobody needed to. Someone needs to step up and have Megan's back in this because you two have a habit of reacting to shit before thinking things through."

"Whatever, Zero," I mutter, sounding like a sullen teenager, which pisses me off even more. I lean over the desk to snatch the bottle back. "Isn't it better to ask for forgiveness instead of permission? We're bikers for fuck sake."

He glares at me, his own anger rising. "And how many times, exactly, is she supposed to forgive us, huh? How many times are we going to hurt her before she decides we aren't worth it anymore?"

I don't say anything because despite my anger and confusion over everything, I know he's right.

"What happened?" he asks me calmly with zero condemnation in his voice.

"Truthfully? I have no fucking clue. She mentioned having kids and a house—"

"And you freaked out? I thought that's what you wanted?"

he asks, confused.

"It is what I want and I don't freak out, asshole. I'm the president of an MC," I feel the need to remind him. "I don't freak out. Ever. I just wanted to make sure she was making this decision because she wanted to and not because we were forcing her to stay."

He snorts out a bark of laughter at that, making my head snap up to his. "Please. If she wanted out of here badly enough, she'd be gone. She has the means, the money, and the people behind her to make herself invisible."

"She wouldn't place her family in danger. It could be declared an act of war," I point out.

He rolls his eyes at me. "She knows we won't do jack shit to her family because she would never forgive us. Plus, I'm starting to suspect that she has a far more formidable circle of friends than we were led to believe. I think if we waged a war against Carnage, we wouldn't be the ones walking away victors."

"Wow, nice vote of confidence you have in the club there, Zero," I spit, my pride hurt.

"Oh, fuck off, Viper. We both know that until we can make sure all the traitors are dispatched, we will always be weaker because we can't tell who is friend and who is foe. Now, stop stalling and tell me what the fuck happened."

"She let slip she loved us then refused to say it again. We ended up fucking over the desk where I eventually managed to get her to admit it again, then she had a meltdown and left."

"Did you hurt her?" His voice is sharp like a knife, making me stare and glare down at him.

"No, I didn't fucking hurt her."

He frowns up at me, confused again. "I get you can piss her off like nobody's business but that doesn't sound like Megan. What happened before that?"

"Nothing. As I said, I wanted to make sure she was a hundred percent sure she wanted to commit to a life with us because she wanted it and not because we forced it on her, so I told her she was free to leave and—" Zero jumps from his seat with a look of disbelief on his face.

"You told her she was free to leave!" he yells.

"Yes! I want her to want to be here and clearly, she doesn't," I add the last part with a grumble.

"Yeah," his voice takes on a hard-sarcastic edge, "and did you tell her that too or did you just tell her that she was free to leave?"

Whatever he's putting down I'm not picking up. I try to wade through the whiskey-glazed memories of that conversation and view it again. I picture myself saying those words and see what I didn't process the first time around when I was so caught up in my own exuberance. Pain. Humiliation. Devastation.

I open my eyes and stare at Zero in shock as the picture starts to make sense. Like the last couple of moves of a Rubik's cube, everything begins to slot into place.

"Fuck!" I pick the bottle off the desk and launch it at the

wall, watching as it shatters and the remaining amber liquid drips to the ground.

The door slams open to reveal Grim breathing heavy like he ran back here.

"The apartment is still empty. She's fucking gone," he tells us, looking like he's two minutes away from ripping this room apart. I'm suddenly stone-cold sober as the knowledge dawns on me that she's gone. I fucked up so bad she left.

"No. No, fuck that. She isn't going anywhere. Call church. I want her found. She's pissed, I get that, but she's ours and she isn't going anywhere," I say vehemently.

He nods and disappears as I grab my phone off the desk and text her number, mentally pleading with her to reply. When I hear a vibration, I look at Zero to see if she's replying to him because she's still pissed at me but he shakes his head.

"It's not mine, man." He walks over to the desk and bends down. There, under the chair, is Megan's phone.

"Fuck, it must have fallen out when we were fucking. There goes plan B. Can't track her if she doesn't have it fucking with her."

"Jesus, fuck. I feel like I'm coming out of my skin. Find the prospects and see if she has someone on her. She fucking knows better than to disappear without one of them watching her back."

"On it. I'll see what I can find out and meet you in church." I don't answer as I follow him out, heading back to our apartment to double-check. I find it empty like Grim said.

"Where else could she go?" I muse to myself, thinking about where she has felt most comfortable since she got here. It would need to be somewhere quiet or she would have already been spotted.

I look around at all the buildings, many of them apartments belonging to people Megan would never turn to for help—at least not yet. Plus, nobody is stupid enough to hide her and risk bringing down the wrath of their president upon themselves.

That leaves the woods. They go on for miles in each direction, offering her a million places to hide but it will be getting dark soon and my girl is not stupid. Being stuck out there with no sight and no hearing is asking for trouble.

A frisson of worry works its way through me. Even though I know she wouldn't take that risk, it doesn't stop me from imagining her out there hurt somewhere. Once it gets dark, nobody would find her. Hell, there isn't even another property around here except for... the cabin. Shit.

I run over to my bike, not bothering to let the others know what's going on because if I'm wrong, I don't want to divert them from looking for her.

The prospect waves me through the gate as I make the ten-minute drive in four. I've barely stopped the bike before I'm off it and slamming my way indoors. I know as soon as I'm inside, it's empty. It's too quiet and none of Megan's subtle fragrance permeates the air. It just smells stale from being closed up and a thick layer of dust coats the table and countertops. I toss the place anyway, checking every space that could be big enough for her to hide, even though I know that's not her style anymore.

The little girl that used to hide in the shadows is a thing of the past. Now Megan is full of fire and wrath and passion. She would far more likely swing a punch at me than hide in the fucking closet I'm searching through. I slam the door shut, frustrated.

"What the fuck am I doing?" I mumble to myself. I'm acting like a lovesick fool and not like the president of a motorcycle club. Time to think with the other brain for a minute.

She wouldn't hide. She wouldn't run unless she was in imminent danger and I know, despite my colossal fuck up, that she knows I wouldn't ever lay my hands on her in anger.

That leaves me with her licking her wounds somewhere before she comes back swinging a baseball bat. Besides, she wouldn't leave Conner here if she was gonna run—

"Fuck."

My phone rings in my pocket, and a flash of disappointment hits me when I see it's Zero and not Megan.

"You found her?" I answer.

"Not yet. Prospects haven't let anyone in or out of the gates except you in the last few hours so she's here somewhere. She has Conner with her so she's not going to do anything stupid like try to scale the fence," he says sardonically. I take a deep calming breath and let the tension ease from my body.

"I'm overreacting," I state. It's a fact, not a question.

"You and Grim both," he mumbles as I head back to my bike.

"But I suppose you had good reasons. Grim will always act like this because of losing his sister. You just reacted to his panic because it was your fault she was missing."

"Thanks for that, asshole."

"You're welcome. Now get your ass back here so we can find our girl. I'm going to enjoy watching you try to dig yourself out of this one."

"You know I could take your patch, right?" I remind him as I straddle my bike, playing the president card.

The disrespectful motherfucker just laughs at me.

"Nobody else would put up with your cranky ass. Plus, I'm Megan's favorite," the lying sack of shit tells me before hanging up.

I start the engine just as I hear something that makes my blood run cold. I turn it off and listen again, almost convinced my brain is playing tricks on me until I hear it a second time.

I'm off the bike, heading toward the woods at the back of the property when I hear the same noise again, only this time it comes from behind me. A shard of white-hot pain steals my vision for a second, making my legs buckle, my body crumpling to the ground as I fight a losing battle to stay conscious. All I can think about as the darkness swallows me whole is my missing girl and the sounds that caught my attention.

The sound of gunshots.

CHAPTER TWENTY-ONE

Megan

I'd stormed away from Viper, swiping the tears from my eyes as I tried to get it together. I headed straight for the apartment, stripping out of my clothes as soon as I closed the door behind me and climbed into the shower. I turned the dial as hot as I could bear and let it wash down over me, cleaning the remnants of our lovemaking—I snorted at that—fuck session away. I dressed in black jeans, a black V-neck T-shirt, and a cropped black leather jacket. I didn't worry about drying my hair, opting instead to braid it before heading over to the diner to collect Conner.

I pasted on a fake smile, pretending everything was okay to Grim and Zero, not being able to bear the thought of them taking Viper's side and agreeing that it was my time to leave.

Whether they believed that to be true or not, I don't know if they seemed happy when I mentioned getting a bigger house for future fictional babies but they would never go against what their president wanted. The MC was all about the brotherhood. Hell, hasn't Diesel said those very words to me once before?

I was all too aware of where I sat in the hierarchy of things and unfortunately, having a pussy meant I would always be considered lesser than the dick-swinging assholes in my life who wore leather.

Luckily, they got caught up talking to Trip so I made my excuses and brought Conner back to the apartment so I could plan my next move.

Which brings me to now, sitting cross-legged on the bed while Conner watches a cartoon about a young girl dressed as a ladybug who saves the world.

With Jenna and Wyatt moving into my place and being so settled, I wasn't about to go invade their space or ask them to move out, so my apartment wasn't an option.

I could head to Carnage. Conner has two brothers to meet but there's a part of me that just can't handle the thought of explaining everything, only to have to listen to their I told you so declarations.

Stupid fucking bikers. I couldn't have just fallen for teachers or something, could I? I flop back and pull a pillow over my face, wanting to scream bloody murder into it but not wanting to traumatize the kiddo sitting at my feet.

Talk of the devil. I look down at him when he taps my foot and watch as he points at the door.

"Great," I grumble, climbing off the bed, ready to snap at whoever's brave enough to knock on my door. I know it's not one of the guys as they would have just barged in using their own key cards. However, that does not change that I have so much anger swirling inside me needing an outlet that whichever poor schmuck decided to knock on my door is going to regret it.

I swing the door open and realize two things straight away. One is that I had grown too complacent living here. I forgot the number one rule about women's safety. Always check to see who is on the other side of the door before you open it. The second thing that slipped my mind because I had been too wrapped up dealing with Viper's bullshit was that hell hath no fury like a woman scorned, which is exactly how I found myself staring down at a gun pointed directly at my stomach.

"Of course, my day could only get worse." I sigh. "Wanda, you really don't want to do this. The second you pull that trigger, a swarm of bikers will descend on you and what they will do to you will make you pray for death."

She pushes the gun harder into my stomach, forcing me backward until she is able to step inside and close the door. "Do you really think I care? I have nothing left to fucking lose thanks to you," she spits. Her eyes look around the room, making my skin crawl. If she touches Conner, I'll kill her.

"Where is he?" she asks. I look behind me and see that Conner has made himself scarce. Thank fuck for smart kids.

"I don't know who you're talking about. With the number of guys I have living here, you'll have to be more specific than that. Either way, they will be here any minute," I tell her, hoping like hell she'll leave.

She walks around the room, never moving the gun away from its target, before stopping on the other side of the bed. If I were alone I could make a run for it but I don't know where Conner is so I won't risk it.

"You couldn't just stay gone, could you? Everything was fine until you showed back up. Why the fuck do you and your mother always have to ruin everything?"

"I guess we're just talented like that. Just putting this out there, Wanda, I was dragged back here even though it was the last place on earth I wanted to be."

"I should have just gotten rid of you when I had the chance. So fucking stupid." She starts banging her head with her free hand, making me swallow as my bravado starts to slip. There is no reasoning with crazy and something tells me this woman is as batshit as they come.

She bends down, making me tense and ready to take any chance I might get to wrestle that gun away from her. Before I get the chance, she smiles a cruel-looking grin of victory before standing and showing me what the bed had been hiding from my view. Conner. He must have climbed underneath when he heard her voice at the door.

I step towards them but for the first time since she got

here, she turns the gun away from me. When she points it at Conner, I step back and raise my hands in defeat.

"Always the same. He used to hide under the bed when he got scared at home. I figured he would grow out of it eventually but I guess he's more like you and your pussy mother than I realized."

She pulls his back to her front and keeps the gun aimed down at him as he cries out my name. I don't need to hear his voice to feel his fear. It's beating against me from across the room like a barrage of relentless waves threatening to drown me.

"Let him go, Wanda. It's me you want. He's done nothing to you for Christ's sake, he's just a little boy."

"I don't think so. You don't get to call the shots here. Now, I want what I came for, then you can have this kid back. He means nothing to me anyway. He was always just a means to an end." I swallow down the rage at her words, praying this will all fade into the fuzzy memories in the young boy's mind as he gets older.

"What do you want?"

"What do you think I want? I want the money that should have been mine. I was his old lady. You aren't even his daughter. Give me the money and I'll be gone."

I sigh, wondering how she even knew about the money to begin with. "He didn't leave me any money, Wanda. The trust fund came from my mother and my maternal grandparents' side of the family."

"Lies. That bitch was nothing but a biker whore." I bite

my lip and swallow it down while she still has Conner, although the gun is now pointed back at me, which is better.

"My mom came from old money. She inherited it from my great-grandfather. She might have turned her back on that life when she fell in love with King but she was still entitled to her trust fund when it kicked in," I explain to her patiently as I edge closer, hoping to get myself between her and Conner.

"Fucking King," she snarls, her anger so palpable the gun shakes in her hand. "He was mine, but she had to come along and rub her pussy all over him. He was mine. Mine. Mine."

"You knew King?" I ask, taking another step closer, hoping to keep her distracted. I must admit I'm a little curious about how she knew the former president of Carnage and my brothers' father.

"I was King, Joker, and John's favorite girl. They were going to make me their old lady, I just knew it. I was this fucking close. Then Melinda came along and King didn't see anyone but her. Even Joker and John pulled back for a while until they realized she didn't feel for them what she did for King.

"She broke them apart like Yoko-fucking-Ono. When John left, I went with him, showing him where my loyalty lay, and he made me his old lady. I had two kids from a drunk deadbeat father but John took care of him for me. He loved me and I loved him. All I wanted was for a man to take care of me and I finally had it all. Until she came back.

"John became obsessed with her. His hatred was so vast,

he loved that he now had King's favorite toy to play with. She ruined everything," she says vehemently, leaving me in stunned shock. I never knew any of that part.

"Now he's gone. Everyone's gone." Her eyes are haunted, showing me just how broken this woman really is before her face hardens again and her sneer returns.

"Melly owes me. I want that money or I'll take the life of her son just like she did mine," she tells me, her voice devoid of all emotion as she points the gun back at Conner. I believe her. She's right, she really doesn't have anything left to lose.

"I have a copy of John's will. It was mixed in with my mother's things that Rock gave me that day at the hospital."

"What! What will? There wasn't a will, I searched everywhere," she yells.

I gesture for her to calm down. I speak again, hoping my voice sounds quiet and even. "He left the compound to you. That's why I hid it. I didn't want you to have it because you were always so mean to me." I try to make myself sound small and scared, mimicking the memory of what my voice sounded like when I was younger and she belittled me.

"You selfish bitch. I knew you were just like your mother. Where is it? I want it now!" she demands, reminding me of that awful child from a Roald Dahl story I loved as a child.

"It's in the time capsule I buried here as a kid. I didn't know what else to do with it when I got back here and I didn't want anyone else to find it. It's in the woods in mine and my mother's favorite spot near the cabin."

"Cabin? Gettie's old place? Fine, let's go but no funny business or I'll shoot him. Climb out the back window and head over to the tree line so nobody can see us. Remember what I said."

I reach for my boots where I tossed them on the floor earlier but she screams at me to leave them. She smiles at me, getting a kick out of the fact that she's about to make me trek through the woods barefoot but I don't bother to argue. She's too unpredictable and I won't put Conner at risk.

I slide the window open and climb out, holding my arms open to Conner. Wanda all but tosses him to me and climbs out behind us. She keeps the gun leveled at us but I feel better having Conner in my arms.

I hitch him up on my hip, breathing in his comforting little boy scent as we trudge through the forest. I block out Wanda behind me and concentrate on the path ahead. I know this route like the back of my hand but over the years the undergrowth has grown wilder and more unkempt. Trying to navigate it in nothing but a pair of socks is a nightmare, a painful one, but I refuse to show her that, knowing she would enjoy my suffering.

Thorns scratch against my legs, making me thankful I opted for jeans after my shower. I trip over the wayward roots and stumble to make my way over them, knowing the slickness I can feel on my soles is blood.

It doesn't matter how many times I stumble through, I refuse to fall. I stay on my feet and don't lose my hold on

Conner even as my arms begin to burn and shake from carrying his weight for so long. He might be small for his age but he's still extra weight I'm not used to carrying.

Finally, we stumble into the clearing. I take a deep breath and slide Conner to the ground, keeping a tight grip on his hand. I lead him to the woods on the opposite side of the cabin, which now looms before us. An unexpected kick to the back of my leg has me tripping. Thankfully, I catch myself before I can fall and drag Conner down with me.

I turn to face Wanda, who is huffing and puffing like she has just climbed Everest as opposed to walking for twenty minutes. "What?" I snap.

"Where is it?"

I point in the direction I was heading.

"If this is a setup, I swear I will make you watch as I empty this gun into him." She indicates Conner, who cowers behind my leg.

"He's just a little boy. How can you hate someone you helped raise, who is truly innocent in all this? I just don't understand. When you tried to stop me outside the diner from taking him, for a moment I really did think it was because you loved him. What a fool I was."

She cackles and laughs as if I have just said the funniest thing she has ever heard, making me want to rip her ratty hair from her head. "Love? You thought I loved him?" She dissolves into laughter again, tears escaping her eyes as she struggles to catch her breath. "I didn't keep him because I loved him. I kept him because he's my trophy," she tells me, her face twisting into an evil sneer.

"A trophy?" I choke out incredulously.

"Do you know how old he is?" She smiles and there is nothing friendly about it.

"Six," I answer the age he told me earlier as something inside me warns to brace myself.

"Ah, yes, that's correct," she tells me with a giddy clap. Even though I was right, everything in this moment feels wrong.

"Conner, tell Megan when your birthday is," she barks at him, making him cower even farther behind me.

"Christ, you are so fucking stupid. Didn't you even question why you hadn't noticed Melly was pregnant? No, of course not. You were too busy leading my son around by his dick." She shakes her head at me and rolls her eyes. "Stupid fucking girl," she mocks but I'm getting ridiculously lost in the latest plot twist of my life.

"Look, do you want this fucking will or not?" I yell at her, wanting this over with, knowing instinctively I don't want to dig any deeper into whatever she is trying to explain to me.

She gestures for me to continue onwards. I do but my unease is growing the closer I get.

When I finally find the tree marked with my initials, I bend down next to the little mound of earth that has recently been disturbed. I take a deep breath and blow it out, sending up a silent prayer of thanks. If I get out of this in one piece,

I'm buying Oz and Zig a fucking Lamborghini each for Christmas.

She stands over us to watch me dig but that's not going to work. I need to distract her. Despite every single neuron in my brain telling me I'll regret this forever, I speak. "What were you talking about before, about my mother? I don't understand." I continue digging with my hands but keep my eyes on Wanda, who smiles big.

She moves away and starts pacing as she gears up to tell me with a dramatic flourish. She spins in a circle for a moment like a child playing before leaning against a tree opposite us. With the gun in her hand pointed at her feet, she stares at me without seeing as she loses herself in her memories.

"I couldn't have any more babies after my boys. There were complications and they had to remove my ovaries. That's probably the thing I hated your mother for most. She could give John the one thing I couldn't. A son by blood. But I showed her." She laughs, making me want to scream at her to shut up just as my hand hits plastic. I slide my fingers over it until I find the opening, feeling around inside until my hand finds what it's seeking. I manage to keep the bag hidden within the hole I had dug as I work to get the gun out one-handed.

"Tell her when your birthday is, Conner," she must scream it, because the little boy crouched beside me jumps.

He stares at me, fear evident on his face as he mouths the word "Christmastime," before hiding his head against my shoulder. His words are enough to carve my heart to shreds and leave me bleeding out on the floor.

Now I understand what she was inferring and I wished I had listened to my instincts that told me to run. "She died in July," I tell her, but I know. I know what she's going to say.

"Did she?" she questions.

The tears run down my face. I hate that I'm giving her the satisfaction of seeing me cry but my mind just can't process the level of evil contained within one person. She laughs again, enjoying the pain she's inflicting. Now I know what she means by Conner being a trophy. Every time she looks at him he's proof that she won.

I pull the gun-free and flick the safety off, hoping like fuck they loaded it because I'm only going to get one shot at this.

"She didn't kill herself. Fucking hell, she was too much of a coward for that. Besides, she wouldn't leave you or hurt her precious unborn child. I kept her locked up in her room in the basement under our house. Nobody but us knew about it. As you know, John had it soundproofed so her screams wouldn't disturb the rest of us. I kept her down there until she went into labor and then I took her kid. Oh, it was the best day of my life. Finally, after everything, I managed to break her. Every time I looked in his eyes, I got to relive it over and over again. She took my son from me so I took her son from her. It was poetic justice if you ask me.

"She didn't last long after that. She curled up into a little ball and died a little more every day until finally—poof—she was gone."

She looks at me then, coming back to herself. "And now that you've done the hard part, I'm going to be gracious and finally reunite her with her children. I'm nothing if not benevolent."

"Fuck you," I spit out. "You will always be a poor man's version of my mother. A watered-down wannabe. She was pure class and the bravest person I knew. She'll live on in the memories of the people who love her but you, you bitter shrew, will be forgotten in the blink of an eye." I wrap my arm around Conner and bury his head in my shoulder before lifting the gun and firing it at her.

She crumples to the ground, a look of shock on her face as the bullet wedges itself in her chest.

"Keep your eyes closed for me sweetheart," I whisper to Conner before pulling away from him and standing up. I walk over to Wanda's prone body and smile.

"See you in hell." I fire another bullet into her skull and watch the life drain from her eyes.

I sag in relief and drop the gun. I run for Conner and pull him into my chest as we sob together for all we've lost and all we've been through. I don't know how long we sit there before our tears run dry but when I pull back and place a kiss on his forehead, I tell him something he needs to know. "Our mother, your real mother, was an amazing woman and she loved you so fiercely and so completely. I know this because she loved me exactly the same way. I'll tell you all about her, I swear."

"Okay," he offers me a wobbly smile. Okay. Just one simple word but it's enough.

"Everything will be okay now."

I didn't realize I spoke too soon until Conner's eyes go wide a second before something collides with the back of my head and everything goes black.

CHAPTER TWENTY-TWO

Zero

The minutes roll by mocking me. When an hour passes with no sign of Viper, or Megan still for that matter, my usually calm demeanor starts to fray around the edges.

All of the brothers finish funneling in, barring Viper and the prospects manning the gate. We've gathered in the large room at the back of the compound where we hold church while waiting for Viper to get here to begin. The prospects are usually excluded from church but I want everyone on this.

The same instincts that kept me and my brothers safe across the ocean scream at me now that something is wrong. As VP, I step up and call a halt to all the chatter as people take their seats, commanding the attention of everyone around me.

One look at Grim tells me he's feeling the weird vibe too.

"Any news from the prospects?" I ask him.

"No sign of Viper or Megan yet," he confirms.

"Fill us in here, Zero. Something going down we should know about?" Trip asks from across the table.

"Megan and Conner are missing. Viper went out looking for them but he should have been back by now. Any other time and I would chalk it up to coincidence but my gut is telling me something else is going on here."

"She wouldn't just run away. Not after everything," Trip muses. "You thinking foul play?" He scowls at the thought.

"Could be she's just hiding out after her fight with Viper," Rock adds from beside him.

"How do you know she had a fight with Viper?"

Rock snorts, his seat creaking as he sits forward.

"I was in the bar when she tore out of his office in tears. I asked her if she was okay but she tore my head off, muttering about asshole bikers so I let her be." He shrugs.

"Pissed off women are nothing if not determined. If she doesn't want to be found, she won't be," he adds.

A few of the guys nod in agreement, the tension in the room easing a little but not from me.

"And what about Viper?" I ask him.

"That I don't know. Could be he's found her and they're making up." He winks, making the guys laugh but his blasé attitude is making my skin itch. Then again, what did I expect from the man who was happy enough to leave Megan on the streets to defend herself for years?

"How long's he been gone?" Rock asks.

"An hour," I admit, making Rock laugh out loud.

"Christ, Zero, he's not five. Cut the guy some slack." He's right but his words are still grating on my patience.

"Last I checked you were no longer the president or the VP, Rock, so how about you lay off trying to give me orders," I bark and the room goes quiet again at my unusually frosty attitude.

"Trip," I address the man who I know adores his old lady. "If Honey was missing, especially if she was upset and in a place that still doesn't feel like home, what would you do?"

"I'd tear this place apart brick by brick until I found her to make things right," he answers without giving a single fuck what anyone else thinks.

"Grim, text Kaz and Wizz to head over to the cabin to look for Viper. That's where he was the last time I spoke to him. Everyone else, I want you to fan out and find Megan and Conner. There are only so many places she can be with a small boy and wherever she is, she's on foot. I want all available eyes out looking until they're found."

Everyone leaves to begin the search. Even the ones who think I'm overreacting do my bidding without a word of argument.

I try Viper's phone again and again until finally, after another fifteen minutes, he picks up.

"Thank fucking Christ. I'm going to kick your

motherfucking ass when you get here," I yell at him, signaling for Grim that I've got a hold of him.

"It's Kaz, Zero. Viper's been shot. An ambulance is en route but it's bad, man," he tells me, making me freeze solid in place.

"I'm on my way—"

He cuts me off before I can continue. "There's more. Wizz searched the surrounding area and found Wanda dead with a bullet to the stomach and one to the head. I don't know what the fuck happened but he's doing a clean up now as this place will be crawling with police unless you can get a lock on it."

My breathing comes out in ragged pants, my anger making my skin feel like it's splitting at the seams. I can hear the siren of the approaching ambulance through the phone and Kaz yelling that he's over here.

"Gotta go. I'll keep you updated but, Zero, you gotta know one last thing. Someone has carved 'Carnage' into his chest." He hangs up just as my anger detonates.

"What is it?" Grim's voice has me turning to face him. Whatever he sees has him taking a step back.

"Viper's been shot. He's on his way to the hospital now. Wanda's dead," I tell him, not recognizing my own voice.

"What?" I turn to face Rock and Cougar, who walk back through the door together, both of them halting at my words.

"The word 'Carnage' was carved into his chest."

"That bitch!" Rock roars before throwing a chair. "I know she hated Wanda but what the fuck did Viper do?"

I step towards him, ready to rip his head off at what he's implying but Grim holds me back.

"Are you suggesting that Megan shot Wanda and Viper before carving him up?" I ask him incredulously. "Are you out of your fucking mind?" I roar.

"I get it, Zero, but you have to admit it's a hell of a coincidence that your girl disappears without a trace and the two people who she clearly has an issue with are suddenly shot. The word 'Carnage' sounds like she's leaving a message about where her loyalties truly lie," Cougar comments quietly, keeping himself between Rock and me.

"If my nephew dies, I'll kill the bitch myself," he spits.

This time it's me holding Grim back.

"Get the fuck out of here, Rock." When he doesn't move I yell again. "Go!"

He shrugs off Cougar's hold. "Tell me one thing. What the fuck are you going to do about this, VP?" He spits "VP" like it leaves a bad taste in his mouth. If I wasn't so preoccupied, I'd cut his fucking tongue out for this disrespect he's showing.

"I'm going to start a war," I tell him ominously and watch as his shoulders drop along with his head. He offers me a nod, a piss poor job of an apology if I ever had one, then leaves.

"Zero," Grim says my name like a warning but I ignore him, looking straight at Cougar.

"I'm taking Grim and all but two of the prospects to

Carnage with me." I raise my hand when he tries to speak. This isn't open for discussion.

"She is our old lady. We'll deal with it. The prospects are expendable so I'm taking them. I'll leave two on the gate but I want you and Rock to gather every single member and old lady in here while we're gone. We're going on lockdown. Go find Rock and fill him in. Nobody comes in or out while I'm gone, got it?"

He nods and leaves to do my bidding.

I turn to face Grim once were alone.

"Zero, this isn't right," he reasons with me, but I shake my head. I don't want to hear it.

"Hospital first. I need to check on Viper and talk to Kaz and Wizz. I need you with me on this, Grim. I'm asking as your VP to follow my orders without question but I'm asking as your friend to trust me."

He searches my face, for what I don't know, but eventually, he agrees, giving me the green light to put my plan in motion.

⋆ ⋆ ⋆ ⋆ ⋆

KAZ IS in the waiting room when we pull up to Mercy General, his head bowed, blood still coating his hands.

He looks up when I place my hand on his shoulder. "Any news?" I ask him quietly, keeping my emotions locked down so I can get on with the job at hand even as the sterile smell of antiseptic and floor cleaner invades my senses, threatening to crack my fortitude.

"Doc says it was a through and through. Went through his shoulder and hit his collarbone on the way out. It was a sheer fucking miracle that nothing major was hit. The main issue is the amount of blood he's lost."

"He's a fighter and the most stubborn bastard I know. He'll pull through," I inform him, knowing it will take more than a bullet to keep Viper down.

"I'm swapping you out with Eight Ball and Karma. I want you and Wizz with me. You up for that?"

He nods without question, offering me his loyalty, which is why I'm thankful to call this man my brother.

"So what's the plan?" Grim asks from beside me. I spin around to face him and the rest of the guys. The grin that spreads across my face has the nurse who was offering me a seductive smile from behind her desk going pale and turning away.

By the time I've explained my intentions, everyone is wearing similar expressions.

We walked in here to check on one of our fallen but we walk out united in our determination to live up to our names and rain down chaos on those who have earned it.

CHAPTER TWENTY-THREE

Megan

The pounding in my brain pulls me from my sleep. It feels like a dozen ice picks are smashing their way through my skull, making nausea swell inside me.

Holy shit, did I get drunk? I search my brain for memories but they feel foggy and out of reach. Every time I try to reach out and grab one, they dissipate like vapor.

I keep my eyes squeezed shut and concentrate on the last thing I do remember, which is arguing with Viper. His words cut me like knives, giving me every reason to drink myself into a stupor but it's unlike me to drown my sorrows. Try as I might, I can't remember anything beyond telling him I hoped it was worth it.

I push up on one hand and nearly faceplant as a wave of

pain so intense steals my breath and has me lying back down. I open my eyes and see nothing. Panic washes over me as the darkness stretches out before me. Not being able to see after losing my hearing is my worst nightmare. As my chest heaves, I have to fight to remind myself to take deep breaths before a panic attack swallows me whole.

When I finally calm my breathing enough, I focus on my other senses. The space around me is cold and damp, the air stale and acrid smelling with a metallic, almost copper tasting, tang in the air letting me know wherever I am it's inside a building of some sort. My throbbing arm is a reminder not to place any weight on it so I sit up again, but slowly this time. I use my uninjured arm to feel the floor around me.

When I try to get to my feet, I feel pain slice through me as I place my weight on them. I also feel something pulling at my ankle. Reaching down, I feel a set of cuffs attached to my ankle. Using my fingers, I figure out pretty quickly that the other end is locked around some kind of pipe running up the length of the wall. I give it a hard shake but it's solid, not budging an inch.

I slide my cold hand under my T-shirt and slip my fingers under the edge of my bra, fiddling around until I find that little seam at the edge. I pick at it, pulling the frayed edges, working at it until it finally loosens enough for what I need. Slipping my hand between my breasts, I use my thumb to push the edge of the wire through the small hole I've poked in the fabric and then maneuver it through the hole until I can snag the end of the wire between my fingers and pull it free.

Leaning down, ignoring the throbbing in my arm and shoulder, I slip the wire into the lock of the cuffs just like I did when Zero cuffed me to the bed all those nights ago. Thirty seconds later and the cuffs open, allowing me to pull myself free.

Every inch of my body hurts, each spot even more painful than the next. Nothing, however, compares to the skull-splitting headache. As much as I want to curl up and die, I know I can't. I don't waste any more time feeling sorry for myself or trying to figure out where I am. I search the floor around me, hoping it's relatively clear so I can make my escape. When my fingers bump into something, I instinctively yank my hand back before I can begin to try and figure out what it is.

Taking a deep breath, I reach out my shaking fingers and wrap them around the object that I belatedly realize is a leg. A child's leg. That breaks through the foggy haze and has me pulling my aching body over to the little boy who is lying far too still.

I shot Wanda. Conner's look of horror. The pain in my head and then nothing. The images spin on a loop over and over in my brain. Shoot, horror, nothingness.

"Conner?" I can feel the wobble in my voice as I run my hands over his body, trying hopelessly to check for injuries without being able to see him.

He doesn't move, making the vomit I had desperately

been trying to keep down crawl up my throat. I turn away and lean over, throwing up everything inside me. Each wretch of my stomach compounds the stabbing in my brain.

When there is nothing left to bring up, I wipe my mouth with the edge of my sleeve and crawl back to Conner. I slide my fingers up his neck to feel for a pulse. When I find the steady *bump, bump* under my fingertips, a sob of stark relief escapes me. He's alive but I don't know how long for. I have to find a way to get us out of here.

My first instinct is to scream but then I remember that someone put us here and swallow it down before a sound can escape me. If I draw their attention they might come and finish the job or worse, do something else to Conner. Whoever it is has proven they have no issues hurting a child.

Okay, think Megan. I slide my jacket off gingerly, biting back a scream when I pull it free from my arm, which I'm guessing is broken. I use the jacket to cover my little brother before I climb once again to my unsteady feet. The motion makes my head spin again like I'm on a ride at a fairground spinning around and around at dizzying speeds. I don't know much about head injuries but I don't need to be an expert to guess that I have a concussion. Not that it changes anything other than I have to fight harder to stay on my feet.

With my good arm out in front of me, I take a shuffle forward and wait until I bump into something. Thankfully, there doesn't seem to be anything in my path to trip over before my hands encounter the cold smooth stone wall. Keeping my hand on it, I follow it until I reach a corner and then turn to follow it across the other side of the room, hoping I'll be able to gauge how big this space is.

I've taken only six steps before I smack my head on something hard and collapse to the floor in a heap. My hands naturally go down to break my fall, which means I land awkwardly on my sore arm. A scream rips from my throat before I can stop it. I can't move, the pain is so debilitating it hurts just to draw air into my lungs. I don't fight the tears as they flow freely down my face, instead focusing all my energy on trying not to pass out. I allow myself a moment, just one second, to consider the merits of curling into a ball and waiting for someone to rescue me. Then I think of that little boy lying somewhere in the dark depending on me. I climb to my feet again as determination floods my system.

No, fuck being rescued. This time I'm going to rescue my damn self.

Lifting my hand in front of my face, I reach out to see what I hit and feel... wood? Sliding my hands lower my heart starts to pound when I realize what it is I'm touching. Steps. Old wooden steps. I scramble around until I feel the bottom step and maneuver myself as carefully as I can up them until I encounter a door.

I fumble around some more until I find the handle and give it a yank. It's locked, naturally, but I can tell by the feel and shape of it what kind of lock it is. More than that though, I'm actually familiar with these locks as I've been picking them since I was a kid sneaking down to see my mother. I'm still on Chaos property, I'm just—"Fuck." I press my forehead against the door and breathe in through my mouth and out through my nose slowly.

I know exactly where I am. I'm in the basement under the house I grew up in with Wanda and John. I'm in the room that held my mother prisoner. I close my eyes, which is ridiculously unnecessary, but it helps me concentrate on the picture in my head of the basement layout from when I was a kid.

There is one entry point to the basement, a large wooden door that leads down from the back of the kitchen. The kitchen sits at the back of the old 70s style house with a large archway leading to a sitting area. We will have to make our way through there to get to the hallway that leads to the front of the house. I've never given much thought to the layout of this house before but right now I'm cursing whoever designed it. My only hope is that the house is empty or that I can find a weapon of some kind. There is no way of knowing what I'm going to be walking into, but staying here isn't an option.

Knowing where I am means I don't have to worry about being quiet because this place is soundproofed. It also means that if someone comes back to finish us off, nobody will hear us scream. The house is set at the back of the lot near the woods. If I can just get us outside, we can find coverage in the trees and make our way back to the clubhouse.

I take another deep breath through my mouth, the thick cloying scent of rot and mold making my stomach turn again. I don't know what this room has been used for since my mother's death. Something tells me I don't want to know but if the smell is anything to go by, I doubt it has ever been cleaned.

I bite my lip hard, shutting down that thought before it can spiral. Knowing this is the place where she died is something I'm not ready to deal with. I can't fall apart. There will be time for that later. Right now, I've got to get my shit together.

I close my eyes and picture the room as I remember it when I was little, back before I realized it was a cell. Even when she was given free rein of the club, if she wasn't servicing someone she was expected to sleep here like a dog in its kennel. She had nothing and yet somehow, she made it look pretty with what she had. As a kid, I never looked beyond what I could see. My only concern was why couldn't I stay with her when I hated being upstairs with John and Wanda.

With the childlike blinders off, I can now picture the cold stone walls beneath the dog-eared posters of sunny beach scenes, majestic forests, and wild jungles. All the places she would never get the chance to see. The stone floor remained permanently ice cold with only a single small rug that had been salvaged from the dumpster behind one of the other apartments to break up its bleakness. The far left corner used to house a small single bed covered with a thin threadbare blanket dusted with a little red rose pattern that had faded over the years. Beside it, there had been a rickety bedside table in a retro-style wicker with a small off-white battery operated desk lamp upon it that had been the only source of light in this now dark room. There are no electrical light sockets or outlets down here in the room only ever meant to have been for storage.

That's all I remember about the contents but every time I snuck down here, she lit up like she had everything she could possibly need and I guess in a way she did. I was her greatest treasure which unfortunately turned me into the perfect target for them to use as a manipulation tool with threats of violence.

I bite my lip hard enough to draw blood, bringing me out of my memory, forcing myself to focus on the task at hand. I know I can pick this lock. I've done it a thousand times before. The problem is, I know I'm hurt pretty bad. Do I head to the exit and try to get help and come back for Conner or do I attempt to get him out of here myself, hoping like fuck I don't pass out in the process?

I don't know what I'll be walking into, I don't know which is the best choice, but I just can't bring myself to leave him here even if it's to get help. What if he wakes up terrified? What if he hurts himself? No, I can't leave him behind.

With my decision made, I slowly descend the stairs, retracing my steps until I find Conner exactly where I left him. After giving his body another once over with my hands, I'm pretty sure he doesn't have anything broken. At this point, it's a risk I'm going to have to take.

I grit my teeth and use every ounce of strength I have left to pick him up with my good arm. He's heavy, making my already unstable body pitch forward. Having a useless arm doesn't help matters but I manage to stay on my feet by will alone.

"I will make it," I tell myself. There is no other option. Either we both get through that door or we both stay because I'm not leaving him.

I work my way back around the same route as before, far slower than last time, stumbling occasionally but I make it back to the steps and that's all that matters. I place my foot on the bottom step and center my weight. As I start to take the next step, Conner moves. Slowly at first as he wakes, then his moves turn frantic and I feel him slipping from my grip. With no other option, I drop to my butt and cradle him in my lap. His flailing limbs make him smack against my injured arm, making me scream out. He stills his movements instantly before I feel his little arms wrap themselves around my neck as recognition sets in. A second later, I feel his hot tears scorching the skin of my neck.

"Conner, Conner, sweetie, I need you to calm down for me, okay? Shh... it's okay, I got you but I'm a little hurt so I need my favorite little man to help me out. Think you can do that?" Shit. I feel useless not being able to see or hear him. Frustration beats at me again but I refuse to let it break me.

"You know my ears don't work properly and I can't hear you right? Well, because it's so dark in here I can't see you either, which means I don't know if you're talking to me." I fight to keep my voice from breaking. He needs my strength right now, not my tears. "We are going to have to stick with yes-no questions for the moment. To answer yes I want you to tap my shoulder like this." I lift his hand and tap it against my shoulder.

"Only this one though, as the other arm is hurt, okay?"

I wait a moment, then feel him tap my shoulder once.

"Good boy. You are so freaking smart and brave. Right, to tell me no, I want you to feel around for my ear and give it a tug. Now this question is super important, all right? I want you to really think about it before answering. Are you hurt anywhere?"

I wait a moment before he taps me on the shoulder.

"Shit," I curse, balancing him in my lap and placing my hand in his.

"Can you place my hand on what hurts Conner?" I feel him tugging my hand and lifting it until I can feel his soft hair beneath my fingers.

"Your head hurts?"

He moves his fingers to my shoulder and taps once.

"Oh, baby so does mine. Do you hurt anywhere else at all?"

A tug on my ear has me sending up a silent prayer of thanks.

"This is what we are going to do, Conner. You are going to wrap your arms and legs around me and hold on as tight as you can and I am going to get us the heck out of this place. I know it's scary in the dark but I am so impressed with how brave you are being that I can't wait to tell everyone how you helped to rescue us, my very own little hero. We need to move now so climb up and hold on tight."

He does as I ask and I can tell he's trying to be careful of my bad arm, making me smile for the first time since waking up down here. He has our mother's fearlessness. I kiss the side of his cheek as he buries his head against my neck and wraps his little fingers in my hair.

I make my way up the steps. Each footstep is agony as the added weight of Conner pulls on the last reserves of my energy but I fight through it. We make it to the top in one piece, thankfully. I lower Conner to the floor slowly so I can grab the wire tucked in the back pocket of my jeans.

Bending down, I use my fingers to feel the tiny opening of the lock and slip the wire into the mechanism. It's harder with the use of only one hand, taking a little longer than usual to get it open. Eventually, I feel it click and the door handle pushes down with ease.

Slowly, I crack the door to look out and am met with my worst fucking nightmare.

I freeze on the spot and try to stifle my sobs so I don't scare Conner but my whole body shakes with the force of them trying to break free. I bite down so hard to stop myself from screaming that blood pools in my mouth.

It's not what I can see that has me on the verge of a panic attack, it's what I can't see that has my mind spiraling at the possible connotations of what this will mean for me. It's as dark up here as it is down in the basement, the blackness so encompassing it's suffocating me.

The difference between up here and down there is that this isn't normal.

I reach out a hand, find the counter, and feel my way across it until I feel the sink. It's exactly where I can picture it in my brain. Above it is a huge bay window that looks out onto the woods. This whole room is usually bathed in light and it probably is now. The problem is, I can't see it. I can't see anything.

The blackness is not coming from the room I'm standing in, it's coming from me.

I squeeze the counter with my fingertips as I start to sway when another wave of pain moves through my head. Conner's small hand slips into mine, reminding me that I can fall apart later but right now I have to get him somewhere safe. I lean against the counter for a moment, letting it take my weight as I picture the layout and find my bearings.

"Okay, Conner, we're nearly there." I bend down and turn to where I assume he is.

"Conner, is this the house you lived in with Wanda?" I ask him, making sure I'm not losing my mind on top of everything else.

A tap on the shoulder reassures me that I'm not crazy just yet.

"Something is wrong with my eyes so I'm going to need you to guide us outside. Do you think you can do that?"

A tap on my shoulder has me smiling despite myself.

"Fantastic. You are my hero, little man. I couldn't do this without all of your help."

I grip his little hand tightly and use the counter to pull myself back up. I hold on to it for a second before doubling over and puking, hopefully in the sink.

Conner's hand in mine is the only thing keeping me grounded and when he squeezes it harder, I know he's scared. I wish I could wrap him up in my arms and run with him, to keep going until I find Viper, Grim, and Zero who I know would keep us safe, but I don't think I'm even going to make it through the front door.

"It's okay, I'm okay. Let's just go. Nice and slowly now."

He tugs me along and I follow, concentrating on staying upright. I catch my foot on something, smacking my bad arm on the wall and hitting my hip on the corner of the table that wasn't there before. It doesn't matter, I don't feel any of it anymore. My body is shutting down at an alarming rate but I won't stop moving until Conner is out of this house of horrors.

Finally, after what feels like hours, we make it to the door. I pull it open, surprised to find it unlocked, before finally allowing myself to sink to my knees.

"I need you to listen to me now, Conner. I need you to be brave for just a little longer for me okay? I need you to run to the clubhouse. Don't stop for anyone except Viper, Grim, or Zero, no one but them. You get them to come and help me, all right?"

I feel his hands on my arm tugging me, his movements jerky and filled with panic.

"I can't come with you, Conner, I won't make it that far.

Come here." I tug him into my arms, my eyes growing heavy, but I fight through it as hard as I can. "I am so lucky to have you as a brother. I love you. I'll be waiting right here for you to come back. I'm going to be fine, I promise," I assure him, feeling my tears slide down my cheeks at my lie.

"Go now, you have to hurry. Remember what I said. Only trust Zero, Grim, and Viper."

A hesitant tap on my shoulder makes me smile even as I lose the fight to stay awake. I feel a soft kiss on my cheek just before my eyes close and then I feel… nothing.

CHAPTER TWENTY-FOUR

Grim

"Everyone in position?" Zero asks me. I give him a nod to let him know we're ready. I hope he knows what he's doing because there is no coming back from this. "Let's move out," he orders.

I give the signal for the others and we make our way through the gates, the prospects doing nothing to stop us. We fan out around the compound, knowing everyone is already inside. The loud talking and bright lighting give them no indication of what's about to go down.

I slam open the door and push myself ahead of Zero, offering him protection even though the dozen or so other people heading in behind us will ensure his safety.

"What the fuck?" someone yells as the screechy voice of some 70s rock song stops abruptly.

"Where is Megan?" Zero roars at the room at large.

People start moving for their weapons but they pause when all the people at our backs point their guns at them.

"Do not make me repeat myself," he grits out to the room. Half of them look shell-shocked, the other half betrayed. I shrug indifferently. All I care about is finding Megan. Nothing else matters beyond that and Viper pulling through.

"Prospects? You fucking fool. Prospects aren't trained like the rest of us. We could take them out before you blink," another voice yells.

Kaz has him out of the chair he was sitting in and unconscious on the floor in less than three seconds.

"These guys aren't just prospects," I tell them, scanning the crowd and watching the sea of faces.

"These are our brothers from our unit," Zero chimes in. "They have saved our asses time and time again, making our trust in them unbreakable. That's more than can be said for the rest of you, isn't it?"

"One of you knows where Megan is," Grim bites out. "One of you is responsible for shooting Viper and we aren't leaving until I find out who did it so I can return the favor."

"You're a fucking traitor." Rock stands up, kicking his chair over in the process.

Orion, Gage, Halo, and Diesel step up beside us with faces etched with fury.

"A traitor? For calling on their old lady's family? Or

because he knew if we were going to take out your president we would have been a hell of a lot smarter about it than to leave the word 'Carnage' carved into his chest," Orion seethes at the once president of Chaos.

"The only traitor as far as I'm concerned is the rat within Chaos who tried to break the truce between our two clubs and start a war using my sister as a fucking scapegoat. Well, not this fucking time," he tells them.

The Chaos Demons stare at us in confusion. Having been put on lockdown by their VP, only to find themselves being held at gunpoint by the same man will do that to a person.

"They came to us because they can't trust you. That doesn't make them weak or traitors. It makes them smart. They avoided a war with a club that is a fuck of a lot bigger than yours and a group of mercenaries that would happily slaughter you all in your sleep without you knowing.

"I've despised this MC for what they did to my mother but I have a hell of a lot of respect for the men who are trying to turn it around," Diesel tells the crowd before turning to look first at Zero then at me.

"You're still not good enough for my sister though," he grumbles, making my lips twitch. "But I will put any plans of mass murder on halt for a while," he tells me begrudgingly.

"Appreciated," I say dryly.

"My nephew is lying in the fucking hospital thanks to some fucker—" Rocks tirade is cut off as a commotion takes place behind us.

"Hey, stop you can't go in there," I hear one of the

Carnage guys yell a second before something collides with my legs, making me stumble.

"Holy fuck," Zero says.

I look down and see Conner wrapped around my legs, shaking. I bend down and wrap my arms around him, holding him to me tightly as he struggles to get his words out.

"M... Megan," he stutters, a sob ripping from his throat as the room goes wired.

"Hey, it's okay. Take your time," Zero reassures him, crouching down, rubbing his hand soothingly up and down his back.

"She's at my house," his shaky voice whispers, making us look up at each other sharply.

"Wanda's place?" I ask Zero. He shrugs and nods for a couple of the prospects to head out and check. I'm itching to go myself. I need to see her with my own two eyes.

"Conner. I want you to stay here for me, all right. I'm going to go and fetch her and make sure she's all right." I stand up and turn him to face the room. He looks up at Orion and Diesel, who look down at him in shock.

"Holy motherfucking shit," Halo whispers from his spot beside Orion.

"Explain," Orion barks at me, making me want to nut punch him even if I do understand where he's coming from.

"No time. I need to get to Megan but we will explain it all later. In the meantime, this is Conner, your brother. Conner, these are Orion and Diesel, the big brothers your sister was telling you about."

Conner looks up at them in wonder before something over Diesel's shoulder catches his eye, causing what little color he had to bleed from his face.

"Hey, what is it?" I look to see what he's looking at and find Rock staring at us.

"Conner?" Conner looks up at me, his eyes wide with fear.

"He hurt Megan." He points at Rock, making me whip my head around in surprise.

Gage and Halo are one step quicker than me though and have Rock on the floor with his hands behind his back and a foot pressed down between his shoulder blades.

"You fucking prick," I sneer at him just as my phone rings. I pull it out and see that it's Delta, one of the prospects sent over to Wanda's place, and answer it before it can ring again.

"She there?" I bark, the room going quiet once more, all except for Rock screaming obscenities from the floor.

"Fuck!" I hear yelled into the phone and a scuffle of some kind before words are yelled that make my blood run cold. "She's not breathing!"

I don't hear anything else. I hand Conner to Kaz and run. I hear footsteps behind me but I don't stop until I come upon a scene that will haunt me for the rest of my life.

I thought nothing could be worse than losing my sister

but watching Delta do chest compressions on the woman I love is more than I can bear. I rush over and crumble to the floor beside her. Orion, Diesel, and Zero following suit.

I stare at her as tears flood my eyes, willing her to hold on, to fight.

Orion takes over for Delta and I watch on helplessly as he tries to restart his sister's heart. Zero strokes her hair and I'm dimly aware of Diesel muttering some kind of prayer but I'm frozen solid staring down at the woman I can't live without. No. I refuse to live without.

I lie down beside her, careful not to get in Orion's way, even as I hear the sound of sirens in the distance. I place my lips against the shell of her ear and whisper words I know she couldn't hear even if she were to magically wake up.

"Hold on, Raven. Don't you dare give up on us now. I love you, we love you, and we need you here with us, dammit. Conner needs you, your brothers and Luna need you." I feel the tears fall then as I plead with her to stay with us. "Please baby, please. You promised us a lifetime together."

Orion's movements stop as his head bows, grief stark on his face. "She's gone," he whispers but it sounds in the air like a gunshot.

"No." I sit up, refusing to believe him.

"Fight, Megan. Goddamn you, Megan, fight," I scream, collapsing back down beside her, my head on her fragile shoulder. I suck in a ragged breath that feels like I'm inhaling broken glass when I realize I can feel something.

I look up at her face and see tear tracks running down her cheeks.

"Baby?" I slide my hand around her neck and feel a flutter under my fingers.

"Fuck. She has a pulse," I tell the guys looking down at her in disbelief.

Everything after that is a shock of activity as the paramedics get there. I don't take any of it in, not their words, not the guys around me, nothing. All I focus on is my girl and how she fought like a fucking champion.

"Thank you, baby," I whisper as I watch the lights of the ambulance disappear before running for my bike.

* * * * *

I FIND myself back in the waiting room of Mercy for the second time today, waiting for news about someone I care about. It's filled with people who care about both Megan and Viper but all this waiting has me feeling like I'm about to come out of my skin.

When we all took off running, Halo and Gage locked Rock down tight in the basement and posted a couple of their own guys to watch over him. They have zero loyalty to the guy so we don't have to worry about someone busting him lose. In fairness, once the treachery was revealed, most of Chaos was—well, in chaos. People were left reeling that yet again, Megan had suffered at our hands.

I don't know what's going on back at the club. Fuck, I don't even know if there will be a club to go back to after this and right now I don't give a flying fuck. Megan has suffered enough. No fucking more.

"Hey, man. Here." I look up and see Rebel, a brother from Carnage, holding out a cup of coffee to me. "You okay?"

"Not even close. I guess this is karma, huh, for all the shitty things I've done." I shake my head and take a sip, watching Luna lean her head on Diesel's shoulder as she sits between him and Orion, her hands clasped firmly in each of theirs.

Oz and Zig are in the corner with Wyatt, who is, believe it or not, even bigger than them. Curled into his side is Jenna, her eyes red and puffy from her tears.

"Nah, I don't believe that," Rebel tells me, dragging my attention back to him. He takes a sip of his drink and winces. He's quiet for a moment before he speaks. "I don't agree with what you did, sneaking into Carnage and pretending to be something you weren't, but I get why you did it. Family is…" He trails off, looking around the room, an odd mix of Carnage and Chaos united together in their grief.

"Family is everything," I finish for him, watching Zero talk to Gage and Halo as Honey walks over to them and hands out coffees. Her old man, Trip, is on the floor in the corner reading a story to Conner, who has fallen asleep in his lap.

Thankfully, Conner was checked over and given the all-clear. He had traces of chloroform in his blood, which explained the headache he complained of to the doctor, but otherwise, he escaped relatively unscathed—at least physically. Mentally, well that's something else entirely.

After naming Rock as the one who hurt Megan, Conner shut down and hasn't spoken a word since.

"Family of Megan Cooper," a young-looking doctor calls from the other side of the room. She takes a step back when the mass of us descend on her like she's prey, almost losing her footing in her sensible brown suede heels.

"We're her family," Orion tells her. She looks over at us all and swallows.

"I meant immediate family," she answers.

"As I said, we are her family. We are all her brothers, sisters—" he catches my eye as he continues— "and husbands."

"Right, okay." She gives in, which is just as well because Orion can be a stubborn fucker when he wants to be.

"She has multiple cuts and contusions across her body and feet, a dislocated shoulder and elbow from, if I had to guess, being dragged, and a couple of fractured ribs from the chest compressions. They will all heal in time. Our biggest concern is the head injuries she sustained. She has a fractured skull and swelling on her brain. We have put her in a medically-induced coma while we try to bring the swelling down. She is being taken to the ICU now. I'm sorry, but the next forty-eight hours will be critical.

"Fuck!" I hear curses and crying around me and gasps of despair. It isn't until I hear my name called, I look up and see Eight Ball coming towards me.

"It's Viper. He's awake"

CHAPTER TWENTY-FIVE

Viper

Sitting beside Megan's bed, I watch the rise and fall of her chest and listen to the rhythmic beating of the machine next to the bed. I reach over with a wince as the movement pulls on my chest and slide my fingers through hers, careful to avoid all the wires and tubes.

I know I'm not supposed to be here. Christ knows nurse Rachet will have a shit fit if she finds me out of bed and back in here again, but I don't give a rat's ass.

My girl's here because of me. Because I have a big fucking mouth and don't think before I speak. If I had just gone after her sooner. Or told her I loved her too, things might have turned out differently. I shake my head in frustration, shutting down that train of thought before I smash something and get myself kicked out once again.

The guys filled me in on what they knew, but with Megan still in a coma and Conner refusing to speak, we still had way more questions than answers.

I keep replaying our last moments together over and over in my head on a loop. Picking apart each word and action that I missed. I hurt her, then this fucking club that is supposed to have my back, and worse still, my uncle hurt her. My own flesh and goddamn blood.

I stand up and walk gingerly over to the window and look out at the city lights illuminating the night sky. People are at home now going about their normal lives completely unaware that mine has ground to a halt as my heart beats outside my body on a hospital bed in a cold sterile room.

The doc reluctantly says I can leave and as much as I'm ready to get out of here and deal out Rock's retribution, I'm loathed to leave her here alone.

I climb onto the bed beside her, ensuring I don't pull on any of the wires and tuck myself as close to her as I can without hurting her. Resting my hand over the top of her breast, I feel the cadence of her heart—*thump thump, thump, thump*—and let it lull me into a dreamless sleep.

***

LEAVING Megan was the hardest thing I've had to do but Luna

and her brothers are with her, swearing they will call if there is any change. Honey hands me my new cut. I slip it on and give her a nod of thanks.

"I'm getting the other one cleaned for you. I'm a whiz at getting out blood stains but you are on your own with bullet holes," she frowns, making me smile.

"Thank you. Go on home. I'll send Trip back when we've finished."

She nods before turning tail and heading back to the apartment she shares with Trip.

"You ready?" Zero asks from beside me. I look from him to Grim, who is waiting with his hand on the door.

"Yeah. I want this shit sorted today. There will never be another day where Megan isn't safe here even if I have to strip everyone except us three and the prospects of their colors.

"I'm with you brother, you know that," Grim states.

I turn and face Zero. "I don't think I would have made the call you did. And I would have been wrong. You stepped up and kept a level head while making an impossible decision. I couldn't ask for a better VP. Thank you." I hold my fist out for him to bump, which he does without hesitation.

"Jesus, do you two need a little longer? Perhaps you want to braid each other's hair or something?" Grim bitches, making me flip him off.

He pulls the door open wide and steps inside, Zero and me following behind him.

All the club members are here apart from Rock, who is chained up downstairs. I look over at the two Carnage prospects guarding the door and signal for them to approach, which they do without complaint. The rest of the room is quiet, watching me avidly to see what my next move will be. Or maybe just to see if I'll keel over. The day is still young so I guess time will tell.

"Thank you. You guys can go now. Orion said to head back to the Carnage compound. He and Diesel are at the hospital."

They don't speak but incline their heads in a show of respect before heading out.

I turn to face the room, ignoring the nausea that swells as I forget myself for a moment and move too soon. The doctor was not happy for me to be leaving just yet but I managed to talk him around in the end. I refused to let this shit fester a minute longer.

"Demons," I drawl, addressing the room.

"Good to have you back, boss man," Trip calls out. A few of the other brothers call out with shouts, happy for my return too.

"I wish I could say the same thing, Trip." The room quiets again, the moment of joviality gone. "When a man gets shot, it would have been nice to have been able to lean on my family. Imagine my surprise to find out it was family who pulled the trigger."

I stand still, looking over them as Zero and Grim flank my sides.

"I always wanted to be the president, you know. Not because of the notoriety or for the power trip but because I believed in this brotherhood and what it stood for. Shame the rest of you didn't feel the same way."

"We didn't know half the shit that was going on here, Pres, or we would have stepped up," Cougar protests.

"There was a lot of shit going on here that nobody seemed to know anything about. Now, Grim, Zero, and I had an excuse. We'd been gone for over a decade but when we came back, I knew straight away that something wasn't right. I brought on my unit as prospects and before you bitch about that, they weren't given any preferential treatment, much to their disgust. I brought them on because I needed men at my back I could trust and I knew two minutes after stepping in that door that I wouldn't be able to trust all of you.

"I thought it was the fact that you had now had a succession of three presidents in a relatively small time frame.

"I thought you might just need an adjustment period. I mean, I get it. You devote your loyalty to one man, then you're expected to switch loyalties at the drop of a hat again and again." I stop talking to pull out my phone when it beeps and glance at the screen. Halo and Gage have arrived. I text back to let them in and to direct them over here.

"It's on me that I underestimated you. I have to live with the fact that the woman I love," I gesture to the guys next to me, "that we love, is in a fucking coma because I failed to act on the rot within this club from the beginning. That ends today."

The door behind us opens and Halo and Gage step through. I walk over to them and offer each a handshake before turning back to the men in the room who look uncomfortable once more.

"I'm going to head downstairs and deal with Rock. You are to stay here." I nod to Kaz behind the bar, who picks up the remote from the counter he is leaning on and flicks on the huge television screen above the pool table.

The screen lights up, showing a naked and visibly bleeding Rock hanging from a hook in the ceiling in the basement below us.

"You are all going to get a front-row seat to what happens to traitors and of what happens when you hurt one of mine."

"So we're prisoners in our own club now?" Flow calls out, sounding pissed off.

"This is my club and I will do what I fucking want with it. To answer your question though, no, you are not prisoners. I want men who choose to have my back and each other's instead of someone willing to shove a knife in it when that back is turned. When I've dealt with that piece of shit below, you'll be given a choice to stay or to go. Choose fucking wisely because if any of you even think to cross me and mine again I'll make what I'm about to do to Rock look like an episode of *Sesame Street*."

I walk off and leave them to stew on what I said, knowing the place is surrounded and the prospects, who have more than earned their cuts to make them fully-fledged brothers, will keep them contained.

I open the door to the room holding Rock and scrunch my nose up at the smell. "Smells like the dude shit himself. Some fucking president he must have been," Halo mutters from behind me.

I make my way down the steps, moving aside for Gage and Halo to pass. They stand against the far wall, watching on behalf of Carnage as vengeance is met for the woman who is loved by both MCs.

"You sure you're up for this?" Grim asks quietly from beside me so only I can hear him.

I glare at him until he holds his hands up in capitulation. "Just try and stop me," I grit out.

"Fair enough. Mind if I take first shot?" he asks. I shake my head and indicate for him to go for it, moving to stand by Zero so we can all watch him work.

"Hmm... where to start?" Grim muses to himself, walking towards the table where all of our favorite tools are laid out.

He picks a scalpel and a bottle of water off the table before walking over to the swinging man. Uncapping the water he takes a sip before spitting it in Rock's face. Rock's eyes snap open in shock for a moment and widen even further when he sees all of us.

"Hello, Uncle. Surprised to see me?" I call out to him.

"Viper. You guys have made a mistake. This has all been a misunderstanding," he tells me, the begging note in his voice grating against my skin.

"Is that right?" I mock.

"You're taking the word of a traumatized kid over your own flesh and blood?" he stammers in disbelief.

"Well that little kid didn't drag Megan to the fucking house of horrors by herself now did he?" Grim points out. "Want to know what I find interesting? In a room full of hostile bikers all pointing guns and half of them wearing different club colors—big scary strangers to Conner—the only person who terrified him that night was you," Grim finishes before dragging the scalpel down the sole of Rock's foot. Rock screams as blood drips on the floor beneath him.

"What the fuck?" he screams again as Grim slices into his other foot.

Rock tries to swing himself away but hanging a couple of inches off the ground makes it virtually impossible.

"Megan's feet are shredded to pieces. I'm letting you know what that feels like. For every second of pain you caused her I'm going to return it to you."

"But that wasn't me!" he yells as Grim makes another cut and another. I watch the blood pool on the floor below him, finding sick satisfaction in watching it puddle there.

"Really, then who was it?" Grim asks with a creepy as fuck smile on his face.

"That was Wanda. I didn't know anything about it until she texted me to say she was in the woods with Megan and the kid," he pants as Grim takes a break from his slicing and walks back over to the table of tools.

"And why did she take her?" I ask, wondering how Wanda played into all this.

"Megan told her that John had left the deed to this place in his will, which Megan had buried in some secret hiding spot. It was utter bullshit, of course, but Wanda wasn't replying to my messages. I fucking tried to tell her not to go there, that it was a lie, but she didn't pick up her fucking phone," he grunts out, agitated.

"How do you know it was a lie?" Zero speaks up. "He could have left a will leaving it to Wanda. Stranger things have happened," he goads him.

"I know it was a fucking lie because I was there when he made his will out. I told him it was a stupid fucking idea and that he should have left it to me as I would be president if he croaked but the paranoid bastard thought that would give me an incentive to kill him myself."

"It's not paranoia if it's true though, is it? My guess is John recognized something in you that the rest of us missed. A coldhearted fucking killer," I tell him. He stares at me but doesn't answer.

"If he didn't leave it to Wanda or you, who did he leave it to?"

Rock glares at me as Grim picks up the blowtorch, his face going white before rushing out his next words. "He left it to Melly," he answers. "Which was fine because she was none the wiser and would never get the option to leave here and start asking questions."

"But then she died," Grim adds, walking over with the torch in his hand.

"Fucking Wanda pushed things too far. I was so busy stepping up as president that I didn't notice. By the time I realized Melly was dead, it was too late to do anything."

I look at Zero in confusion before taking in Grim, who seems just as lost.

"What did Wanda have to do with Melly's death? She shot herself," I tell him something he already knows but when a grin spreads over his face I feel the hairs on my arms stand up on end.

"Did she?" he asks.

Grim turns the torch on and presses it against the heel of Rock's foot, causing him to bellow in pain.

"Always with the torch," Zero mutters.

I smile in spite of myself.

"Nothing like the smell of crispy fried traitor to wake you up in the morning," Gage quips from the other side of the room.

"I'm not a fucking traitor. Everything I did was for this club," Rock yells, delusional.

The asshat probably even believes his own bullshit.

"What happened to Melly?"

"She killed Crogan. The penalty for that should have been death but she was pregnant and Wanda wanted that fucking kid. I never could tell that stupid woman no."

"Holy fuck. You were in love with Wanda," Halo curses, coming to the same conclusion I just did. I turn and glare at the asshole. Silence from the peanut gallery would be nice.

"It didn't matter. She only had eyes for John. Even when he was out of the picture, she just couldn't let that piece of shit go." Something occurs to me while he speaks, something that's blindingly obvious now that the facts are in.

"Melly didn't kill John," I speak out, thinking back on his words about how Melly had shot Crogan and should die. He never mentioned John.

"You told everyone she killed herself and used her as a patsy."

"Shit," Gage spits, knowing, I'm betting, how much Orion and Diesel are going to be pissed.

"He didn't deserve her and he was running this club into the ground. I stepped up and made the hard choice."

"Oh, spare me. You wanted the keys to the kingdom, the crown, and the queen by your side but you found out the hard way that not all that glitters is gold."

He carries on talking, my words not penetrating his unstable brain at all. "Wanda kept Melly locked up in the basement of her house. When she went into labor, she took the kid and kept him for herself. Wanda lived to taunt Melly with him every chance she got until eventually, Melly went to sleep and didn't wake up. I didn't know she was dead until Wanda came ranting to me about what the fuck was she was going to do with the kid now. As you know, she eventually sent him away to school. Out of sight out of mind."

"You didn't answer my question about who this land

belongs to now," I remind him as Grim switches the torch back on and presses it to the bottom of Rock's other foot.

His screams are like music to my ears. When he looks like he's on the verge of passing out, I signal for Grim to stop.

"Tell me," I order.

"Megan. It's Megan's land," Rock gasps out in pain.

"Fuck." She spent two years on the street when all of this was hers. "Does she know?"

"I didn't think so. I watched her for two years sleeping in doorways and dumpster diving for food. I figured if she knew, she'd have claimed what was hers and have us all kicked out."

Zero walks up to him, pulls back his fist, and smashes it into Rock's face.

"You weren't looking out for her, you were watching to see if she was going to make a move," Zero spits at him.

"I had to protect the club," Rock yells. "She could have taken everything."

"She should have. We took everything from her," Zero tells him with nothing but hatred in his tone. "Why did you give her the money, her inheritance? She didn't know about it, after all."

"A lawyer showed up here the day of her birthday and said she could now access her trust fund. It had nothing to do with Melly's death. It was old money left to her from her grandparents. I couldn't access it," he explains, letting us know he damn well tried. "I figured if I gave it to her she would move on and forget all about the compound. And she did until you guys came back," he growls.

"I assumed she didn't know about this place being hers, but when she told Wanda John had left it to her, I knew Megan had played me. I tracked Wanda's phone to your mother's old cabin," he regales me without remorse. "You were fucking around with your phone, so I stayed in the shadows until I heard gunshots. I figured Wanda had found out she had been tricked and killed Megan. I couldn't let you hurt Wanda, Viper. You have to understand I loved her..." His voice trails off, his implications clear.

"So you shot me?"

"I wasn't thinking. I just reacted. I carved 'Carnage' into your chest so that eyes would be off of us for a beat and we could make a run for it but it didn't matter anyway." He looks away as grief coats his features, only for it to quickly be replaced with hate.

"Wanda didn't fire the shots. Megan did. She killed the woman I love," he screams. Good. I'm fucking thrilled.

"So you hit her." It's a statement of fact. I squeeze my fists so hard my hands turn white.

He shrugs, unremorseful. "I walked up behind her and smashed my gun into the back of her head. She obviously didn't hear me shoot you or me coming up behind her." He laughs.

"The kid just stared at me before fainting or some shit. I tossed him over my shoulder and dragged Megan through the woods to Wanda's place. It seemed fitting that it should all end there. I tossed her into the basement, grabbed some chloroform Wanda kept there when she wanted to mess with Melly, and placed Conner down there with her. I had nothing against the kid but I couldn't leave any loose ends."

He lifts his head to look at me. "I guess you can see why."

I shake my head in revulsion at the man I was once proud of.

"One thing bothers me though. Why step down as president?" Zero asks, running his fingers over the tools on the table.

"I wanted to take Wanda and leave, and we were going to, but then you brought Megan here and Wanda just couldn't let it go." His head drops forward in defeat. "Just kill me, Viper, and get it over with."

"Tut, tut old man," I tsk, walking toward him like a panther who has his prey in sight.

"Did you really think it would be that easy? Oh, no, you won't get an ounce of mercy from me."

I look to Grim and then to Zero, who has picked up a power drill and smile my first true smile of the day. "Do your worst but make sure he lives. I think we'll keep him down here for a while so he knows exactly what it feels like to be trapped and in pain."

"You don't want a shot?" Zero asks, walking over to Rock with the drill.

"If I touch him, I'll kill him. He doesn't deserve the sweet release of death. I'll give Doc a call and have him on standby. He can patch him up just enough to keep him alive."

Zero nods in understanding before pressing the drill against Rock's kneecap.

I walk up the steps to the soundtrack of ear-piercing screams and the unmistakable sound of shattering bones.

When I walk back into the main room, there is a huge smile on my face. If the guys weren't wary of me from watching the TV screen, my smile soon changes their minds. "Now, if Chaos is in your blood, come and stand beside me. If you can't handle it, then get the fuck out of my club."

CHAPTER TWENTY-SIX

Megan

I open my eyes, blink and open them again but it didn't change anything. All I can see is darkness. I try to sit up but something is on me. There is something in my arm that pulls when I yank, before I can feel liquid running down my elbow.

My brain dimly makes the connection that I'm lying in a bed but it doesn't feel like mine. When I feel hands pushing me back down, I fight back even though my limbs are too heavy and my movements are sluggish at best.

The hands are relentless though. As I feel skin against skin, someone grabs my arm, my brain flashing back to another place and time where there were hands on my skin, darkness, and pain.

I do the only thing I can. I scream. I scream as loud as I can until a sharp prick on my arm makes me jump. Then everything starts to feel fuzzy. My movements stop because I don't have the energy to move anymore.

Maybe I should just go to sleep again. Maybe this is all just a nightmare that I need to wake up from.

* * * * *

THE NEXT TIME I wake up my head is clearer. Unfortunately, that means I can feel the pain more acutely. I don't think there is a part of my body that doesn't hurt and that includes my hair.

I open my eyes slowly this time and suck in a quick breath as my new reality sinks in.

This isn't some fluke, a sick joke, or even my mind playing tricks on me. I'm still trapped in the darkness. My breathing picks up and even as I recognize the start of a panic attack coming on, there is little I can do to prevent it.

I jump when I feel hands on my face and try to pull away, but when I feel lips on my forehead I still.

I know that smell.

"Zero," I sob out. He kisses my cheeks, my eyelids, my nose. Letting me know he's here. It helps but it also hurts like hell too.

"You should go," I tell him as tears run down my face.

He squeezes my hand but doesn't let go. Probably his way of telling me he isn't going anywhere.

"I can't be your Raven anymore. I'm sorry, I'm so, so sorry but I can't live the rest of my life in the dark. Please don't ask me to."

I feel movement before he climbs onto the bed beside me and wraps his arms around my battered body so carefully it's as if I were made of glass.

"I love you. I love you all, but you have to let me go," I cry him as his hand reaches down to take mine.

Instead of holding it, he lays his hand over mine with his two middle fingers bent. I try to pull away, but he presses against my palm again, his hand in the same position. Thumb, index, and pinkie finger up and his middle two bent down.

I gasp when I finally understand what he is trying to tell me and proceed to burst into body-wrecking sobs again—and they are body wrecking. Each twinge of movement feels like a dozen knives digging into my skin and flaying me wide open.

I focus on his hand and on the message he learned so he could tell me.

I don't know if this is the extent of the sign language he knows but if he was ever going to learn anything this was a good way to start.

He does it again, pushing the symbol he's made against my palm.

"I love you too," I choke out.

I feel him twist a strand of hair around his finger as I drift off again in his arms, my body beyond weak and tired.

When I wake up again, he's gone but there is a rough scarred hand holding mine. I don't know if it's one of my guys or someone else so I start to panic, especially when I feel the blanket being pulled away from me but when they lean down and place their face against mine, I can tell it's Viper from his aftershave. I calm a little until I feel soft hands that don't belong to him lifting my nightgown.

"No, get off me. Stop touching me," I scream, causing Viper to move back. "Nooo... no, Viper, don't leave me. Make them stop touching me please, please," I beg him.

I don't know what's happening but the soft hands stop touching me. They get replaced with what I now know are Viper's hands. I feel him drag something wet up my thighs and between my legs, making me flinch before my brain can catch on. He pauses for a moment before continuing but I can't stop my tears as my humiliation burns brightly.

He's washing me. I'm guessing it was a nurse's hands I could feel earlier when I freaked out and now Viper has taken over.

"I'm sorry. I'm sorry about our fight and everything I said before. I'm so sorry but, Viper, this was so much more than you signed up for." I can't speak anymore. Instead, I close my eyes and will myself to just die already. I don't want this to be my life from now on.

I won't become their burden.

I don't speak as he finishes up. I don't speak when he tucks the blankets over me. In fact, I don't talk at all anymore, scared that if I open my mouth my wail of despair will escape. Instead, I settle for screaming in my mind until I feel something on the edge of my bed a moment before a pair of small hands are placed on each side of my face.

"Conner," I breathe out, my relief that he's safe overriding everything else.

"Are you okay?" I ask him. When he taps my shoulder once in yes, a sob erupts from me.

He hugs me tightly, letting me breathe him in for a moment before I feel a large hand pulling us apart a little. I fight to hold on to him but I realize they aren't taking him away just sitting him up.

A large hand taps my shoulder. When I don't say anything he does it again.

"I don't understand," I tell him, frustrated until Conner taps my shoulder again.

I gasp. "You want to know how Conner and I are communicating? Tap my shoulder for yes and tug my ear for no.

One tap on my shoulder tells me I was correct.

"Okay. Oh, god. I have a million things I need to say. Did you find who hurt us?"

One tap.

"Stupid yes no questions means you can't tell me who," I growl out, frustrated.

"I can't see, Viper. I'm so afraid. I don't want to live alone in the darkness like my mother did."

One tug on my ear.

"No? No, what? Crap. Hold on, let me think. Are you

trying to tell me something? Jesus, I sound like I'm talking to a Ouija board."

One tap yes.

"Is it to do with me not being able to see."

One tap.

I open my mouth to ask him the only thing that matters and snap it shut again, scared beyond belief of what his answer will be, but I have to know.

"Will I ever be able to see again?" I can feel the tremor in my voice.

One tap.

I freeze, sure I must have read that wrong.

"I'll see again?"

One tap.

"Oh, my god." I bury my face in my hands and cry. I don't know how long this will last and I can't ask but the fact that it's temporary gives me a flicker of hope.

"Do you... do you promise? Swear it on my life?" I ask, feeling the tears drip from my chin.

One tap. And it's the best thing I've ever felt in my life.

* * * * *

THE ROAD to recovery was a long one. There were times I just wanted to lie down and give up but my stubbornness had nothing on Grim's, Viper's, and Zero's determination to get me well again.

When days turned into weeks with only occasional

flickers of light and shadows, I started to believe they had lied about my prognosis. Until one morning, months later, I woke up and right there in front of me was Grim's sleeping face.

My strangled gasp must have woken him because his eyes flicked over me before he pulled me close and tucked me beneath his chin.

"Why do you have a black eye?" I ask him quietly, swallowing down a wave of emotion as I look up at his face.

He answers me with his eyes closed out of habit I guess, making me wonder how many times he has spoken to me over the last endless amount of weeks before remembering I couldn't hear or see his words.

"Sparring with Zero yesterday. I was distracted thinking about your ass in those yoga pants," he tells me before his eyes pop open and all sleep disappears from his face.

"You can see me?" he questions.

"I can see you," I confirm with a sob before I find myself once more crushed against his chest.

Hands-on my hips have me turning my head to look behind me. Viper's dark eyes stare back at me like unfathomable pools of emotion. "I'm sorry, so fucking sorry. I've been waiting for you to look at me with those big blue eyes of yours so I could say that. I love you. I only set you free so you would, hopefully, chose to stay. Turns out I'm not great with words," he says somewhat bashfully, making me laugh.

The look on his face would bring me to my knees if I wasn't sandwiched between the two of them in bed.

"I overreacted. I'm sorry too," I tell him, running my hand along the scruff of his jaw. "It's so good to see you." My eyes blur with unshed tears but this time the happy kind. "I have so much I want to ask you. I've missed so much."

He pushes me onto my back and climbs on top of me.

"I'll tell you anything you want to know but first I need to fuck you. I want your pretty little eyes on me the whole time okay?"

My pussy spasms at his words.

"Okay, Viper," I whisper.

He dips his head and sucks a nipple into his mouth, making me gasp with pleasure. The guys had stopped putting nightclothes on me as they inevitably ended up on the floor. I had missed a lot of things being trapped in the dark but sex wasn't one of them.

Once I was healed, all of them looked for any excuse to touch me. It was the only thing that kept me connected and fed my bond with them. They anchored me in place when I felt like crawling out of my skin and as the touching turned to more, I yearned for those moments when they brought me such exquisite pleasure that I swear for brief moments I saw stars in my darkness.

I turn my head to Grim, who leans over and takes my lips in a hot kiss that speaks promises of the dirty things to come.

At this point, I think they know my body better than I do myself.

There had been an element of recklessness, a taboo almost, to making love with them when I didn't know what they were going to do to me or when. It was like being permanently blindfolded while being seduced by three scorching hot guys who had become my whole world.

Viper's hand slides down between my folds finding me slick and needy. He smiles at me before lining up his hard cock and pushing inside. Grim dips his head to work on my breasts, one of his hands balancing him while he slides the other up and down his cock. I grip Grim's hair with my hand, holding him in place as I gaze up at Viper and bite my lip.

Viper's movements speed up, the feel of my eyes on him bringing him closer to the edge. He reaches between us and rubs my clit, making me arch up into Grim's mouth.

"Oh, yes. Harder," I beg.

Viper complies, thrusting into me harder and faster than before. Grim mimics him, speeding up his own movements of his hand gliding up and down his cock.

So many things I want to see, to watch but my brain feels overstimulated and a wave of pain moves through my head.

I close my eyes, not wanting to ruin the moment and gasp again as Grim bites down on my nipple.

Viper picks that instant to pinch my clit as he plants himself inside me and comes, making my own orgasm wash over me, my headache forgotten.

"I love you both," I manage to mutter before I fall asleep.

Hands-on my body wake me a little while later but these

hands aren't exploring. They are coaxing, trying to pull me from my slumber peacefully.

"No... go away. I'm comfy," I grumble before a large hand slaps my ass, making my eyes shoot open.

I glare at Viper, who is grinning down at me without remorse.

"Zero is bringing the cage over." He frowns at the word cage—what my bikers hatefully call cars on account of feeling trapped inside them.

I roll my eyes at him. "It's a car and you have no idea what it's like to be trapped," I tell him, making him halt. "What, too soon?" I shrug awkwardly. "If I don't joke about it I'll go insane, Viper. The things you guys had to do for me, I can't—" I'm cut off by his lips on mine, soft and sweet.

"I'd do anything for you Megan, we all would. Besides, you would do it for us if the situation had been reversed."

My shoulders slump at his words. Of course, he's right but it doesn't mean I have to like it. "Fine. You're right. I swear from here on out if you ever find yourself both randomly deaf and blind I will change your tampons for you every month." I smile sweetly, making him shake his head in exasperation.

I get what he's saying, I do. But it's going to take time for me to deal with everything that's happened to me lately.

Just then the door swings open and Zero walks in.

"Fuck, I forgot how pretty you are," I tell him, making him stop and look at me with wide eyes.

"You can see?" he asks, sweeping me up into his arms and spinning me around before I can answer.

"Urgh, gonna puke," I groan, making him lay off the spinning.

"Shit, sorry."

I get dizzier far easier since my attack and still tire quickly.

"I'll forgive you if you do that thing I like with your tongue later," I suggest with a smile, trying to lighten the mood. I'm afraid if I start crying now, I'll never stop.

"You've got yourself a deal there, Raven," he agrees, making my facade crack.

"Hey, what's wrong? Are you hurting?" I shake my head and then wince. That shit hurts too if I shake it too rigorously. Apparently, having your skull cracked open like a hard-boiled egg takes it out of you.

"I'm fine. I just missed my nickname that's all."

"It's not a nickname, sweetheart. A raven is who you are. Fearless and strong even when shrouded in black."

I nod my head, gently this time, at his double meaning. I didn't feel strong, not at all but I'm standing here now, so that has to count for something.

"Come on, get dressed. We can argue over how awesome you are later. We have somewhere we have to be."

"What? Where?" I rarely leave the apartment anymore.

"Luna's in labor and she's asking for you."

I RUSH into the hospital room, shoving through the wall of leather and testosterone and make my way over to the frazzled blonde on the bed.

"Megan," she cries out, tears springing to her eyes, shocking the shit out of me.

I wrap my arms around her and hold on tight as she cries against my shoulder for a second before pulling back and resting my forehead against hers while she calms herself down.

With a shuddering breath, she looks up at me and blinks before slapping my arm.

"Hey, what's that for?" I yell at the crazy lady.

"You can see and you didn't tell me," she wails.

"It's new. It literally just came back," I tell her.

"What, as you were walking in here? Because anything else is unacceptable," she scolds me.

"Well, no, I mean I was going to but then Viper stuck his dick in me and I forgot," I answer with a shrug.

"No, Megan, I warned you about the perils of magic peen. They make you lose your mind. I swear one day you're just walking along merrily and then next thing you know, there's a bun in your oven." She shudders and sniffs. "I'm baking a freaking human for god's sake. What am I doing? I'm going to fuck this up.

"I can't do this Megan. I don't know how to be a mother. Fuck, I don't even really remember my own. I need to try harder to be better but what if I mess my kid up so bad they grow up to be a serial killer or something?" she babbles, making me snort.

I look around the room and see my guys followed me in and are standing on the left looking amused while Luna's guys are gathered over by the window. Their expressions range from panic to pride.

Any beef and hostility between the two clubs have been put aside over the last few months. The two clubs might never be the best of friends but they are allies and any remaining hostilities have been forgotten at the sight of the pregnant woman softly sobbing before us.

"If your kid grows up to be a serial killer then they will be the best goddamn serial killer this country has ever seen."

She looks at me in shock for a moment before laughing, gripping her belly hard when a contraction takes hold of her. When it passes, she waits for me to continue.

"You have a room full of fathers in here," I remind her, pointing behind me at Halo, Orion, and Gage. "And a corridor out there lined with uncles. Nothing is going to happen to this kid, I promise. Even without all that you are forgetting one very important thing."

She stares at me with a pensive look on her face.

"You are Luna fucking Cartwright, badass bitch owner of a group of mercenaries and the reigning Queen of Carnage. You have got this. You are fierce, loving, and loyal to a fault. So your white picket fence is topped with barbed wire, who cares?" I shrug nonchalantly.

"The kid has three dads. I think they will know that their

mama thinks outside the box. Don't try and make yourself smaller to fit someone else's ideal. Be exactly who you are, the woman they love, the queen the club respects, and the mama who will go to battle for her kiddo."

She takes my hand as another tear escapes her. I think of my mother and all she endured to protect me and feel nothing but proud that I have her strength in my blood.

"I got this," Luna repeats my words before looking out over the room, her eyes falling on Zero, Grim, and Viper.

"I'm sorry. These hormones are freaking killing me. One minute I'm an emotional wreck and the next I'm horny as fuck. Those are the only emotions I feel anymore."

I laugh as she looks at her guys, her eyes trailing over them seductively.

"And I'm back to horny," she mutters, making me shake my head with a smile.

"You might want to pop that kid out first."

She scowls at me, pissed that I have the audacity to get between her and her biker sandwich. "I just need a little dicking." She pouts. "Just the tip, really."

"Shut it, whorzilla. Baby out then cock in." I put my hands on my hips as she gives me an evil look.

"It's probably for the best. You really don't want to see your brother's colossal cock." Oh, you bitch. I gag before smiling sweetly at her.

"You'll need his colossal cock after that baby's stretched you out." I run away when she flings the pillow at me. Orion decides to step in then before I fling it back. He wraps his arms around me and hugs me tight.

I hold on to him, my mind always settles when he and Diesel are close by. I freaking love having brothers.

"Thank you for visiting me even though I was pretty fucking boring." He snorts at that, placing a kiss on my forehead.

He lets me go and signs slowly, making tears prick the back of my eyes. *I missed you.*

"You learned to sign," I choke out, overcome with emotion that he would do that for me.

"Of course I did. You're my sister but it's not just me, all of the guys are learning. Oz and Ziggy have been teaching us. We can't let the Chaos boys outdo us, now can we?" he teases.

My guys have been learning how to sign so they could try and sign against my palm. It was hard going and more than a little frustrating but it also solidified just how much I love them.

"How you feeling?" he asks me.

"I'm okay now. I'm sorry I've been such a pain in the ass. I just… it was a lot to deal with you know?"

He nods in understanding. "You don't need to apologize. I'm fucking awed by your strength. I don't think I could have handled it for a day let alone months. Just don't overdo it too soon now, okay?"

"I won't, I promise. I'll wait outside with the guys. We can talk some more later. I'll come back after we grab Conner from school. Right now, it's time to become a daddy," I tell him just as the doctor walks in with her clipboard. She startles a little when she looks up and finds herself surrounded by bikers but she relaxes when I offer her a smile.

"Okay, Luna. I need to see how far dilated you are. Anyone who isn't supposed to be here needs to leave." I can't see the doctor speak but thankfully, Luna signs for me, so I indicate for the guys to head out.

I give Gage and Halo a quick hug before turning back to Orion. He lifts his hands and signs for me. I stare at his hands before turning to face Luna who is attempting to look innocent while fighting back her laughter.

"Now that's just mean," I tell her when she can't hold back her laughter any longer.

"What?" Orion looks to Luna before facing me again. I see the moment it dawns on him what she's laughing at. He straightens up and crosses his arms over his chest. "I didn't sign 'take care, I'll see you soon' did I?" he asks, cursing.

"No." I snort. "You just told me you like to take it up the ass."

His eyes widen in horror before he turns back to Luna. I can't see what he's saying but whatever it is makes the doctor blush. I take that as my cue to leave and head out into the corridor, the lighthearted moment disappearing as the three Chaos members find ourselves surrounded by Carnage.

"Back off guys. We are here because Luna wanted us to be. This isn't a dick measuring contest to see whose is bigger." I gag again, a look of disdain on my face, I'm sure.

"Although apparently, Orion wins that title and it was more than I ever wanted or needed to know about my own brother."

The tension eases with my words and I catch some smiles. I spot Diesel and run towards him. He opens his arms so I fling myself into them and hold him tightly.

I went years not knowing they were out there. It only took me moments after meeting them for me to realize that I could never go back to that.

"You can see?" he questions when he sets me down again.

"So everyone keeps telling me." I laugh.

"Damn, I'm so happy for you."

"I'm pretty happy for me too." I look over at all the guys waiting around for Luna to deliver the next generation of Carnage, spying my guys talking to Rebel and Lucky.

"You did it, you know?" Diesel tells me when I turn back to face him.

"Did what?"

"United two MCs. I mean, I still think they're assholes who aren't good enough for my little sister but I guess you could have done worse," he grumbles.

I look at my guys and think about how they have washed me, dressed me, and heck even took me to the bathroom without even flinching.

"They're perfect."

He fake gags. "I think I just threw up in my mouth."

I laugh at him and give him a shove.

"They're far from perfect." He shakes his head but smiles

and dips his head closer. "But they're perfect for you." He kisses me on the cheek before walking over to give Grim shit. He just can't help himself.

Oz and Zig collapse into chairs opposite me.

"Yes, I can see, before you ask," I tell them with a huge smile.

"Thank the lord. Nobody should miss out on all this awesomeness." Oz indicates his rather large body making me throw my head back and laugh.

I sober for a minute, taking in their handsome features. "Thank you."

They know what I'm talking about. Nobody else has asked about the gun I used to shoot Wanda. It hasn't come up yet, so I've kept it to myself.

"It wasn't enough." Zig shakes his head angrily.

"I'm here, aren't I? Trust me. It was enough." They both look at me for a moment before nodding their heads to accept my thanks.

A large body sits down next to me, pressing a hard thigh against mine. I look up into Grim's handsome face and grin, staring at him boldly just because I can.

"I'll never get tired of looking at you," I breathe out reverently.

"Trust me, Raven, I know the feeling." He slips his fingers through mine before turning to face Oz and Zig, a look of apprehension crossing his features that has me frowning. When his leg starts to bounce up and down I start to worry until he blurts out what's bothering him.

"I want you guys to help me find my sister," he tells Oz and Zig.

"Why us?" Zig asks him curiously.

"I've exhausted every other avenue but I won't give up, I can't. I hear you guys specialize in this kind of thing." When they don't speak Grim carries on. "What would you do if it was your sister?" he implores.

"Everything within my power," Oz answers him honestly.

"You find anything that might help, a place to start?" Zig asks, slipping into work mode. I watch Grim's face tenderly, knowing how hard it was for him to ask them for help.

"Only a name. A big-time arms dealer who calls himself Gemini. He's the person who I think has my sister, but the guy is like a fucking ghost—" He cuts off when I squeeze his fingers so tight, I must be close to snapping them.

"Jesus fuck, Megan. You've gone white as a sheet. I knew this was too much too soon. Let's get you home." He shifts to stand but I grip him hard.

"What is your sister's name?" I don't know what my voice sounds like, but I have Grim, Oz, and Zig's full attention now.

"Why, what's going on?"

"What is your sister's name?" I repeat with gritted teeth.

"Vida. Vida Roberts."

"Viddy." The words rush from my mouth in a breath of air. I haven't seen her in forever. She had some trouble and went into hiding only leaving Wyatt untraceable emails to let him know she's okay.

"What the fuck? Viddy? Your Viddy is my Vida? No, that

can't be. It has to be a coincidence, unless— wait, do you know who Gemini is? You know where he has my sister?" he asks in disbelief, drawing the attention of the rest of the guys in the waiting room.

"Viddy isn't with Gemini, Grim." I swallow and drop the bomb.

"Viddy *is* Gemini."

"Well, fuck."

The End... kind of.

Viddy's story is coming soon in the spin-off Novel Ricochet. Book three in the Underestimated Series will continue with Reign of Kings.

SNEAK PEEK: THE QUEEN OF CARNAGE

*Want to see where it all began?
Read Luna's story in The Queen of Carnage Book One in The Underestimated Series.*

**The Queen of Carnage
By Candice Wright**

My grandpa always told me there were times in our lives where we should stand and fight and there were times when we should run and hide. Running when you knew the odds were stacked against you didn't make you a coward, it makes you smart. This is one of those times.

I'm wearing little silver ballet flats and a knee-length navy blue sundress with spaghetti straps. Although the dress does amazing things for my legs, it doesn't give off a particularly intimidating vibe. Not that a five-foot woman with white-blonde hair in crazy ringlets and blue eyes that are a touch too big for her face could ever really be described as intimidating. Badass maybe, but not intimidating. The hulking biker chasing after me certainly doesn't seem to find me intimidating in any way.

The gorgeous huskie beside me is keeping pace despite the pain he must be feeling from the swift kick to the ribs he received earlier. A kick which ultimately led to my current predicament.

LET ME BACK UP A BIT. My name is Luna Cartwright. I'm twenty-eight years old and I was born to two awesome parents, James and Kate, who were the very definition of hippies. Now, before you laugh at my name, you should know I have two older brothers named Ziggy and Cosmic. Yep, you read that right, Ziggy and Cosmic. I happen to love my name, largely because I know it could have been so much worse.

The five of us lived in a tiny town in Ireland, just outside Dublin, up until the summer I turned eight. That's when both of my parents were killed in a car accident, leaving my brothers and myself in the custody of my wonderful, yet slightly insane, grandpa.

Gramps was a retired Vietnam War vet who lived on a

farm deep in the wilderness of Tennessee. My mother had left home as soon as she could get her student visa and study abroad, which is how she met my father. But me? Well, I loved it here. We were taught to hunt and shoot and tend the farm and I was treated just like one of the boys. In fact, the only girly thing I owned until I was about seventeen was a box of tampons. When I was eighteen, my brothers enlisted, so I decided to move closer to the city. That's where my love of all things girly came from. Seeing shop windows filled with everything from beautiful dresses and intricately designed underwear to soft fluffy throws and pretty trinkets meant my little studio apartment had looked like the center page of a women's magazine. But it was also how my business got started. I began to make custom gift baskets as presents for my friends and family—baskets full of goodies for moms-to-be or bottles, blankets, and bibs for baby showers.

When Gramps got sick, I moved back in with him, staying by his side until his frail body eventually gave out. By then I had my own website and, although I still deliver the odd thing personally, most of my stuff is shipped online. There are even a couple of shops in the neighboring towns that have started stocking my goodies.

This is how I accidentally met my furry friend beside me. I have, as a general rule, no sense of direction and without the use of GPS, I'm pretty sure I would have ended up in the wrong state a time or two. I was making a delivery to a cute little shop that had opened in Neavsham, which is a twenty-minute drive from where I used to live, when I got turned around and my GPS decided to have a meltdown on me. Even with my lack of direction, I still managed to figure out pretty quickly that four lefts had me turning in a circle. After a fair bit of cursing, I had pulled over next to a large industrial building that was partially hidden by trees, to text Megan, the shop's owner, when I became aware of a dog whining. I got out of my truck and followed the noise until I came upon a huge white and gray huskie on the other side of a six-foot chain-link fence. He heard my approach and growled at me a little, not in an I'm-going-to-rip-your-arm-off kind of way, more in a back-off-and-leave-me alone-I'm-having-a-shitty-day kind of way. I sat on the grass on my side of the fence, pulled some beef jerky out of my pocket (don't judge) and poked a piece through the fence for him. He whined a little but wandered over, scooped up the jerky, and lay down right in front of me. In a moment of bravery or stupidity, I stuck my fingers through the fence and started stroking his beautiful coat until his tongue lolled out and he was panting. That day I fell a little bit in love with him and anytime I was in the area making deliveries, I came to visit.

That's how I happened to witness a tall wiry man with a pockmarked face and long greasy black hair kick the shit out of the poor dog when he hadn't respond fast enough to the asshole's commands. I felt my blood boil beneath my skin. No way was I going to leave him there to be subjected to that kind of treatment. I made my delivery to Megan's and then asked her if I could leave my truck there for a little while. She kindly agreed, so I pulled wire cutters and old gloves from the toolkit in the cargo bed, courtesy of my brothers, and retraced my steps on foot to save my furry friend. It was getting late by the time I got there but he was waiting by the fence, sitting in the humid evening heat when I returned, like he knew I was coming for him, and my heart melted a little more. Using the cutters, I made an opening in the fence big enough for him to get through without scraping himself on any sharp edges, when I heard a shout from the side of the building. I dropped the cutters, urged the dog through the fence, and then I took off like a shot through the woods with my escaped prisoner.

Which brings me to now—huffing, puffing, and stumbling over the uneven terrain as I run blindly through the woods in ballet flats. Not my finest hour, for sure. Out of nowhere, I find myself wrapped up in leather-encased arms and pulled back hard against someone's chest. The dog snarls ferociously at my captor but calms when the voice behind me, with a Texas drawl, tells him to settle.

I wiggle and kick my legs, trying to gain some leverage, but with my arms pinned to my sides, my movements are limited.

"Settle down, sugar," the deep voice rasps out.

His arms are firm, his grip strong, but he isn't hurting me. He isn't using more force than necessary and he isn't trying to grope me in the process, so I calm myself down and take stock of the situation. I have always been able to read people, ever since I was a kid, and something is telling me this guy isn't going to hurt me. He loosens his grip as he feels me relax and leans down to speak softly into my ear.

"Want to tell me why you're stealing our dog?"

I'm about to answer him when the pockmarked asshole who started this whole thing by kicking the dog comes running toward us. He must have circled around and come from the other direction.

"You fucking cunt," he shouts. He surprises the shit out of me and the biker at my back by swinging his arm out and slapping me across the face with the back of his hand.

Now, let me tell you, that shit hurts like a bitch. Before I can even get my bearings, I find myself facing the burning deck of cards logo on the back of biker man's jacket as he places me behind him. Before either of us can say or do anything else, though, my furry friend is on the pockmarked biker, dragging him to the ground, pinning him with his teeth in his shoulder and growling a warning that if he moves, he's dead.

I smile as my face throbs, taking a small amount of satisfaction from the fact that the dog now has the upper hand. The biker that grabbed me calls him off, unfortunately.

"King, heal," he commands.

King, huh? Great name. It suits him. Oh, right, focus.

King obeys immediately, clearly trained and familiar with my pseudo protector.

Biker dude steps forward, then bends down and, I kid you not, he picks up the pockmarked asshole around the throat like he weighs nothing. If I wasn't so busy looking for a way out of this mess, I would be totally impressed. Okay, so I'm still a little bit impressed.

"Do you want to tell me what the fuck you think you're doing?" he growls—the biker, not the dog.

"That bitch stole our dog," the idiot with the hand wrapped around his throat manages to reply, which is actually quite impressive as his face is turning an alarming shade of purple.

"You never put your hands on a woman in anger, you piece of shit," my biker tells him. He pulls back his right arm while still holding with his left and sucker punches the guy in the face. The pockmarked ass drops to the ground like a sack of bricks and doesn't get back up.

Biker man then turns to me and, holy shitting hell, this man is pretty, although I probably wouldn't say that to his face. He looks a little like Chris Hemsworth with his blond hair in a man bun, his faded denim eyes, and chiseled jaw covered in day-old stubble. He's taller than me, but then, everyone is, but at around six feet two he towers over me and he's built in a way that screams "I work out." I didn't even know men this gorgeous existed in real life. I'm tempted to pinch him just to make sure I'm not dreaming. He ignores me checking him out and gently runs his thumb over my cheekbone, causing me to wince and him to frown.

"Come on, let's get you to the compound and get you cleaned up." He grabs my hand and starts pulling me back through the woods with King following behind us. I'm so busy marveling at how hands that size could be so gentle, it takes a while for his words to penetrate my thick skull.

"Hey, um, yeah, I'm not going anywhere with you. Thanks for sticking up for me back there, but I'm going to just go now." I pull my hand free and manage to take a couple of steps away from him before I find myself upside down and over his shoulder.

"Hey, put me down."

He slaps my ass, hard enough to make it sting, effectively stilling my movements. "Settle down. I don't want to drop you and cause any more damage to that pretty face of yours. You stole our dog, sugar, I can't just let you go. Besides, you need to tell my president what just went down."

We walk, well, he walks, I bounce, for what seems like forever but is probably closer to five minutes, while I mentally berate myself for getting trapped in this situation to begin with. We end up at a huge gated entrance to what I'm assuming is their compound. It's hard to see much from my upside down angle. He slides me down his body and shouts over my shoulder to the guards, I'm guessing, to open the gates. I'm thinking this is a very bad idea and I can tell he has noticed my train of thought because he places both hands gently on either side of my face.

"Nobody is going to hurt you in here, sugar. Your punishment will more than likely be a favor of some sort."

My eyes must be the size of my head as I guess what kind of favors they could ask of me. He takes one of my hands in his and tugs us toward the door.

"Not what you're thinking, sugar. Nobody here would ever put their hands on you without your permission, okay?"

I nod because what else can I say? Despite my small stature, I'm quite good at defending myself but unarmed and in a compound filled with god knows how many bikers, I'd be screwed. I just hope that doesn't mean literally.

ALSO BY CANDICE WRIGHT

THE UNDERESTIMATED SERIES

The Queen of Carnage: An Underestimated Novel Book One

https://books2read.com/u/47EMrj

THE INHERITANCE SERIES

Rewriting Yesterday

https://books2read.com/u/3JVj6v

In this Moment

https://books2read.com/u/bxvnJd

The Promise of Tomorrow

https://books2read.com/u/bowEy1

THE FOUR HORSEWOMEN OF THE APOCALYPSE SERIES

The Pures

https://books2read.com/u/mdGl1y

THE PHOENIX PROJECT DUET

From the Ashes: The Phoenix Project Book One

https://books2read.com/u/bO65pN

ACKNOWLEDGMENTS

Jodie-Leigh Plowman – Designer extraordinaire. Thank you for my beautiful cover.

Tanya Oemig – My incredible editor - AKA miracle worker, who goes above and beyond.

Missy Stewart - Proofreader and lifesaver.

Gina Wynn - Formatting Queen.

Sosha Ann – My amazing PA and friend. You are one of the strongest people I know, and I adore you.

Aspen Marks, AC Wilds and Isobelle Carmichael – My girl squad. I'm blessed to have such amazing, strong and talented women in my life.

Julie Melton, Rachel Bowen, Sue Ryan - My Beta Angels. You ladies are the bee's knees. I will never be able to tell you how much I love and appreciate everything you do for me.

Thais Neves – There isn't enough words in the dictionary to express my gratitude for everything you do for me.

My readers – You guys are everything to me. I am in awe of the love and support I have received. Thanks for taking a chance on me and on each of the books that I write.

Remember, If you enjoy it, please leave a review.

ABOUT THE AUTHOR

Candice is a romance writer who lives in the UK with her long-suffering partner and her three slightly unhinged children. As an avid reader herself, you will often find her curled up with a book from one of her favourite authors, drinking her body weight in coffee. If you would like to find out more, here are her stalker links:

FB Group https://www.facebook.com/groups/949889858546168/

Amazon amazon.com/author/candicewrightauthor

Instagram https://www.instagram.com/authorcandicewright/?hl=en

FB Page https://www.facebook.com/candicewrightauthor/?modal=admin_todo_tour

Twitter https://twitter.com/Candice47749980

BookBub https://www.bookbub.com/profile/candice-wright

Goodreads https://www.goodreads.com/author/show/18582893.Candice_M_Wright